PRAISE FOR C

"Beth Uznis Johnson's debut novel *Coming Clean* is a sharp, sexy, pressure chamber of a book. Earthy and carnal like the work of Lisa Taddeo, darkly complex like Ottessa Moshfegh's *Eileen*, Dawn is a cleaning lady with a lot going on in her head, and a keen interest in what boundaries she can push as she makes a kind of peace with grief. In these pages, we find the razor's edge where everyday life tips over into art. Read it once for what happens, and then again for what's earned."

—Ashley Warlick, author of *The Arrangement*

"*Coming Clean* sneaks up on the reader in the same way that hard truths in the novel sneak up on Dawn, the protagonist. At first it seems we're spying on Dawn's customers along with her, that she is our window into those complicated lives, but gradually our gaze shifts to Dawn herself, and the houses she cleans become our windows into her. This is a smart, funny, thoughtful novel about a young woman on the cusp of starting over. We see that cusp before she does; the tension we feel is the fear that she won't recognize it in time."

—Susan Perabo, author of *The Fall of Lisa Bellow*

"Regret, guilt, grief, the secrets of private lives put on display, and a chance at redemption. Beth Uznis Johnson's debut novel, *Coming Clean*, illuminates as much as it titillates. Johnson has such a grasp on how our contemporary world has affected our relationships. Her empathy for her characters, often flawed and nearly broken, is striking, and her unique vision left me eager to keep turning the pages. This is an impressive first novel."

—Lee Martin, author of the Pulitzer Prize Finalist, *The Bright Forever*

"Raw and unflinching, *Coming Clean* exposes a young woman's guilt and grief over the loss of her fiancé. Dawn cleans other people's houses, peeking under the sheets and peering inside closets, revealing the most intimate secrets of families vastly different from herself. Her tenacious quest for these hidden truths evolves into a search for her own self-acceptance. Dawn is witty and sharp, brave and impulsive, and through her journey, readers will discover there's a little bit of Dawn in each of us."

—Carla Damron, author of *The Orchid Tattoo* and *The Stone Necklace*

"*Coming Clean* is a book you don't want to miss, turning inside out classic themes of guilt and betrayal, and giving us, in no uncertain terms, the glorious middle American version of *Remains of the Day*. This book is practically an instant classic, it is that good and that smart and that brave and that unsettling."

—Fred Leebron, author of *In the Middle of All This*

COMING CLEAN

Beth Uznis Johnson

Regal House Publishing

Published by
Regal House Publishing, LLC
Raleigh, NC 27605
All rights reserved

ISBN -13 (paperback): 9781646034154
ISBN -13 (epub): 9781646034161
Library of Congress Control Number: 2023934870

Cover images and design by © C. B. Royal

Author photo by Edda Pacifico

Regal House Publishing, LLC
https://regalhousepublishing.com

The following is a work of fiction created by the author. All names, individuals, characters, places, items, brands, events, etc. were either the product of the author or were used fictitiously. Any name, place, event, person, brand, or item, current or past, is entirely coincidental.

Printed in the United States of America

To my late grandmother, Evelyn R. Uznis,
for believing girls should get chances.

And to Ken, Alex, and Kevin

TOP 100 WAYS TO MESS WITH CUSTOMERS

1. Organize sex toys
2. Mismatch socks
3. Toss random condom in a drawer
4. Toss condom wrapper in trash
5. Switch lamps between rooms
6. Change soap brand
7. Sprinkle flower seeds in garden
8. Swap canned food with store brands
9. Rearrange furniture
10. Add appointments to wall calendar
11. Refold underwear
12. Smear chocolate skid marks
13. Sort closets by color
14. Hang TP wrong direction
15. Rearrange silverware
16. Overstarch one sleeve
17. Hide prescription meds in back
18. Slide hemorrhoid goop to front
19. Switch junk drawer contents
20. Set clocks fifteen minutes ahead
21. Set clocks fifteen minutes late
22. Write anonymous love letter
23. Move knickknacks between rooms
24. Re-hang artwork
25. Unscrew light bulbs
26. Random hair on pillow
27. Change speed dial numbers
28. Switch salt and sugar
29. Move XLax to Imodium bottle
30. Microwave milk jug
31. Try on formalwear

32. Read diary
33. Take bubble bath
34. Relocate nail clippers to silverware drawer
35. Speak only in robot voice
36. Replace family photo with similar family
37. Add peroxide to shampoo bottle
38. Add deer urine to perfume
39. Drink best booze
40. Replenish bottles with cheap booze
41. Luxuriate in expensive skin care routine
42. Transfer golf clubs to attic
43. Apply layer of shampoo to toilet seat
44. Re-sort important papers
45. Drop phone number into pants pocket
46. Erase programs from DVR
47. Smudge lipstick on shirt collar
48. Relocate passport to basement desk drawer
49. Short sheet guest bed
50. Eat all but one cookie
51. Replace goldfish with bigger goldfish
52. Defrost freezer items in fridge
53. Subscribe to porn magazine
54. Replace spare keys
55. Disconnect light switches
56. Reprogram thermostat
57. Record fake checkbook deposit
58. Leave fake adoption records for kids
59. Saran wrap toilet seat prank
60. Rip butt seams on pants
61. Loosen door hinges
62. Reprogram garage door
63. Hijack Facebook; post conspiracy theory
64. Hide car keys in basement desk drawer
65. Swap coffee to decaf
66. Swap decaf to regular

67. Replace fancy coffee with instant
68. Hide dead fish in milk chute
69. Reorganize fridge
70. Alphabetize bookshelves
71. Replace cough medicine with maple syrup
72. Flip batteries in remote control
73. Display pictures of first wife
74. Slip dirty magazines into rack
75. Move fancy towels to basement bathroom
76. Replace vitamins with Viagra
77. Squeeze Nair into shampoo bottle
78. Jam drawers to open 1 inch
79. Flip cups in dishwasher
80. Flip knives in dishwasher
81. Erase phone contacts
82. Delete laptop files
83. Blast volume on TV
84. Release vacuum seal on pantry items
85. Lower fridge temp to freezing
86. Write dirty messages in bathroom steam
87. Reorganize kitchen cabinets
88. Tape over telephone receiver to lower volume
89. Replace light bulbs with lower wattage
90. Mismatch DVD cases
91. Swap book jackets
92. Set all clocks to different times
93. Set alarm clock for 3:37 a.m.
94. Leave voicemail from Sunset Massage Parlor & Escort Service
95. Superglue plugs into outlets
96. Move hanging tennis ball in garage
97. Hard boil every other egg
98. Reset the sprinkler timer
99. Disconnect doorbell
100. Stir sand into Vaseline

Monday: Exposure

Turn on lights and look for what's dirtiest.

One of the best parts about cleaning other people's houses was she got to fuck with them. Dawn wiped Barb Turner's TV cabinet until the grain of the wood gleamed in its most pristine, dustless state. Then she replaced the silk daisies in the same lopsided line as usual. Each flower grew from a rigid copper stem sprouted from a brushed-nickel pedestal. Barb, who seemed equally rigid, preferred: yellow, orange, pink, orange, yellow. Dawn left them any way but that.

It wasn't that Dawn didn't like Barb Turner. Or her décor. The colors brightened the room and, despite being old enough to have lost the sheen of newness, she dusted the petals and brought some shine back to the copper. The fake flowers were trendy, maybe even hip.

What bothered Dawn was how a perfectly clean square appeared when she lifted a flower, the havoc of the Turners' week having settled around each base. What difference did it make if your stuff was clean or dirty when you didn't seem to notice it in the first place? All that time and money spent on decorating only to fade into the backdrop of the day to day. People should notice what they had before it was gone because everything became gone eventually, be it from fading trends in home design, normal wear and tear, old age or sudden, unanticipated destruction.

The flowers would be forgotten were she not to move them around, left untouched and ignored amid the family commotion. So, Dawn slid the yellow flower to the center and staggered them a little—forward, back, forward, back—for added effect.

Barb restored order to Dawn's chaotic line of flowers week after week. Neither spoke of this game they'd been playing for nearly a year, a back-and-forth push like checkers, with each player refusing to lose. She pictured Barb standing in front of the cabinet every Monday night, arms crossed, ready to make her move, wondering whether to say something to the goddamned cleaning lady about putting things back like she'd found them.

She imagined Barb thinking: *Maybe she didn't do it on purpose, the cleaning lady. Maybe she thinks the flowers look better with the tall orange one on the end. Do they?* Barb would be forced to see the life she had created for herself, right there in front of her, in her decent-sized house in a decent neighborhood in upstate New York, exactly the way she'd wanted.

Dawn swung her plastic jug of Magic on the way to the living room. She knelt in front of the coffee table and used both hands to squirt a line of her cleaning concoction from one end to the other. She sat back on her socks. The wood discolored beneath the wet part. She didn't know enough about furniture to say whether this happened because of the high quality of the finish or because it was cheap. It didn't matter as long as she wiped fast enough. She'd never live in a house this nice or this big anyway so it seemed safe to assume that even a veneer finish was the real deal. One advantage of mobile home living was not knowing the difference, or giving a shit for that matter. Dawn's choices to create her future were diminished when Terry died, cut by half at least and fucked over in triplicate by her injuries from the accident.

She ripped a couple paper towels from the roll knotted to her belt loop with twine. The Magic disappeared as she worked it to a thin lather, flipped the towels, and dried the tabletop.

Magic with a fresh citrus scent. Her customers loved it, raved about it, begged to know her secret. She'd yet to discover a finish—wood, vinyl, granite, porcelain—that didn't gleam after a wipe down. *Make yourself invaluable*, her father always said. He didn't care she cleaned houses as long as she did her best.

As sure as Dawn ran her cloth over the smooth legs of the Turners' coffee table and along the creases where grime tended to collect, her father polished the copper rails at his Key West bar so they glimmered like new pennies. People should pay attention to their belongings and take care of those they cared about. Her cell phone quacked as though he knew she'd thought of him. "Hey, Dad. What's up?"

That bad feeling rose through her, as though he could only be delivering crushing news. It had to be about the accident, like her father's health insurance wouldn't cover her after all. Or Terry's parents had finally sued. She'd lose the trailer, her father the bar. Her heartbeat pulsed through the grafted skin on her elbows. The bad feeling, which hadn't been quite so bad lately, seemed to swallow her whole. A person had no control over a body when trouble called. Trouble still owned her: her elbows, her brain, thoughts, heart, everything.

She sat cross-legged on the floor next to the bottle of Magic. The paper towel roll stuck out like an awkward appendage. Her hair blanketed her neck and shoulders so she twisted it into a knot and tucked the ends, willing the curls to stay put for once.

"Shawna quit," her dad said.

The news didn't make Dawn feel better. In the end—really—pretty much everything was about the accident anyway.

Sweat rolled down the edge of her face and melted into her hair near her right ear. Deep breathing, she reminded herself. The doctor said it helped ease the anxiety.

"You there?"

"I thought Shawna was the best waitress you had," she said.

"What matters is I need to hire another waitress in time for the holidays. The job's yours if you want it."

Her father had sold most of his possessions years ago and moved to Key West. He opened a dive bar that served hamburgers atop wax paper in red baskets. *Best local burgers*, his chalkboard sign said. Vacationers wandering off the cruise ships believed him.

"But my cleaning business," Dawn said. She'd filled all five days of the week. The routine of the expected had allowed her mind to settle into the ease of autopilot, at least until she got home each night. Still, hearing herself say the words stunned her. Autopilot wasn't close to enough. Her father was silent for a beat, confirming her response lacked the enthusiasm he'd expected. "I won't argue with you about all the reasons you should or shouldn't come. Say yes and get down here."

"I can't, Dad. Not right now."

"Why not? Cleaning houses doesn't interest you. It's not your passion. Think of this as a new experience to try. It's a solid business, Dawn."

"Terry's mom is holding a candlelight vigil next week for the holiday."

"What?"

His tone held the amount of incredulity she'd expected from this admission, possibly a little more. Any father would be skeptical. After so many years tucked snugly into the fold of the Folly family, Terry's mother's silence seemed to him a betrayal. Dawn hadn't been so sure. It got complicated, understanding who had betrayed whom, and this included her father, who had been happy to parent in the casual manner required when a person lived 1,500 miles away.

You lost as much as she did, he'd insisted. *She should be helping you heal. How dare his mother pin this on you!*

Dawn watched a tiny ant scale the Turners' wall, traveling the edge of the floor molding like a long road. She knew it was heading toward the crack near the front door. It must lead to freedom.

"How do you know about this…vigil? What is that, praying?" her father said.

"She called me. She asked me to come."

"Sandy Folly? When did you start communicating again? Does your mother know about this?"

"I didn't tell anyone. But she was nice, Dad. I feel like I should go."

"Go so everyone can blame you?"

"Thanks a lot," Dawn said, even though she knew he was one of the few who didn't.

"Saying no to this job means I'll hire someone locally. It'll get snatched up. The tips are great. You need a fresh start."

Dawn remembered the way the sunlight hit her face and

how the smell of the ocean blew past before she pulled open the door to the bar and walked into the blast of air conditioning and reggae music. The dim lighting contrasted with the bright outdoors, as though coming in gave you permission to notice less of the world. Inside the bar, only the pulse of the music and burn of the whiskey mattered. The idea of such a reprieve seemed more than she deserved.

"A new job in Florida is not something you decide on the spot," she said.

She heard voices and clattering on her father's end, pulling her father's attention away from the phone. Relief filled her body like warm sunlight. She couldn't believe herself. An invitation to Florida with a free job on the other end would have equaled hitting the lottery a few days ago. Had she really wanted to hear from Mrs. Folly that badly? Had she been waiting for it all those months? One phone call from Terry's mother and she was sucked back in like they'd never blamed her for the accident in the first place.

"The rum guy's here. Talk it over with your mother. Call me back later," her father said.

"Okay. I will."

"Don't be manipulated, Dawn. There's no way Sandy Folly invited you out of the goodness of her heart. She's fishing for info. Plotting."

"You don't know that," Dawn said.

"Nothing good comes from moving backward. Talk later," her father said and ended the call. Her father *offered* her the job.

Dawn knelt beside the Turners' Christmas tree and removed the red- and green-wrapped packages underneath. The stacks rose, two wobbly towers. Red lights covered the tree and twinkled like miniature video cameras. Dawn gave them the double bird. Imagine if someone really were watching. Not that Barb and Fred Turner had much time to spy, considering their herd of kids and the magnitude of the mess they generated.

Her father *offered* her the job. She'd wanted him to offer her a job, an escape, and now he had.

But attending the vigil didn't have to mean moving backward. That was an assumption. Wanting a peaceful relationship with Terry's mother had nothing to do with a job in Florida. She couldn't help the timing. It was the holidays, for God's sake.

She remembered it was Monday. Matthew wanted to begin shooting for his grant project.

Matthew! Oh, thank God. She'd made a commitment to him. Not officially, but she'd always known she'd tell Matthew yes. She reached for her phone to text her dad. *Photography with Matthew this week. Today till Friday. He needs a model.*

Her father responded immediately.

An excuse or are you telling me you'll leave at the end of the week?

Dawn paused. Her mind overflowed. Her father didn't usually push. Maybe it *was* an excuse, but it was also true. The deadline for Matthew's art grant was the end of the month. She knew better than to tell her father he'd be taking her picture in the houses she cleaned.

He responded before she did.

Call me Friday with a yes or a no. Might be your last chance, kiddo.

The kiddo stung. She liked to think of Key West as an anytime option. For the future. Like if her mom finally got on her last nerve or her cleaning business didn't work out. The kiddo implied her father, who generally treated her as an adult, thought excuses were childish.

Okay.

She speed-dialed Matthew. A rush of adrenalin replaced the bad feeling. She could think about her father's invitation later.

"Hello, D-lightful."

"Matt," Dawn said.

"Don't call me Matt."

"The answer is yes."

"Really? The whole week?"

The rising pitch of his voice rang like a kid on Christmas morning. Dawn couldn't help smiling. Anything to further his art brought Matthew happiness, the kind that resulted in an in-depth analysis of symbolism and meaning and sudden hand gestures, like he was about to cover his ears but shifted to jazz hands.

"I've got no one to answer to. Let's do it," Dawn said.

"I thought for sure you'd leave me hanging."

"I knew I'd say yes. That's what friends do. As long as you remember it's my first time. I might need some coaching."

"Whatever you say, D-ceiver. Should I come over now?"

"You better. I'm almost out of here for the day."

"Got it. Bye," he said and hung up.

She stashed her phone, found her bottle, and aimed. She squirted Magic around the Christmas tree skirt and wiped it clean. Twenty-seven presents already and still two weeks until the holiday. How on earth could the Turner kids understand the meaning of gifts when they got all of that? That's how it worked, whether it translated to toys or money or sex. Or sex toys. Barb had an impressive stash of vibrators hidden in her underwear drawer, a variety of torpedoes in an array of sizes and colors, some with feelers and ticklers. Matthew would love that; he was most interested in the things people wanted to keep secret.

She'd show him the way Fred Turner kept his socks stacked in rows in his top drawer, unpaired. And the way he draped his only fancy tie—branded with an extravagant Italian label on the back—over the first shirt in his closet to trick you into thinking all his clothes were that nice.

Dawn knew the more you had, the less the overall value of the thing. Not that the Turners were wealthy, they weren't. It might be nice to be somewhere in the middle, in the place where poor people thought you were rich and rich people knew you weren't. A house like this, Dawn thought, could totally be enough as long as you didn't make it too much. One thing she knew for sure, she'd never let her life get this big or this messy. No matter where she lived.

Barb had fanned the Christmas presents in anal-retentive piles according to the pattern on the wrap. Candy canes for Bobby. Snowmen for Susie. Snowflakes for Johnny. Dawn replaced them in the same manner you'd deal a hand of poker.

She worked her houses from top to bottom, always taking care to remove cobwebs from the corners of the ceiling with a broom, dust between the slats of the window blinds, and douse the knickknacks with Magic. She scrubbed floors until her knees went numb. She stood on countertops, for God's sake, to reach the dust on top of cabinets. She wiped drips and spills from refrigerators. Her efforts made it easier to take liberty now and then. With a thing or two. Here or there. Really, probably every domestic servant got retribution for the annoying habits of at least one customer.

She'd never go as far as stealing. And Matthew's photography project, so what? The idea of studying the Turners' private life seemed like a mandatory perk of the job. They'd never know. Figuring out a family's deal was far from a crime.

Come on, Dawn. You have a look. It's the right look. The cleaning concept is perfect. You can't argue with that, Matthew had said.

I could probably argue, she'd said.

She backed into one of the Turners' fat velvet chairs. Everyone should have a Matthew. She liked having a male friend, someone she could tell anything, and she especially liked the change in his expression when she talked about the future and he wasn't in it. Matthew was a friend first. Everyone knew that. He dated other women—Jen, the latest. Still, Dawn could tell her friendship held significant worth to him. It mattered to her that she mattered to him. Whatever flashed across his face made her feel wanted.

Modeling for Matthew could help her get unstuck. So many aspects of her life had become sticky: living in the trailer, cleaning houses for a living, staying in upstate New York.

Only you can get back on your feet, her father had said. *Sometimes it seems like you're hanging around waiting for him to come back.*

Dawn knew by now that being dead meant not coming back. Her fiancé Terry no longer existed and the engagement ring he'd given her seemed better suited for the little box tossed somewhere in her closet. Getting used to her finger without the ring took longer than she expected, considering she'd only worn it for a fraction of her lifetime. But being asked to be someone's wife had changed her. Family was essential to the Follys. And they had chosen her. Terry always tried to please his parents, especially his father. He wouldn't have asked without their approval. Dawn saw her future with the Follys so clearly, she wanted to believe she could still have it, even without Terry. That was ridiculous, she knew now.

Her bare hand came to represent everything that changed with Terry's death and she became an adult she'd never envisioned, someone who visited the trailer park to inquire about availability and rent, someone who used the library computers to create an account on Craigslist to advertise cleaning services. She became the woman alone at home with the back of her hand pressed to her mouth in moments of grief or anger or fear or guilt. If she happened to catch a glimpse of the little ring box in her closet, it seemed like jewelry that didn't belong to her. That was someone else's life.

Enough time had passed now for Dawn to see that neither of the potential lives—the one married at twenty-one to Terry, or the one she lived at twenty-two, cleaning houses and going home to a trailer park—were like she'd dreamed about. She'd pictured herself as a college student at NYU, in the smells and sounds of the city, at a bar with other students, drinking whiskey, and discussing intellectual subjects. Or in jeans and a T-shirt on campus at Syracuse, walking down a shabby street to someone's house for a study session. They'd smoke and watch football. She'd envisioned herself in Key West with her dad, working at the bar and going to community college, assuming there was one.

No one pictured herself getting engaged at twenty, but Dawn knew how situations could evolve that transformed you into a different person. Or perhaps you realized the person you were wasn't the person you thought. Maybe it was impossible to know whether Terry had changed her into the person willing to envision a totally different future or if Dawn simply hadn't known herself before that moment at the Folly family reunion when Terry put his arm around her and Dawn watched Mrs. Folly nod at a group of cousins as though all had fallen into its right place.

Nothing mattered more than making him happy. Thoughts of NYU and Syracuse dissolved. Life changed course. She gripped the arms of the Turners' chair and let her palms slide forward and back against the grain of the velvet. She stopped thinking about it here, she had to. The very idea that an event might put into motion Dawn having a life like Barb Turner, or any one of her customers, overwhelmed her with its infinite possibilities. More so that anything in motion could stop and restart. Stop forever. Restart again. And again. Stop.

Dawn craved a cigarette. She weighed the pros and cons. Smoking at the Turners' required too much effort and who wanted to stand in the cold, in full view of the wannabe neighbors, tapping ashes into her palm? Not her, not today. The Chens were the only ones who smoked and they weren't until Thursday. Sometimes Dawn vacuumed there with a cigarette in her mouth just because she could. Sometimes Wei Chen followed her around with her own cigarette, yapping away though Dawn couldn't hear.

Every house she cleaned offered a different kind of satisfaction. She took what she could get. Who didn't? No one, that's who, and she guaranteed that every other cleaning lady spied, snooped, or stole. People who handed house keys to hired help had it coming. The clues couldn't be ignored: clinking vodka bottles in the trash, a crumpled bank statement on the kitchen counter, a magazine under his side of the mattress. Every house told a story.

Focusing on their stories kept her mind off her own.

So if Mondays were imitation middle-class comfort, and Tuesdays were old-school money, and Wednesdays were uptown condominium enormity, Thursdays were smoke-soaked white carpet, and Fridays were a vast cedar deck overlooking the forest. No one saw a thing on Fridays. Except for Dawn because she saw everything. Fridays were the Letwinskis. If she wanted to be anyone, which she really didn't, it would be them. She took a lap around the first floor, dropping the bottle of Magic next to her supplies—bucket, mop, broom—waiting near the front door. Her gaze drifted to the yellowing gouge on the leg of the table in the hallway. That was the problem with the Turners. Each possession seemed scarred: the frayed edge of the carpet, a burn on the linoleum from a dropped pan, chipped paint on the doorframes. As though Barb were being punished for each and every one of her trendy desires.

Dawn came to expect the imperfections. When the living room got freshly painted, a dent appeared a few weeks later from a child's toy or book thrown across the room. The few times she'd encountered Barb in person, there had been salad shrapnel covering one of her front teeth, a run down the back of her pantyhose, a sick kid clutching her leg and making awful whining noises. Not that Dawn was perfect or close to it, but aside from keeping her scars covered, she knew Barb saw her as someone, if not enviable, at least reliable and under control.

Dawn ripped the Velcro straps on her kneepads and tossed them in the bucket. She massaged her elbows and longed for the tight red skin to be more elastic, forgiving. It had been a year and a half, for God's sake, would they ever get better? The doctor said maybe, maybe not. Everyone said movement was the best solution. Movement. Motion. All she did was move. She'd become a moving target without a clear sense of who was aiming at her in the first place.

Pointing her elbow toward the ceiling gave the best view. Red and wrinkly, but taut too, like a shirt that comes out of the dryer in a ball and won't smooth no matter how much you iron it. The red patch burned and pulled as though her elbow might pop through the skin. She almost wanted it to. That skin belonged on her thigh anyway. The grafts would settle in, the doctor said, and eventually blend to be less obvious. Now, when she rotated her shoulder to see it with her arm straight, the skin rose a little and puckered. She imagined she could peel it off like a sticker. Until then, she thought, just keep moving. At least Dawn could make the Turners' place gleam and smell nice.

Invaluable, Dad, just like you said.

She'd been doing this for nearly a year and had never lost a customer.

Dawn thumped upstairs to the Turners' bedroom. Late afternoon had settled into the house, from the sunshine that broke through the clouds and warmed the slices of space it occupied to the clicks and creaks of west-facing walls that relaxed as the day wore on. The last time she passed through the kitchen, the digital display on the microwave said it was quarter past three. Dawn tried to think back to a time at the Turners' when someone came home for the day. Nothing came to mind, and she was almost positive she'd stayed until five. The kids must have latchkey or afternoon activities.

She paused in the Turners' bedroom doorway and waited for the silence to wrap around her. The rigidity of the room came into sharper focus under the glare of the overhead light: the stacked books on the shelf, the precise angle of the photographs on the dresser. Their bed, too small for the large room, a queen. Each week, Dawn avoided the damp outline of Fred Turner on his side of the mattress. The fitted sheet had wrinkled beneath his weight and faded. She couldn't bear the idea of touching Fred's place for confirmation that it was, indeed, moist. The rate at which she tore the sheets off the bed might break records.

Barb's side of the bed, dry and barely mussed, edged so close to the perimeter it was hard to believe she didn't fall out. The Turners' marital bed solidified everything Dawn believed about marriage, mainly that it made no sense. Her own parents, divorced since she was six, couldn't think of one positive trait about the other after sixteen years apart. Her mother simply raised an eyebrow (leaning over to tap her cigarette on the side of the ashtray) and scrunched her mouth into a knot.

Oh, Dawn, I don't know what I saw in him. There must have been some kind of attraction there.

The Turner's bed, now that it was clean and fresh with new sheets and the comforter pulled up, gave no indication that within a day or two, a silhouette would appear to depict a couple sleeping separately with little, if any, crossing over the dividing line. She knew Barb took antidepressants, Zoloft, and had once drawn a complex diagram of all the reasons a person's fingers could be dangerous: *tickling and grazing,* whatever that was. *Sweeping,* though she assumed not a floor.

Dawn moved to the threshold of the Turners' walk-in closet. At least she could look for something to wear. She scanned the section of robes and nighties—some classy, others skimpy—hanging on the rack between the shelves of Barb Turner's sweaters. The drawers contained her underwear and other unmentionables, like the vibrators and a travel-sized bottle of K-Y Warming Jelly. The way they were shoved to the back and buried, she doubted Fred knew they existed. Dawn stepped into the small room, disturbing the perfectly groomed carpet. One of her trademarks was backing out of a room with the vacuum so her customers walked in each time leaving fresh footprints.

She appraised the robes with her hands in the back pockets of her jeans. She wanted a garment to appeal to her by sight, not texture. Matthew took pictures, after all, so the feel of whatever she wore could only be visualized. Assuming he wanted her in a garment. She released her curls from the knot and smoothed her hair. Were anyone to judge, it wasn't like Dawn cared.

Despite herself, she reached forward and fingered the lapel of a floral kimono. She could be art wearing a kimono like that. Its pinks, reds, and blues shimmered under the lights. The pure white background seemed as clean as the flesh inside a coconut. She pulled the belt from its loops and circled her neck like a scarf. Glorious, the feeling of silk on skin. It slid off and fluttered to the ground in a coil.

None of the lingerie in Barb's closet looked used. Some still had store tags affixed to the label or sleeve. What a waste. Dawn remembered the nightgown on the back of the closet door. She swung it shut. There, the navy-blue, plaid flannel from Lands End hung in a thick, matronly line. That one she wore.

Dawn picked up the belt and snaked it back through the loops. She left it untied like she'd found it. Matthew probably wouldn't want her in clothes like that anyway. Too classy. The purpose of art was to make you feel, he said, and the type of feelings stirred up by Matthew's photos had nothing to do with class. Dawn hadn't been lying when she told her dad it was a serious project: a Krindle visual arts grant was twenty-thousand dollars.

She pictured the way Matthew's fingers wrapped around the edge of his camera and recalled the first time she'd noticed them: the last time he took her picture, in the hospital. That was for his day job at the newspaper. Now that they were friends, Dawn knew Matthew's hands were soft for a regular man, but not for an artist. He bit his fingernails badly. He'd almost told his boss to fuck off instead of going to the hospital to take Dawn's photo, but he needed the job.

Matthew reminded Dawn of the boys from middle school: not fat, not thin, not defined, just regular frames with a hint of baby fat waiting to melt away to form the men underneath. His voice, neither loud nor soft, had the midrange tone of any other guy she knew. His limbs, proportional to the rest of his body, were neither flabby nor lean. Yet despite his lack of physical presence, his art was far from weak. You'd think he'd choose a beautiful kimono, but he wouldn't. No doubt he wouldn't. He'd cut that thing to shreds.

Matthew stood in the Turners' bedroom with his camera bag between his Doc Martens. The fresh, cold smell from outside had followed him in, along with a hint of cigarette smoke and weed. He scanned the room, pulling his hair back from his forehead to keep it from obscuring his vision. He kept nodding,

going back to the doorway, and rechecking for significant miss-
es. Matthew always did this upon arrival. It reminded Dawn
of those painting sheets from childhood when you dampened
the paintbrush to activate the watercolor drawing on the page.
After enough passes, the full picture appeared. Matthew swept
two fingers into his front pocket and came out with an elastic
band, which he snapped around his curls to free both hands.

"I'd almost forgotten the feeling of civil disobedience,"
Matthew said. "We're sneaking around someone's home. Like
spies. It's euphoric." He patted a drumbeat on the worn den-
im of his thighs. "Daily life is basically the same as any other
house, but at the same time it's completely new and unknown.
It's like we're all the same person, living basically the same life
in separate houses. You know?"

"Yes, I think so, but we need to hurry. I should have called
earlier."

"Think of a serial killer. A person that twisted might sleep
in a bed just like this one, with the exact same bedspread from
the mall. Maybe he'd have a wife next to him. That guy might
feel more content with his life than the guy who lives in this
house. Perceptions of what makes a good life are all over the
place. Someone here could feel like a complete failure or a total
success."

Dawn nodded. Matthew got how a person's past could taint
what came next, be it abusive parents, neglect, or overindulgence. It didn't matter *what*, but the *what* mattered to the future.
He always did a good job summing up situations in a way that
confirmed what Dawn subconsciously knew. Like zooming in
on an object and enlarging it for a better view.

"If I walked into this house as a kid, I would have thought
these people had it all," Matthew said. "In a way, I still do, but I
can spot all sorts of details that make this life hard."

He stepped to the bookshelf and slid out a book, turning
the title so Dawn could read it: *Surviving When They're Depressed.*
He put the book back and picked another: *Incest Impacts Families.*

Dawn, who had dusted the books every week, never once

stopped to notice what the books were about. She nodded, impressed by the discovery.

"Look what this is next to," Matthew said. He replaced the book and showed her *Fifty Shades of Grey.* "Reality versus fantasy."

"This is the perfectionist lady. The one who's afraid of fingers. Remember?"

He observed the room, tapping his fingertips together. The sudden freshness of the moment gave Dawn a sense of being lighter. The day no longer included only work and home, it encompassed creativity and imagination. She and a friend were putting their minds together. Sometimes life expanded in that way.

"Do you think she's afraid of her own fingers?" Matthew said. "Imagine being afraid of a part of you. You're forced to live with it."

"Probably not. It's like tickling. You can't tickle yourself. On you, your fingers are safe. On someone else, they're not."

"Interesting," he said. "I'll bet you're right." He lifted a glass paperweight from a stack of books and set it back down. "One of life's greatest contradictions is how you can hate something, but on you it's okay. Like conservative politicians who are against abortion, but their mistress gets one when she gets pregnant. People are such hypocrites."

Dawn turned to the underwear and bras she'd arranged on Barb Turner's bed: a pair of white cotton underwear, silk granny panties, and a frumpy bra, followed by some middle-of-the-road lingerie. Stuff like she—Dawn—would wear: silk panties with good coverage, bras with a hint of lace, but not enough to itch. She fingered a red lace bra on the bottom right side of the bed and doubted Barb had ever worn it. She wondered what had prompted her to buy it in the first place.

Dawn re-sorted the underwear into different piles. Her choice to become a maid suddenly struck her as hypocritical. She used to say she wanted to go to college and major in psychology. Everyone—friends, family, mere acquaintances—said she had a knack for analyzing and understanding people. She knew she could be a damn good therapist. Yet she hadn't gone to college. She wasn't a psychologist. She cleaned other people's houses.

She could have gone back and started again, gone to school and accomplished goals she'd set out to achieve, but she hadn't. Healing took too much time. Healing from the accident hurt so much she had to push those old interests aside.

"What about suicide?" Matthew asked. "That's got to be the most dramatic proof you can hurt yourself with your own parts."

Matthew didn't understand. You couldn't kill yourself with your own parts. There had to be extraneous tools like rope or a tailpipe spewing car exhaust or a weapon like a razor blade or a gun. You couldn't just hold your breath and wish yourself dead. Matthew stepped beside her, his presence strange and looming in this bedroom she'd only experienced in isolation.

"What do you think of these?" Dawn said.

She held up a pair of pink and white panties, thinking they might have suitable ass coverage. Truth be told, which she'd never tell Matthew, she hadn't thought through the full impact of taking her clothes off. Matthew wouldn't know this; Dawn talked a good game and always perused his portfolios with the most casual of attitudes.

"I like that they're sexy yet reserved, because they aren't too revealing. That seems to be what this lady is about, right? She pretends to be perfect despite being far from it." He took the panties from her and rubbed the fabric. "Nice. You could cup your breasts with your hands. You know, fingers stretched as wide as they go. To emphasize the fingers."

"Who's going to know she's afraid of fingers?" Dawn asked. "How would anyone tell by a picture?"

"It's not that we want them to know, D-vine. We put the fingers into focus in a way that's uncomfortable."

He scanned the lingerie on the bed and lifted another pair of panties, a red thong.

"What about this?" he asked. "Don't you think she'd convey fear if she were more at risk? So the fingers will only reinforce the discomfort she'll transmit because of some underwear that's not safe?"

"Not safe?"

"You know, out of her comfort zone," Matthew said.

Dawn nodded, imagining how the small, lacy patch might look against her thighs. For as much as she enjoyed a conversation with Matthew about deep topics—like how a person's fear might influence her choice of underwear—she sensed a kind of irony that she was getting ready to leave her own comfort zone.

"Someone who's been traumatized would feel exposed in this," Dawn said.

Matthew held the thong close to inspect the lace.

"I think we're on to something. Exposure. This feels horrible. It's awful. She'd hate it."

"What's beautiful is always like that," Dawn said. "Never practical. Never comfortable. It's that idea that if it seems too good to be true, it probably is."

"I knew we'd come up with real ideas. This is why I wanted you for my model."

Dawn warmed from Matthew's praise and tried to hold onto whatever it was that caused him to think she was interesting. It only figured that sexy underwear resided in your butt crack and rubbed like sandpaper. Perfection, for Dawn, was not worth the effort and discomfort.

"Do you want me to put on this torture garment or not? Yes? Decide."

"Yes, definitely. I'll get set up."

She swept the thong from his index finger. It seemed natural to glare at him for selecting something so skimpy. She tried, but Matthew was busy pulling back the layers of bedding and checking how the light came onto the bed through the window. He expected her to act like a model, for the sake of art.

☙

Matthew yanked the top corner of the comforter so hard the sheets came with it and the decorative pillows sailed across the bed, one landing on the floor. He stood back for the view and dove onto the bed. He thrashed about, kicking and pounding his fists until the bedcovers and sheets lost any hint of tautness from when, earlier, Dawn had stretched them over the corners of the mattress and tucked the sides.

It seemed unfair and a little cruel to watch the undoing of her hard work. The bed transformed to a mess after only a few seconds. So typical, the way people were forced to take the time to do a job right—paying attention to details, exercising patience, arguing with yourself that, yes, a little extra effort does matter—only to have everything ruined in a fraction of the time.

"Dude! Do you know how long it took me to make it that good?"

She stood with one of Barb's towels wrapped around her and couldn't help playing with the loose threads on one corner. Waiting for Matthew to set the scene took longer than she would have guessed. A pulsing numbness dulled the sensation in her face and hands, the exact same feeling she remembered before opening her mouth to give a speech in high school.

He stopped thrashing to inspect the disarray. His green T-shirt was twisted. Matthew seemed to have little awareness of his body or the clothes he wore. He generally chose some nondescript brand of jeans with a T-shirt. Depending on the weather, he pushed his arms through the sleeves of a plaid flannel. He treated the shirt like a jacket, spring, winter, and fall, even on the coldest days.

"You've got to hurry. I don't want to lose my job over this side project."

He took off the flannel and tossed it near the bedroom door. His eyes stayed on the bed, as riveted as one might be by the scary part of a movie. He paced back and forth, walking several strides forward, stopping, and taking his steps in reverse. Dawn wondered whether Matthew's flannel, now curled on the carpet, ever got washed.

Matthew was the first artist she'd ever known and it fascinated her to see him get lost in his craft. That's what he called it. Dawn envied his ability to concentrate on a project completely. She imagined his thoughts and worries dropping away as he narrowed his focus. Her mind always bounced around from topic to topic, worry to worry, conclusion to conclusion. She watched her friend and decided it didn't matter whether he washed the flannel shirt or not. He looked fine—a decent enough looking guy—and he didn't stink. What difference did it make? An artist shouldn't have to worry about tasks that required little thought, like cleaning or laundry.

"These people get home from work sometime, Matthew."

"I'm thinking, D-range."

A creak in the hallway caused her to twitch and her heart pumped faster.

"It's not going to do any good if they come home and find you here with me wearing her goddamned underwear."

"Okay, okay. On the messed-up part of the bed. Let's start there."

She dropped the towel and sat on the edge of the bed. She swung her legs around. The blunt hammer of insecurity hit her between the eyes, so she disconnected from her body. The numbness from before didn't compare to now. Paralysis crossed her mind, then losing consciousness and passing out. Neither happened so she waited. She wasn't sure she'd be able to follow directions if Matthew asked her to move.

She cleared her throat, taken aback by the stage fright. It wasn't like she cared what Matthew thought about her body. She didn't! He wouldn't come on to her anyway; she'd been clear, after their single, pitiful grief fuck a year earlier that she had no recollection of it occurring and, even if it had, it wouldn't happen again.

Why had she not thought this through? She knew why—she'd been planning to say no until her father mentioned the job in Key West.

The memory of sex with Matthew was so distant she barely

thought about it anymore. As far as Matthew knew, she didn't remember it at all. But now, with her bare ass against the smooth, clean sheets, the image of Matthew's hands tightening their grip around her thighs came to mind. The rest of it followed, even the noise he made when the physicality of it all came over her and she really started to move. He'd leaned his head against the back of the couch and moaned softly—eyes fixed on her face the whole time—in a way that made her feel appreciated, unlike Terry ever made her feel.

Matthew stepped forward and made eye contact. His face reddened and he coughed. She'd nearly forgotten about the flecks of gold in his hazel eyes. She hadn't liked the gentle curve of his shoulders beneath her hands. The soft slope of his deltoids lacked the bulk she was accustomed to with Terry. She hadn't been ready.

Dawn took a breath, though she already had lungs full of air so she exhaled loudly. It sounded like irritation. She ordered herself to be cool. Without Matthew's friendship, she had nothing.

"Well," she said, rolling her eyes. "This isn't awkward at all."

Matthew shook his head and refocused.

"Slide up a little, closer to the pillows. Let's take some this way, but I'm going to want to reposition you to capture the curve of your waist and lower back."

"Keep my elbows out of it. I don't want people seeing them."

"Don't worry about that. Photoshop can fix imperfections."

"Oh, thanks."

"None of the scars will show unless we want them to," he said.

She hoisted herself back several inches. She spread her fingers and cupped her breasts like he'd suggested before. She widened her eyes. "Like this?"

"That's not bad to start. Your hair is phenomenal. The color and texture juxtaposes the smoothness of your back."

He adjusted his camera so the lens extended for a closer

view and then retracted as though repulsed. She watched his index finger sink the silver button and heard the tinny crunch.

She concentrated on his arms and how much a person's arms could tell you about them. Matthew had fair skin and dark hair. The hair on his arms wasn't too much or too little. The muscles of his forearm gently rippled and rolled beneath his skin. *Extensor digitorum. Flexor carpi ulnaris.* Terry used to flex and point them out to her. Unlike Matthew, Terry had very little hair on his body and sharply defined muscles. He liked tanning after the gym because being in shape looked better with a tan. Matthew's T-shirt had probably been washed over a hundred times. The green had faded and the black print of Smokey the Bear had dulled to grey. The sleeves mostly hid his upper arms so she only caught the slightest edge of his *biceps brachii* against the weight of his camera. Terry used to roll up his sleeve. *Deltoid. Triceps brachii.* He wouldn't put his sleeve down until Dawn ran her fingers over the contours.

She imagined Matthew being the starting point, the shape of a man before the weights and the workouts. Terry would call Matthew a *pussy*. Somehow Dawn knew Matthew wouldn't care. Matthew lived outside his body. He focused on the world, not himself. She diverted her gaze to the photograph of Barb and Fred Turner on the dresser. She didn't want to think about what Matthew would have said about Terry.

"Look here, into the lens," Matthew said. "Like it's trying to kill you."

"Ooh, Matthew, your lens is scary."

Nonetheless, she did as he asked. She liked the idea of living outside herself. Fear shivered up the length of her spine so that, for a moment, she was able to imagine how Barb Turner might feel: anxious all the time despite having tried to create a home and family. People carried their emotional baggage around; Dawn, too, surely would if she ever got married or lived like this. She forgot about being self-conscious. Her nerves were wrought, but she let it go for a few more minutes to let Matthew work.

Matthew was, after all, the artist here.

࿎

Barb Turner's thong with its abrasive lace crept further up her butt. Sitting in stillness brought out every itch and sensation. Dawn wasn't one to wear thongs but now understood the term butt floss. It seemed impossible a person could wear one all day. Her mind drifted to desk jobs and she wondered if sitting still for eight hours ached like this. God forbid a woman chose a thong *and* an office. She tried to remain motionless as Matthew held up a hand to tell her so. He spent several minutes changing the lens on his camera and making adjustments. Dawn allowed her gaze to track a line from the camera, up his arm, across his collarbones, onto the bedroom wall, over to one of the two matching bedside tables.

Fred's alarm clock read 4:55. It was the old-fashioned digital kind that plugged into the wall. Dawn had hated the ancient appliance and its glaring red numbers ever since it went off one afternoon while she was cleaning. The blare sounded like a fire drill, an emergency that would startle the shit out of anyone. Today, the closer the numbers got to 5:00, the more certain Dawn became that it would go off again.

"Matthew!"

He peeked around the camera and raised an eyebrow.

"I practically piss the bed when I hear a car on the street," she said.

The intensity of his eyes without the lens between them made her realize how little she knew—about Matthew, about art, and who knew what else—and how much Matthew put into his work. He probably saw a different world, unique to him, that twisted and changed like the view through a kaleidoscope. He blinked as though he'd forgotten she was in the room.

"I've got a lot to do today," she said.

"Like what?" he asked good-naturedly, disappearing behind the camera as though a conversation might buy him more time.

"Don't imply your work is more important than my work."

"You're done with work for the day." He pointed and grinned as though he'd won.

"I have to call my dad about moving. And I want to go to the library to research Key West."

A twinge of guilt ran through Dawn about dropping the news like a bomb, but someone had to come home soon to fix dinner for all those kids. The room held the odd angles of afternoon sunshine.

"You do?"

He set his camera on the dresser and found the bag. He noticed his shirt on the floor, picked it up, and shoved the collar into his back pocket so it hung down his leg like an oversized bandana. Whatever concentration he'd been absorbed in was gone. He finally moved with a bustle of efficiency.

"Didn't you want to reposition me or shoot my ass?" Dawn said.

"Are you moving to Florida, D-vulge?"

She hadn't meant to tell him yet. It wasn't supposed to turn into a big deal until she'd had at least one night alone to think about it. Other people's opinions always hit hard, like snowballs pressed around a handful of stones that added to the impact. Matthew loved the idea of traveling and trying new adventures, finding yourself perched on a mountaintop or a boulder on a beach.

"I might," she said.

"Since when? Why didn't you tell me? This is huge!"

"No, it's not. I got invited. I need to decide."

"Invited by who? Your dad?"

"He offered me a job."

Matthew brought a hand to his chest and stood there looking genuinely happy for her good fortune. Dawn became painfully aware she was almost naked. She wished he'd toss her the towel. His lack of awareness of her state of undress and apparent delight over the impending move got on her nerves. A chill came over her, making her scalp prickle.

"Are you done taking my picture or what?" she said.

"I got what I needed. Your time is valuable, too, and should be respected. We should get out of here."

"Let me see how they came out."

"No way," Matthew said. He zipped the camera into the bag.

"What do you mean, no?"

She leapt from the bed and grabbed Barb's towel, tucking it around her as she hurried toward him. "Show them to me! How could you make me sit there all that time and not let me see? That doesn't sound like collaboration."

"I'm the one doing the grant application," Matthew said, skirting aside.

"You said *our* project."

"I don't want you seeing photographs you don't like. People get sensitive about how they appear to the outside world. You have to trust that I'll put you in the right light. I promise you'll have a say, just not yet."

"Next you'll tell me I don't get half the money."

"If it's about money, don't worry. You know my word is good. Don't be paranoid."

"Goddamned trailer," she said. "Isn't it always about money?"

"With ten K, you could unload the trailer. Hell, give it away. Especially if you have a job waiting."

"Such stupid decisions I've made."

Dawn sat on the edge of the bed. She regretted the words as soon as they'd left her mouth and, complicating matters, the night she'd spilled her guts about the accident was the same she claimed not to remember. A delicate balancing act, this trying to keep track of what were secrets and what were not.

Matthew tilted his head and opened his arms, offering a sympathetic hug. She didn't move. Times like this she loathed her friend for his undefined physique and insistence on being called by his full name. His eyes enraged her with their kindness.

"Well, doesn't it seem fitting I bought it with the insurance money? So, I own this big burden, this constant burden to remind me."

"D-lux. You don't need to keep the trailer. You can do anything you want. We could go backpacking in Europe. Drive out
west and find jobs. You could move to Key West. I'd miss you
like hell, though."

He hoisted the bag over his shoulder. Dawn noticed the tex-
tured imprints from his boots on the carpet.

Of course she had to keep the trailer. She'd purchased it with
Terry's life. The woman with no ring on her finger lived there
with the ring box in the closet. A cheap Christmas wreath from
the Superstore hung on the door. The space was just enough
to confine her, to keep her away from the world, or protect the
world from her. If she didn't have to go to work, she might
never leave. She found herself drawn to it in the same way a
dog is drawn to an open wound, licking and cleaning it, liking
the taste even if it inflicted pain. Each night, she went home to
it and waited for the sore to open again.

"You going to sit there all night?" Matthew asked. "Wait until the mister comes home to see if he notices the difference?"

"Go downstairs and wait for me."

Once he was gone, she stood and found her reflection in the
mirror. She'd grown heavier over the year and a half since she'd
met Matthew. Her arms, breasts, and stomach were still firm
and tight. Her thighs, hips, and ass had widened a bit, but not so
much she worried about cellulite or stretch marks. She crossed
her arms and rubbed her biceps. She recoiled a little when she
realized she'd become aroused.

"Matthew," she called, watching her reflection.

"What?" she heard him reply from downstairs.

Dawn didn't answer. They'd run out of time anyway.

"What?" he yelled.

She wondered what he'd do if she called him up.

"Want to grab drinks after this?" she said.

"Are you kidding me?"

"What's your problem?"

"You said you had to go home and call your dad."

"Oh, right. I forgot."

"You'd lose your ass if it weren't attached."

She regretted mentioning her dad and Key West, and not just because she really, really needed a drink. Matthew did not know about Mrs. Folly calling or the invitation to the prayer vigil. He had no connection to her old life. She liked it that way. He didn't need to know how close she and Mrs. Folly used to be, or how the sound of her voice had seemed to reach through the phone and pinch off her airway so it took a moment before she could breathe or speak.

Dawn folded Barb Turner's thong into a perfect square, tucking it deep inside one of the closet's built-in drawers where she'd found it. She pulled on her clothes and gave a quick 360 to be sure all the items were folded, placed, and organized. She liked being inside the secure margins of four walls. A room that small meant you were alone, in a good way, without any possibility of eyes on you or sudden noises.

A white rectangle came into focus against the black silk pocket of one of Barb Turner's robes. Dawn reached for it. She'd recognize the bright hospital logo anywhere. Only recently had her hospital statements stopped coming in the mail. She unfolded the page and read before taking a breath.

A collection of deep-rooted phobias resulting from a history of physical trauma.

Then the trauma Barb had endured, listed with bullet points like you'd see on a grocery list.

- *sexual molestation at age nine at the hand of a cousin*
- *date raped at sixteen by a boy she dated for six months*
- *excessive drug and alcohol use throughout college*
- *fear of fingers, causing panic attacks and the necessity for anti-anxiety medication*

Christ.

Dawn scanned the closet. Of course Barb must have her baggage like everyone else. Her eyes found the robe. Strange to imagine Barb in such a garment: alluring, sensual, tempting to her husband. The heartbeat beneath her fingers made her realize she'd brought a hand to her chest.

Dawn habitually flipped through the single pile of paperwork on the Turners' kitchen counter each week. She liked credit card bills that revealed outrageous purchases like the self-help kit either Barb or Fred had purchased for six monthly installments of $89.95. Dawn fed on these factoids like candy, little treats to make the day interesting and explain certain mysteries, like why she routinely found crumpled lists in the bedroom wastebasket of the top ten ways to improve your life.

This find, though. Too much information. Way too personal. To think a moment ago they'd been analyzing Barb Turner as though they had a goddamned clue. How easy it had been to make assumptions and generalizations based on surface discoveries. Hadn't that been the very worst part about being involved in the accident: that friends, teachers, classmates, random strangers passed judgment with virtually no information?

She reminded herself that she and Matthew were exploring ideas for the sake of his exhibit. Possibilities weren't the same as believing something to be true.

The paper shook in her hand. She left the closet and set it on the dresser.

She hurried to make the bed as before, pulling the sheets taut, and smoothing the pillows. Double-checking her work, she acknowledged the hassle of tucking the edges of the blanket and did it anyway. Barb and Fred deserved the clean house they paid for.

"Dawn! A van just drove up the driveway."

"Out the front, out the front," Dawn cried, rushing down the stairs for the vacuum. Matthew stepped out the front door just as the back door squeaked open. Dawn took the stairs two at a time to get back up. She pushed the prongs into the outlet and switched on the machine. Its howl filled the room. Barb's psych report fluttered on the dresser. Dawn halved it, quartered it, and shoved it into the back pocket of her jeans.

She vacuumed her way out of the closet, then the bedroom,

down the hall, and down the stairs. The machine squealed when it hit the wood floor so she yanked the cord to shut it up. In the silence, she realized she preferred the roaring white noise.

Whoever had come home remained mute. She had no idea who was there or where they were in the house. The urge to attend to Barb Turner's fake flowers came over her as strongly as a craving for a cigarette. How she wanted to go back to the family room and arrange them in the right order so Barb didn't have to worry or think about them.

Gooseflesh raised the hair on her arms. Perhaps Barb watched her this very moment, keeping quiet in order to spy on her routine. Fixing the flowers meant risking the game, like she'd be caught cheating. *That's stupid*, Dawn thought. *Barb might slide them into the correct lineup without a second thought. She might barely notice. She might not care.* Dawn rolled the vacuum into the hall closet. She hurried to gather her supplies, as if it were a race. The fear that drove through her was irrational, she knew, but fear was fear. She clattered out the front door, pulling it closed behind her, and hurried toward the car as though she were running late.

Dusk had fallen. She slid her key into the frosty lock of the trunk to store her stuff. Watchers surrounded her: Barb peeking through the living room curtains, Mrs. Folly hidden by a tree, Terry's best friend Nick Pew in the old car down the street, Terry from above. She turned the key in the ignition. A new race began: getting home before dark so she could still see the trees and trailers around hers. She had to get inside before giving anyone a chance to hide in the night.

Dawn pushed into the trailer and locked, bolted, and chained the door. She left the light off. The sight of the cheap black-and-white-checkered kitchen tile would only piss her off. She'd loved it when she picked it out. She remembered considering it urban and cool. The retro-checkered squares seemed more interesting than the pressed laminate fashioned to imitate wood planks. She knew now that the deeply discounted price was most likely because they'd been sitting on a warehouse shelf for twenty years. The sales associate probably got a free vacation for selling them after so much time, or at least a couple rounds of drinks. Despite his own bad polyester pants, he probably joked to his coworkers about her lousy taste. Like she'd known about choosing decor. She'd still never been to the city despite having lived four hours away her entire life.

She'd settled for getting her own place. At twenty-one, a trailer seemed perfect: no yard to maintain, not a lot of space to keep clean, no upstairs neighbors making a racket all night. A perfectly contained little home. No one at twenty-one knew about property value and depreciation. Dawn hadn't a clue about that, and her mother and stepfather, Davis, never gave any indication that purchasing a trailer was a losing investment. They were thrilled to see her up and around, making decisions, and, more importantly, out of their house. Her mother helped her pick out the trims and finishes. *Your very own bachelorette pad. We girls don't need a man telling us what to do. And thankfully Davis isn't like that. You don't think he is, do you? Your father, on the other hand—*

She'd wanted Dawn to choose the pink and black kitchen tiles, but the remaining box was a few short for a single-wide kitchen. Dawn didn't bother telling her mother she thought Davis was very nice, just like her father had been very nice. At least Davis held a semi-decent job and enough inherited money to take her mother to Ft. Myers every winter for two weeks.

When the sales associate informed them of the pink and black tile shortage, Dawn feigned disappointment.

Dawn's purse bumped onto the table as she sat on the hard chair in the corner. She took a moment to let her eyes adjust to the pressed white cabinet doors. Her father wasn't expecting a call from her, but she could check in. The idea of the conversation exhausted her. She sent the call anyway and heard the smooth, tranquil tone of his voicemail message. Probably for the best, as she didn't feel like shouting to be heard over the music and chatter in the bar. Her father liked to sit on the last stool and make conversation with locals, cruisers, vacationers, anyone really. He told people to visit the Hemingway house and climb the stairs of the lighthouse. Dawn hung up without leaving a message.

The floaty, adventurous aspect of a day made different by Matthew's project was gone. Talking to Matthew about the trailer left the prospect of moving away seem unattainable. Everyone would think she was running away.

She kept her eyes on the curve of the bottle on the counter, within reach, that somehow reflected light from a neighbor's place. Dawn's windows came with mini-blinds, but many residents hung old towels or children's printed sheets for privacy. Some kept the windows bare. The people in the trailer park weren't bad. It housed mostly poor families with little kids, some older people living alone, and the onsite manager, Justice. Justice liked her a little too much. But he was nice and cool to hang out with. Not tonight, though. She couldn't walk up to Justice's door and knock every time she wanted company.

By now her belongings were in focus against the grey light. Through the kitchen, the orange velour couch she'd bought resale butted against the wall of the living area. She rarely sat over there; TV didn't hold her attention, despite Justice having somehow spliced her a cable connection. Whenever she watched, she emerged from a state of daydream to find her eyes fixed on a commercial for cheap craft toys—available to purchase from an 800-number in time for the holidays. The few framed photographs on the round table in the corner were representative of the girl with the engagement ring: she and her best friend Katelyn Rice in bikinis on their senior trip to Key West; a forced pose at her mother's wedding to Davis, with Dawn hunched between them, an arm around each of their shoulders, as they sat in the banquet hall for their champagne toast. She'd pushed the picture of her and Terry at prom behind the others to keep it out of sight. Replacing the photographs with more recent shots might help, some from the summer music festival or a party at Matthew's, but the woman with the bare hand couldn't muster the friendly enthusiasm to suggest a photo op. Instead, she let moments pass by and wondered if anyone would include her in a group shot again.

She inched the chair closer to the corner so each shoulder rested against a wall. She held her breath and listened: no movement, people murmuring at a distant residence, the hum of cars on Plant Road. The typical groans and creaks of the settling trailer had become familiar. These sounds no longer caused alarm. Outside, she heard a click and froze. It could have been her car's engine cooling. It could have been the snap of a twig outside the window beneath someone's foot. She considered yelling, "I know what you're doing out there!" She didn't for fear of a response.

Light appeared in the glass pane above her door and traveled the length of the wall as a car drove by. She relaxed. Anyone outside wouldn't just stand there in full view of a passing vehicle. People in the trailer park weren't the best neighbors, but no one would tolerate a lurker. Dawn was sure of it.

She thought about peeking through the blinds and finding Mrs. Folly standing there with a single candle illuminating her face. Terry's mother had supported Dawn for a long time after the accident, but then she'd changed her mind.

I don't know what to believe anymore, Dawn, she'd said.

Another car drove by and slowed, almost to a stop. Dawn heard laughter and recognized the voice of a teenage neighbor, whose boyfriend dropped her off. If only she hadn't told Matthew she had plans. They could have gone out drinking and rehashed the success of the photography session. Later Dawn would simply have to stumble from the car to the door and pass out in bed. Those were the best nights, when she numbed her senses to the point of forgetting Mrs. Folly and the psychic she'd employed, Nick Pew ranting about how Terry wouldn't crash his motorcycle going in a straight line, or the chip in her car windshield that could have been caused by any number of projectiles, including an angry person hurling rocks. And that flat tire she'd gotten last summer—she could have hit a pothole, or perhaps someone punctured the rubber with a pocketknife or nail.

Knowing anything for sure was impossible, whether the box she'd left on the kitchen table had moved to the counter or if her toothbrush had gone from blue to green. Hadn't it been blue? Leaving the lights off helped keep those worries away. With or without Matthew, she knew what to do.

Eventually she uncrossed her legs, unfolded her hands from her lap, and reached for the Evan Williams. She leaned for a juice glass from the cabinet and set it on the table with a click. She tried to let all the thoughts from the day drain out of her mind in the same manner the swirl of soapy water drained from the Jacuzzi tub in the Turners' master bathroom. She liked the way the drain slurped the water and wished she possessed another chamber or force of will to suck the memories from her brain to a resting place that—dirty, clean, foul or fresh—no one, including her, could see or remember after they passed through the grate. Whatever thoughts she managed to force down always bubbled back into view, usually bringing with them remnants of other garbage she hadn't expected or wanted to see again.

She uncapped the Williams and poured her own version of Liquid Drano. She filled her mouth with the strong disinfectant, held it on her tongue long enough to feel the burn, and forced it down the drain to do its magic on whatever needed cleaning. She remembered Barb's psych report in her back pocket. She unfolded it on the kitchen table, but it was too dark to read. Dissecting someone else's problems would wait, as would worrying about how she could have been stupid enough to forget to put the paper back where she'd found it. After four slow and calculated swallows, she filled the glass a second time, sat back in the chair, and waited.

Another good part about cleaning other people's houses was you didn't have to worry about anyone noticing you were late. Or hungover.

TUESDAY: AUTOFOCUS

ONCE YOU FIND THE TROUBLE SPOTS,
START THERE.

Dawn pushed the second key on her ring into the brass dead-bolt and paused. She closed her eyes and held her breath as her stomach clenched against whatever whiskey remained in its lining. Her frontal lobe pulsed against her skull like the knock of a lazy and uncommitted intruder. She'd never drink the rank and rusty tap water at the trailer so she waited until she got to work. Thirst worked as a motivator.

At least Tuesday meant the McIntyres. They had countless options for rehydration, like the water and ice dispenser on the freezer door, a filtered tap built into the kitchen faucet (over-looking the pool, no less), and plenty of other choices. The wet bar outside the kitchen had an ice machine. Dawn marveled at these luxuries: ice cubes you didn't have to crack from plastic trays; a cold stream from the refrigerator door *or* the tap by the sink; the fully-stocked basement refrigerator, lined with bottles of beer, sodas in diet and regular, sparkling water, exotic juices, refreshments she never knew existed. Robert McIntyre offered them up in the nonchalant manner of the moneyed.

She leaned against the mahogany door and stayed there when she realized the warmth against her cheek from the rare December sunshine. She knew Robert McIntyre would be inside. His smiling and small talk made her want to yank one of the antique golf clubs from the bag in the family room and drive it through his teeth. People with the habit of smiling through each and every conversation were the ones whose smiles meant the least. The insincerity of it couldn't be more obvious, like talking about the chill in the air warranted the same expression as discussing the wretchedness of the latest mass shooting.

Dawn wiggled the key for a few seconds to give him time to remember. Some of the heat from the door absorbed into her pant leg and sleeve, and she wondered whether the sun was shining in Key West. Probably it was. Keeping her eyes closed, she found the will to push into the house.

"Hello?" she sang. "Anybody home?"

She never did this at her other customers', but it seemed safe to pretend this entrance was standard practice, this closing of the eyes and calling out to ensure everyone's privacy. After all, who was the intruder here? She wouldn't put it past Robert to call the police. He seemed like the type to get annoyed if you mistakenly walked in like you owned the place. Nothing like a breaking-and-entering charge to keep a person in line.

He sat in his usual spot on the couch with his coffee mug. He squinted toward the television, elbows propped on his knees, watching the conservative news channel on the flat screen.

No plaid for Robert today, but the color of his pants bordered somewhere between red and pink. He'd say red. She'd say pink. Gay people didn't dress as gay as Robert McIntyre, not even Matthew's painter friend José who wore women's silk blouses that revealed his waxed chest. Robert's closet was full of colors, like little girl's dresses on Easter. Today his button-down was undeniably pink, complete with a tie that somehow pulled all the red and pink together. He wore a tweed sports coat that reminded her of a college professor—a gay one—with a pipe. He sat back and regarded her across the room, massaging his leather-patched elbows.

"Oh," he said.

She waited.

"Don. Good morning, Don. Is it Tuesday again already?"

"Time flies when we're having fun," she said.

He raised an eyebrow as though he'd never thought about it that way. Her whole life, one of her biggest pet peeves was people not fully pronouncing her name. It figured a jagoff like Robert wouldn't differentiate between *Don* and *Dawn*.

"We are having fun, aren't we?" he said.

He scrutinized her over his glasses. His brain practically rattled in its search to put her in her place. She smiled with clenched teeth, set her supplies in the hallway, and headed to the bar to fill her water bottle. She passed the library with its collection of stuffed animals: a large lion spread on its belly in the corner of the room, an equally sizable cheetah in the other corner, and a beaver with a leather tail that perfectly matched the couch. Because sometimes the wealthy needed to get their safari on.

"I love this ice machine," she said. "Best invention since sliced bread. Wish I had one at my place."

"I can get you the name and number for the manufacturer if you'd like."

Dawn tugged the door and plunged the scoop into the opaque cubes. She avoided Robert's eyes because after he said stuff like that, he had a tendency to stare, as though accusing you of giving him a chore. Like you couldn't compliment someone on his ice machine without having a secondary motivation of getting one yourself, forcing him to do a bunch of legwork or at least a search around for the owner's manual. She rattled the ice as she filled her tumbler. She rotated the tap and brought the ice under the water so it crackled and popped.

"There's filtered," he said.

"Tap is fine. Big plans for the day?"

"Work. First priority as always."

"Amen to that," Dawn said, taking a long drink that cooled as it flowed through the moon-shaped opening. She forced herself to stop before a brain freeze. "Where is Hilary this week? Asia? Europe?"

He blinked.

"Mexico."

"Oh, Mexico," Dawn said. "I almost went there on my honeymoon."

Her voice caught, but he hadn't noticed. She went to her supplies in the hallway. She began unwinding the ball of twine. Robert McIntyre caused her to make the stupidest admissions. He was the worst kind of person to tell details of your life.

"Mexico?" he said, as if she'd suggested the garbage dump. "Oh no. Where did you get that idea?"

"What's wrong with Mexico?" She stood taller and the artificial sweetness drained from her voice. "I've heard Mexico to
be very nice indeed."

She reached for the handle of the mop to steady herself,
knowing how idiotic she sounded. What, was she British now?

"It's commercial, not romantic." He beamed as though the
conversation were perfectly pleasant. "Peddlers selling junk to
tourists. Not intimate or appropriate for a newly married couple. Let's see. Where's a better place? I'd say the British Virgin
Islands. Or the south of France."

"Thanks for the tip."

Turning her back to his smugness, she leaned over so that he
couldn't miss her ass, small waist, and the swirls of color coming off the tattoo on her lower back—her kaleidoscope, which
she got in honor of Terry to reflect on the past in a happier way.

Like Robert McIntyre knew about intimacy.

And, anyway, Dawn and Terry had had a long list of reasons
for wanting to go to Mexico for their honeymoon. First, it was
rated a top honeymoon spot in the travel catalog. The dance
clubs were popular and the bars had themes, like one had a water slide and bartenders who walked around and poured shots
directly into your mouth. She hadn't envisioned their honeymoon to be a week of partying, but Terry had a point: think of
how many free shots they might get.

Dawn remembered the mirrored glass of the infinity pool
from one of the resort websites. The photograph was so clear it
seemed like touching the screen would dampen your fingertips.
Part of the honeymoon package was you got your own pool
on your own private balcony. She had pictured her and Terry
making love in the water, not fucking or going at it like normal,
but loving each other with eye contact and slow hands and long,
wet kisses. What could be more intimate than that? She and
Terry would have been thrilled for a place to have sex without
one of their parents walking in.

Her fingers found the jug of Magic and she imagined dous-
ing Robert, one giant squeeze to release the lump in her throat.

"I best get to work," Robert said. "Let you get started here." He lifted his mug and pressed it between his palms.

Dawn aimed and spouted a circle around the table. It was already clean. Every house had its trouble spots. At the McIntyres', she washed dishes and did laundry. The rest of the place was easy. She sensed Robert's gaze on her as she dropped to her knees, pulled some paper towels off the roll, and the magical scent of citrus filled the room.

"Hilary says you're the best we've ever had."

He checked the view of Bird Lake out the windows across the room.

"I think it's important to do the best you can. What do you do again, Robert?"

He cleared his throat and returned his watery green eyes, ponds full of scum, to her face.

"I'm an attorney. Harvard Law."

"Aren't they expecting you in court?"

"Mostly consulting these days."

He stared into his cup. Robert's longish fingernails ranged halfway between men's and women's fingernails. She assumed it was a status symbol, some European trend. It irritated Dawn they never seemed to have a spec of dirt beneath them. Finally, he set the cup back on the table and brushed his pants. He walked out the front door, jingling the keys in his pocket.

"Nice chatting as always, Don. Have a terrific day." He pulled the door closed.

"Always," she said to the empty air. "You have a lovely day now."

Once she heard his car start and glimpsed the edge of the Mercedes roll up the driveway, she sat on the couch and sighed. She leaned forward and sniffed the coffee, detecting whiskey and not a little.

"Jesus!" She wiped her nose with the length of her arm. "Stupid drunk."

She carried the mug into the kitchen and threw the remaining beverage into the white sink with a splat that left brown streaks seeping toward the drain. She returned to the living room and dropped the jug of Magic back into her bucket. She collected her cleaning stuff and went out the front door. After locking it, she paused for thirty seconds and came back inside.

"Hello?" she yelled. "Anyone home?"

She paused again, thankful for the stillness.

She kicked the door closed, unloaded her supplies properly, retied the paper towels, and started over.

The cool descent to the McIntyres' basement always surprised her with its sharp smells of leather and felt. The brightly colored paintings on the wall and sophisticated collection of toys for the adult hobbyist lightened up the place. Something resembling a pool table with bumpers and knobs stood in the middle of the room, atop an enormous rug swirled with burgundy, blues, and gold. An old-fashioned slot machine sat on a wooden stand carved like the trunk of a tree, which Dawn found stupid since it had started as a tree trunk to begin with. Next to the machine's chrome handle sat a bowlful of quarters. A cribbage board, some type of marble game, and a contraption with a metal ball and scissor-like arms lined the coffee table.

Dawn had tried all the games, finding the metal ball challenge so infuriating she wasted an hour once opening and closing the arms with a surgeon's precision. These ritzy activities released a competitive streak she hadn't known existed. She'd never cared about winning when she used to play Monopoly with the Follys every Sunday afternoon despite their arguing about property trades and whether to up the pass-go amount to make the stakes more interesting. When she and Katelyn Rice used to hit tennis balls at the park, they worked together to see how many times they could get the ball back and forth over the net. Dawn didn't care about playing to win. But at the McIntyres', she gripped the smooth ivory ball of the bumper game and, without knowing the rules, shot it across the table so hard it bounced over the edge and rolled into the laundry room.

She'd used a hanger to extract it from the space between the washing machine and the wall, remembering all those times she'd told Terry, *Calm down, it's just a game,* when his cheeks burned red after his father inevitably taunted him and walked his Monopoly boot to victory. She'd dusted the ivory ball with one of Robert's dirty T-shirts below the laundry chute.

Laundry wasn't normally part of the deal for a maid, at least not according to the websites on how to start a home cleaning business. When she'd interviewed, Hilary called the position *housekeeper,* which to Dawn sounded more like a full-time obligation, possibly live-in. It turned out Hilary wanted a weekly cleaning lady who'd do laundry.

"What is your rate?" Hilary had asked.

"A hundred seventy-five a week," Dawn said, having already figured out how much to say. She knew it would be cheap by the McIntyres' standards. Ever since her mother pointed out a woman at the mall buying a $400 pair of shoes in every color, she'd trained herself to remember that large sums were not large to rich people. Hell, she was offering to clean this woman's house for the fraction of the cost of a single pair of shoes. But Dawn hadn't accounted for the laundry. She took a breath and added, "Plus laundering."

"Plus laundering?"

"Yes. Thirty a week for laundering, which could be adjusted based on the amount of laundry."

Hilary laughed. Unlike Robert, she did so with a stoic face. She gave a small wave of her hand. The rock could blind a person. Dawn could've kicked herself for not saying sixty.

"The two hundred range would be perfectly agreeable."

"Great," Dawn said. "I have Tuesdays open."

"Please know that we've pressed charges against hired help in the past who took it upon themselves to take our belongings. Not that you don't seem like an honest woman. I tell people upfront."

"Of course. I'd be proud to clean a home as lovely as this. I would never mess it up."

Dawn stood and smoothed the front of the one skirt she owned, relieved she hadn't said the cheesy line about a lovely home until after Hilary gave her the job. It sounded insincere and fake, like she'd say bullshit to get a job. Now she had to show Hilary and Robert McIntyre what she could do with a bottle of Magic and a roll of paper towels.

The laundry hadn't turned out to be a big deal. To be honest, there usually wasn't much. Sometimes she liked the routine of hugging an armful of hot dress shirts, pushing a hanger inside each and smoothing them before flattening them with the McIntyres' fancy iron. Robert's pressed easily because they cost four hundred dollars apiece and, somehow, that high a thread count did what it should.

Not today, though. The idea of sorting, washing, folding, and ironing made her head ache worse than it already did. Every good housekeeper had a plan B.

Dawn stepped onto the tiled floor of the laundry room and slid a garbage bag from the box on the counter. It billowed like a parachute when she shook it open. She began dividing the heap of dirty clothes beneath the laundry chute. Whites in one. Colors in another. Towels in the third. Delicates in the fourth. The delicates at the McIntyres' consisted of beige granny panties—silk of course—white full-length nightgowns and bras the size of bowling balls. Robert wore white cotton boxer shorts.

Pompous jerk. She dumped each basket into the garbage bag. He didn't give her the satisfaction of skid marks to mock. She lugged the load out to her car, hurled it into her trunk, and locked it inside like a dead body. She lit a cigarette and headed to the same-day laundry place.

Dawn waved on a battered minivan at the four-way stop. Little kids bounced around inside the vehicle. The mom drove past without eye contact or a wave. Through the dirty windshield, Dawn spotted the layer of dust on the dashboard. Barb Turner drifted to her mind. Dawn pulled smoke into her lungs. Of course takers of pills and sufferers of random phobias gave birth to children and hired maids. You never knew what a person had endured in the past, Dawn reminded herself, like the popular girl in high school who cried about her parent's divorce every time she got drunk, or Matthew, who only shrugged when asked about the cigarette burn on his forearm and explained his mother had bad taste in boyfriends when he was a kid.

Taking just three people—Barb, Matthew, and herself—she could list some of the most tragic circumstances people could face. Like rape. Like child abuse. Like your fiancé dying. None of the three of them acted any different than anybody else. It wasn't like someone would walk up to Matthew and say, *Hey, man, I can see you've been through some serious child abuse and I'm sorry.*

Dawn wondered whether she'd have let Matthew talk her into posing in Barb Turner's red thong if she'd read the psych report before the shoot. It might have been nice to stay away from the whole fear-of-fingers problem. Matthew would have wanted to push the boundaries and take risks, she knew that for sure, but how quickly they'd abandoned cleaning and focused on the one weird problem Dawn knew of.

For Matthew, pushing the boundaries meant going deep. He would have wanted to stick with the finger fear because it undoubtedly had to do with Barb's history, be it the molestation by her uncle or the date rape. Not because Matthew was mean or making fun. Matthew didn't do that. In pain, Matthew found art. His talent was rooted in the exploration of his subject—or object—for whatever it was that exposed a pulse of pain or a twinge of sadness or, sometimes, an ache so strong you had to look away

Wasn't that the point of the project? Of course it was, she told herself. Today he'd identify something at the McIntyres' and build upon it to tell a story. Who knew what he'd see in their expansive home. His project wasn't about mockery. It was about finding beauty in difficulty, whatever form it took. Maybe the reason Dawn kept reassuring herself it was art was because, in truth, it hurt to be exposed. Reading more of Barb's story on the doctor's note wasn't salacious. It sucked. Matthew had managed to capture some of the sorrow.

She relaxed at the realization that Matthew's focus was on her customers, not on her. Imagine what Matthew would come up with if he'd asked to photograph Dawn in her trailer. Or someone like Mrs. Folly in her home with all those photographs of her lost son. The dude was so fucking perceptive it scared her. Let him study the Turners and McIntyres, anyone but her.

She shook her head and took one last hit of the cigarette before flicking the butt out the window. It threw a little shower of sparks onto the pavement as she watched it roll to the gutter through the rearview mirror. The road behind was clear except for one car, a blue SUV, at least a quarter-mile in the distance. Not a vehicle she recognized. She doubted she'd ever stop paying attention. Karma happened the minute you let your guard down. Whether that meant a police officer with a warrant or being rammed by a pickup filled with Terry's coworkers from the Superstore, she didn't know. All that seemed certain was more punishment.

She remembered her father's comment about not letting Mrs. Folly manipulate her. Dawn wondered: what were the chances Mrs. Folly would invite her to a prayer vigil as punishment? A setup of some kind. A setup for what? They'd crashed. Dawn had gotten hurt too. It wasn't like the woman could stage an intervention with all their friends and bully Dawn to admit to something she hadn't done. But how did Dawn know? Mrs. Folly may have spent the last year becoming more convinced of this theory or that, or growing more despondent now that her son was gone. She may have completely gone off the rails. The possibility existed that she wanted to remind Dawn who was to blame.

Or, it could be that she wanted Dawn to know she forgave her.

Forgiveness—of course it mattered. Anyone who said otherwise was full of shit. The most innocent person could feel guilty by the mere suggestion someone believed they were.

She parked in the lot across the street from the laundry place. The guy stood behind the counter. Thank God. His head was tilted forward so the bald patch gleamed through the thin hair on the crown of his head. Perhaps he didn't have a decent phone and always read a newspaper—like an old guy except he wasn't. It seemed likely he'd someday be an old guy, still working there, still with his paper. He'd have the same job his whole life, only he'd get balder and fatter. The guy made laundry a simpler task for Dawn, unlike the older lady, who acted like Dawn had brought too much for a one-day job. Arguing with her got tiring, especially since the place was never crowded. Plus, the sign said same day, for God's sake.

"Ha ha," said the guy, when she walked in. "Back so soon?"

He folded his newspaper and hoisted himself from the plastic chair. He tossed the paper on the counter. Sports section. The guy had told her he played hockey in high school and graduated five years before Dawn.

"Oh, shut it. I'm tired and there's a lot."

He eyed the clock on the wall, shrugging as though trying to straighten his T-shirt. He sucked in his belly so his chest lifted. At least he seemed to remember how to tell time, which Dawn swore would be obsolete soon. She and Terry had agreed—telling time and cursive writing were both practically useless skills now that everyone used electronics.

"Have it for you at two," the guy said, placing his hands on the counter and leaning toward her. His knuckles were fat with deep creases. He jerked his chin, as if he were asking her to lift her gaze to meet his. His teeth were far more interesting, crooked and stained, so she stopped there.

"Two at the very latest. I'm having company."

"Company at *their* house?"

"So?"

"Getting it on with some guy? You're a piece of work."

Dawn didn't mind the teasing. She gave the guy props for having the imagination to wonder out loud whose laundry she was always doing. The bowling ball bras were sign enough they weren't her clothes. He'd concluded that a maid willing to subcontract her labor had zero morals or integrity of any kind.

"I'm not that cliché. Give me a little credit."

"You don't seem all that credible."

She laughed. The guy seemed clever enough for college. She always noticed the people who were stuck in menial jobs. He must have no money or some other decent reason for not going.

"So. You're dating again?" he said.

The question caught her with a jolt. "I don't date," she said.

"You going to the reunion at the bar? Doesn't matter what year you were. They have it every Christmas when people are in town."

Her hands trembled so she slid them into the back pockets of her jeans.

"You remember Gene O'Toole? He always goes. The dude's hilarious. He makes it fun. And Jackson Park, you know him?"

Dawn hadn't known the guy knew about her. He obviously knew a lot. Dating again. Terry Folly's fiancé. *She doesn't seem like she got all that hurt.* The tremors moved to her arms so she clasped each forearm tightly, careful to avoid the grafts. If the guy knew the Follys, he'd tell Terry's mom Dawn had been in. *She never does the laundry like she's supposed to. She thinks it's funny.* Mrs. Folly would nod, once again convinced the Dawn she'd known and loved deceived her in the worst way.

Dawn shook her head—no—and pretended to read a flyer on the corkboard mounted to the wall. She shifted weight from foot to foot until the letters came into focus. *Estate sale.* She waited for the shaking to stop, but it didn't. She deserved this, or her body wouldn't respond this way.

"I'm going to get a coffee," she said.

She pushed through the door to head to the café at the other end of the plaza. She wanted to ask his name but didn't. Not knowing seemed better.

"Whatever you say, Molly Maid."

"Oh, please," she said, but lifted her hip anyway to show him a little ass. She didn't know why. "Go easy on the tags too. I have to take them all off. See you later."

She heard him laugh as the door eased itself closed behind

her. Her head began to pound so she hurried to get there. She wanted Katelyn, who would have joked to distract her or at least said what a loser the guy had become.

Dawn had never been so aware of herself—the cleaning lady on a coffee run, after being called out by the loser in the laundromat—whose head ached with the shame of her existence, at this cheesy indoor strip mall that smelled like melted snow. Unlike Matthew, she didn't have a legitimate reason, like art, to explain her behavior. She quickened her pace, away from the guy who knew her, toward anonymity. She preferred being a nameless, faceless human.

At least the same-day laundry place came with an accompanying mocha to ease the hangover, or whatever else.

Professional decorators had done over the first floor of the McIntyre home, but upstairs channeled the 1950s with shaggy carpeting and tweedy wallpaper with embroidered gold hexagons. To prepare unsuspecting visitors for the shift in décor, Hilary and Robert never removed the automated chair lift that hugged the curved stairway, dating from the time when Hilary's mother needed wheelchair transportation. Its metal track had lost its luster. Its ancient design and switches gave the foyer the feel of a mental institution.

Dawn sat on the plastic seat with her bucket in her lap and flipped the switch. She clutched the padded handles and watched the front door grow smaller. Perhaps Mother McIntyre had experienced the same sensation she might fall to her death, caused by the grinding motor and rocky ride. The lift bumped at the top and shuddered.

She grasped the railing to stand. Matthew would want to try the chair. He might take her photograph on it. She laughed at the idea of herself in one of Hilary's ghostly nightgowns with its high neckline. Her ankles and feet would show since she towered over Hilary. The cinched elastic sleeves would hug her forearms instead of her wrists. She'd suggest it to Matthew.

Dawn set her bucket on the floor of the master bedroom and moved the jewelry box, coin dish, and wood sculpture to the corner. She fired a stream of Magic across the top of the dresser and wiped. She sized up the coins. Mostly silver. Probably a couple bucks. She'd considered taking change or, better, adding change to confuse them. Or, she could replace quarters with fifty-cent pieces. She'd decided against it since both Hilary and Robert probably contributed and each would assume the other did it. Plus, Dawn didn't exactly have money to throw around.

She sat on the floor and wiped the sculpture, a fat Buddha whittled from chestnut or cherry, sanded, and finished to a shine. A little Magic made it gleam like it had been coated with shellac. She cradled it on her lap to dry and wondered how much they'd paid for it. Probably hundreds, if not thousands. Dawn wasn't inclined to steal but she'd be lying if she hadn't considered how taking one or two trinkets from the McIntyres' could change her whole life.

She pictured herself and Matthew shopping the McIntyres' house like one of those fancy museum gift shops. There were endless items—from jewelry to art to crystal vases—Matthew might like to give to Jen for bonus points. Or they could head to the pawnshop for cash. Anyone, including Matthew, would enjoy the possibilities of how to spend a bunch of money. Human nature.

Luckily, she trusted him to not help himself to her customer's riches, at least not without debate. Matthew was the type of friend who left an IOU for taking one of your cigarettes when you left your pack at his apartment. He insisted on splitting all bills down the middle even if he knew you ordered more expensive drinks or dessert. With the exception of art supplies, he always chose the least expensive products to buy. She could see him deciding to take the least expensive of the McIntyres' stuff to prove he wasn't greedy.

White lines of delicate foam had formed along the outline of the Buddha's eyes. Dawn used a paper towel to dry them.

She dried between the carved drapes of his robe and wondered if the person to steal him would be enlightened by the peace and mental clarity he represented. Surely one of the benefits of having a valuable piece of art included the spiritual riches. Imagine being handed all the answers, as if Dawn were presented with an objective view from above of exactly how the accident transpired without the memory of connecting with the Earth in such a way she almost blended with it. Or without imagining whether Terry was pleased or annoyed in the seconds before the motorcycle went over.

She polished the curves of the Buddha's knees and wished the artist opted to reveal his bare toes instead of cloaking them. What if enlightenment included foreseeing the future? Take moving, for example. Chances were, the same problems would follow her wherever she went. Or, being enlightened might show she wasn't meant to leave New York, she was meant to stay and face her problems.

She'd imagined moving to Key West almost every day since the accident, sometimes before it. Wasn't half the dream tied up in the simple fact it was a dream? To get away. To begin again. That's what her father had done, started over, even if Dawn's mother called it running away from his responsibilities. Her father got that fresh start everyone always talked about.

Plus the climate. Those glorious mental pictures of the ocean waves crashing against the rocks as the sun set. Hadn't she yearned for them? She had. Even now, knowing her trailer sat on the frozen ground a few miles away, and her mother sat at her kitchen table drinking beer and playing solitaire a few miles from that, and Terry's mother sat on the edge of his childhood bed a few miles from that; Dawn longed for the smell of sea salt and the beat of a steel drum. Surely the bright flags catching the ocean breeze and open-air T-shirt displays would inspire her to climb out of bed every day, take a shower, and head to work with a purpose.

She set the Buddha on the carpet and watched the rest of the Magic evaporate. Even the guy from the laundromat knew who she was. Wasn't that another reason to move to Key West to get away? Yet the excuses piled up like roadblocks: the trailer, her business. What would Mrs. Folly think? What would her mother think? She would warn Dawn about her father's "non-existent" parenting style. Everyone would assume she was running away. Plus she had zero savings, probably not even enough for the tune-up and gas to get there.

Fuck enlightenment. Somehow knowing she could go—had a reason to go—took away the dream-like quality, the hope, and wonderment, and left her certain she couldn't. She'd fuck it up just like always.

Dawn replaced the Buddha on the dresser and moved to the bedside table. Outside, the cold waves lapped against the dock. The sailboat nodded in confirmation that, yes, owning a sailboat gave Robert McIntyre the upper hand. At the very least, money gave you the ability to spread your mess more broadly—out onto the lake and across your acreage—instead of being restricted to a small space like a mobile home. The lake spread into the distance, long and narrow, surrounded by bare trees and brick houses with shutters, waterfront porches and pontoon boats, raised and covered. The water glittered. Who wouldn't kill for a view like that?

Robert probably farted, scratched his balls, and headed to the bathroom without even noticing.

Dawn's foot landed squarely on the photograph and pressed it into the carpet with a muffled crunch. She picked it up and flipped the crumpled 5x7. In the photo, a flat-chested, naked woman lay on a bed with her leg dangling over the edge. A Great Dane lapped at her crotch. Behind the dog stood a man, also naked, pressed against the dog's backside. He wasn't having sex with the dog; his erect penis stood taller than the animal.

"Oh, Robert," Dawn said.

She set it on the edge of the bed and pressed her fists under her chin. She leaned in for a closer inspection.

The woman was middle-aged and ugly, with short hair and loose skin. The man was tall and overweight. Love handles. Ri-

diculous hair: bald on the top and a ponytail in back. At least
the Great Dane's shining coat photographed well.

Had Robert dropped this on purpose for her to find?

A wave of ick ran through her. If the guy thought she was
into it, well…gross! She laughed uncontrollably, her reaction
when dumbstruck. She and Katelyn would be in hysterics about
now. She stopped laughing as abruptly as she'd started. Perhaps Robert thought she had hit on him. Their conversations,
exchanged over smiles, always bordered on hostility. He could
have construed it as mean flirting in preparation for a hate fuck.
People hate fucked all the time. Even people who liked each
other hate fucked once and a while.

Dawn dusted the bedside table on autopilot. She'd seen porn,
of course, because she searched for free videos when she got
off with her pipe dream. She'd seen stuff with lesbians, men,
fetishes, brutality. Never, though, had she noticed subheads for
bestiality or animals or people who like dogs, but not how you'd
expect. Sometimes there were news stories about men being
arrested for having sex with farm animals. Dawn doubted these
men lived in houses like Robert McIntyre's.

No way the photo belonged to Hilary.

He might have left the photo on purpose.

She flipped it over and left it. Robert, the house, the perfectly fitted floral bedspread, the lamps with the old-fashioned
key switches suddenly seemed sinister. Dawn backed against
the window frame, half expecting Robert to walk through the
door. She verified no one was peeking around a corner or from
a closet. Video cameras in the room seemed unlikely, as the
ceiling and walls were smooth and unflawed. Décor was sparse
without large or hollow items to hold a cleaning-lady cam. Then
again, cameras could be small. She picked up the Buddha and
inspected it.

She considered sliding the photo underneath Hilary's pillow
or hiding it inside one of her drawers. She'd get Matthew's
opinion on what to do.

Come over at 3, she texted.

Whatever she and Matthew thought up, it had to be good. Robert had to be the fool, even if she and Matthew were the only ones to know. She felt a little guilty about the shoot at Barb Turner's, but this guy had it coming.

Dawn double-checked that Robert's Mercedes wasn't coming up the drive when she left to pick up the laundry. She pivoted on her heel to be sure the garage was closed and he hadn't secretly come home. The idea of his murky eyes and smooth fingernails filled her with rage. It figured someone so rich would be a complete shit. She knew: if she had a house with a pool next to a lake and a spouse who earned a lot of money, she'd never risk it. Ever.

She took the curve of the driveway too fast and squeezed the steering wheel with both hands. Her old sedan lurched to the side and creaked as though the shell might slide off the undercarriage.

You can't trust men, her mother said. *Any man. Except Davis, of course; he's in a category of his own.*

Whether having money resulted in someone being more or less trustworthy, Dawn had no idea. Davis had no problem moving into her mother's two-bedroom bungalow with a tiny patch of yard. No garage, just a carport. Old kitchen cupboards and an ancient china hutch crammed into the dining room. You couldn't open the glass doors to dust inside. Mice resided in the basement storage room and left droppings on the concrete. She doubted Davis lived anywhere better before living there.

But at least their house inhabited decent people. Her mother might not be the most agreeable woman, but she'd never belittle someone else for having less. Davis tended to drone on about how much he enjoyed popping the cap from an old-fashioned bottle of Coke, but he didn't criticize anyone for going to Mexico. He probably wouldn't criticize Dawn's father for fleeing, as the flip-flop lifestyle had made him so much happier.

Imagine, Dawn thought, just imagine what Robert would

have thought if he saw Terry. Or her trailer. Somehow, he made
you hate what you had when you wanted it. He made you want
things you didn't. Like now she—Dawn—drove in a fury because she couldn't go to Mexico with her dead fiancé or afford
to live in Robert's creepy house.

Her mind drifted to the dangerous place where she envisioned a life with Terry: she and Terry by the McIntyres' pool in
chairs side by side, connected by intertwined fingers. Icy drinks
dripping onto the cement. Wedding rings touching. She and
Terry hadn't set a date, but they'd be married by now. Definitely.
They'd invite friends over to enjoy the pool. Katelyn and Nick,
because, of course, her best friend and Terry's best friend were
a couple too. They'd take a cooler of beer and go sailing on Bird
Lake. Terry liked adventure and he liked a good tan. She could
practically see him walking down the dock in his yellow shorts,
brown skin glistening, broad shoulders, muscular arms.

Dawn didn't know if she would have been able to trust him
if they had such a life. Even if they didn't.

The heaviness of Terry's loss filled her arms and legs, returning as before with the same sick feeling in her stomach
and pinch near her right scapula. The trailer, it connected them,
and served as a continual reminder, but she'd swore the grief
had become at least more controlled. She'd thought so anyway.
Until Mrs. Folly had called.

Dawn, you kept your number. How is your life?

And then her dad. He was the only person who openly spoke
about blame and how Dawn—as the only person who could be
blamed—had been questioned by the police four times, twice
at the station. Because a road accident had to be more than just
an accident, or, if it was just an accident, had to be discussed in
detail until someone figured out what could have prevented it.
Nick said it to her face, a suggestion more than an accusation,
but still. Dawn didn't care who you were; that shit stuck with a
person. How could it not?

Touching that kimono yesterday had been a bad idea. She
should have known better than to get carried away thinking she

might have had a life like Barb Turner with a walk-in closet and a bedroom with children's photographs on the dresser. All she'd wanted was to feel the luxury around her neck for a moment to see what it might be like to be married and live in a house with lingerie in the closet.

"Stop it!" she said, pumping the brake in the lot across from the laundry.

She clenched two fistfuls of hair and pulled until her eyes watered; she untangled her fingers and crossed her arms to pinch each elbow until she couldn't take it. Pain made it real. She blinked tears onto the steering wheel. It took a while before she could breathe again. When the shocks stopped firing down her forearms and the tears settled somewhere unseen, she switched off the ignition to get the McIntyres' clothes.

Thank God the older lady sat behind the counter instead of the guy.

☙

Matthew stepped into the McIntyres' house from the patio door.

"You're never going to believe what I found," Dawn said.

"What else could it be besides porn? Except bondage restraints or torture chambers, which is just another form of porn."

Dawn closed the door, shaking her head. It figured he got it right on the first guess, as though she might somehow be more in tune with the porn underworld than Matthew. He gave her a long once-over, the kind when a person realized your eyes were red or your cheeks were puffy. She raised her eyebrows, a warning to say nothing.

He pulled a wrinkled joint from the front pocket of his jeans and sniffed it slowly as one might an expensive cigar. Dawn opened the door, ignoring the blast of winter wind. She followed him outside to the bench beyond the pool, facing the lake. She lit a cigarette and closed her eyes. Matthew knew, somehow he always knew when she needed to relax. Dawn had never been one to smoke pot in high school. But the circumstances—and the friend—had changed and it was simply the right vehicle right now. Maybe Matthew was the exact person to smoke with; she wanted to believe their friendship was not fragile.

He leaned toward the lake and lit it with his chin jutted forward. Dawn loved the smell of the burning drugs against the cold. Pot equated warmth. It reminded her of cocoa with a spicy cinnamon stick. Or the smell of a campfire on a brisk morning. Matthew offered the joint, which she took with the other hand. Between the neat, ashy burn through the filter of the cigarette and the effortless torch of the joint, she believed together they offered fortification of some kind.

"Where would you want to go for a weekend trip?" Matthew said.

"Are we going somewhere?"

She passed the joint back. His hands were splattered with red and green paint. The green, especially, stained the skin around his fingernails. He'd been experimenting with mixed media, which meant he often showed up covered in newspaper smudges, colored threads, or dirt.

"No. Like if I were going to take Jen somewhere."

Dawn pressed her palms to her knees. Her fingers were long, her fingernails small and dainty. Taking care of them was pointless, but she kind of liked how they reflected hard labor. Her cuticles were endlessly dry and she'd gashed her left pinky on the faucet in the Turners' spare bathroom so a scab covered the side of her knuckle. Still, her hands were one of the prettiest parts about her. Not that she was ugly, but people were more likely to describe her as striking or smoking.

"How should I know? I could say go skiing in Vermont and she might not like to ski."

Matthew reclined with elbows hooked over the back of the bench. Green paint had splattered in his hair, elfin raindrops, and she envisioned him slapping a canvas with a paintbrush. He leaned to meet the joint in the middle so he didn't have to unhook his arm. He closed his eyes to take a drag. With his legs extended, he resembled a mountain man in his boots and flannel. Sometimes she forgot he was six feet tall. He kept his eyes closed for a moment as though waiting for sunshine to break through the rolling clouds.

"Where would *you* want to go?" he said.

"Mexico," she said, reaching to tap the ashes from her cigarette into the bush where they'd be undetected. She ignored his sidelong glare and exhaled.

"You can't do that for a weekend."

"Leave late Friday. Come back late Sunday."

"You're a pain in the ass, D-stroyer. Clearly you're the wrong person to ask for advice."

"I don't want her hating me for ruining what should have been the best weekend of your lives."

"Okay, fine," Matthew said. "Savannah, Georgia. She mentioned it once."

"People usually know the answer before they ask the question. Have you noticed that?"

His eyes were glassy enough to show he'd smoked plenty before arriving. Still, the way he lowered one eyebrow and peered at her from under it told her he'd caught the familiar line. She'd said it because, in this case, it was true, he *did* know where he wanted to take Jen. She wished she hadn't used those words though. They always ended up in the same stalemate with Dawn insisting it was possible to remember one part of an evening and not another. And who was to say that people didn't use the same expressions whether they were drunk or sober? She stood and brushed the front of her jeans.

"Let's go inside." She pinched off the tip and slid the filter into her back pocket.

Matthew leaned against the kitchen island to unlace and remove his boots. He peeled off his socks and stuffed them into his Docs. She remembered the curve of his big toe and how he trimmed his nails in a straight line. Her mind softened and warmed, as it did after smoking pot. It struck her that of course she remembered his feet. All she'd needed was a reminder.

Forgetting a detail was not the same as not knowing. Matthew stood and spread his toes on the rug.

"Nico dared me," he said, sniffling from the cold, "to take Jen somewhere. He says I have relationship issues. The guy should talk; he's always leering at women."

Dawn nodded. Matthew habitually took risks and dares, like holding the flame of his lighter beneath his palm for as long as he could stand it, taking an extra shot at the end of the night when he'd had plenty, adding ten dashes of Tabasco to his taco because Nico, his boss, said he wouldn't.

Dawn wondered if Matthew had told Jen she was modeling and he'd offered her half the grant money. Jen seemed like the type to object to that. She always went on about the principle of things—the principle! She seemed a little hyper for Matthew, but whatever. Dawn liked the idea she and Matthew had a secret; their friendship still outweighed any relationship he and Jen might be having.

Matthew never dated other artists. He said the biological urge to compete automatically made any artist a bad fit. This included other photographers, painters, sculptors, writers, and pretty much anyone with dreadlocks or wool tights with Mary Janes. He insisted that one artist always possessed more talent than the other and this led to an involuntary hierarchy. Dawn didn't get it. It seemed to her Matthew might appreciate someone like him, someone whose soul he could see brought to life on paper.

Unlike Dawn, who knew his photography moved her but had no clue why. Studying his portfolio left her feeling like someone ripped her heart out at the exact moment she became capable of understanding the world on a higher level. The pale skin of a woman's thigh or the curve of a cheek or the naked branches of a tree at dusk left Dawn wanting to crumble to the floor, pound her fists, and sob for the injustice of it all. However he did it, Matthew saw the truth in its most painful form.

As for Jen, she seemed okay. The dumbest move a woman could make—which Jen didn't—was getting in the middle of a guy and his friends. Friends came first. Some women couldn't handle a guy having female friends, on principle. And despite Jen and all her principles, that one didn't seem to be an issue. The three of them had hung out multiple times in the past— how many?—six months. Had it really been six months? Dawn counted back to the beginning, sometime last summer when they'd gone to the music festival in the park. Holy shit, Matthew had himself a relationship. She remembered how she and Matthew had smoked a joint, but Jen refrained with a wave of her hand that indicated she didn't mind them doing it even if it wasn't her vice. Later, Jen had stood next to Matthew and slipped her hand under the back of his T-shirt—the Zeppelin one—and rubbed his back.

Jen didn't seem to mind Matthew being the starving artist type. She didn't make a lot either. Her job involved finance at a local insurance company where she wore blouses and slacks with pumps. They were the kind of clothes Dawn envisioned wearing had she gone to college to get a degree in psychology. Professional clothes, but not stuffy or corporate. Dawn recognized a lot of Jen's clothes from the displays at Kohl's, which often went as low as 50 percent off or more. She wondered whether Matthew paid for dates or whether they split stuff down the middle. With Matthew, she could see it either way. With Jen, it depended on how she interpreted the principle.

"A place like this, you have to go barefoot to feel all the wonderful pile," Matthew said.

He dug his toes into the rug. Dawn liked the shape of his feet. They were moderately knobby, good since puffy feet were the worst. Her face warmed when she remembered standing up from his couch, directly onto the tops of Matthew's feet. They were smooth. It had shocked her enough to note it before she stepped away to find her jeans, one leg inside out, half on his coffee table.

She wondered now whether Matthew fell into her mother's category of men who couldn't be trusted. Even if Jen couldn't trust him, Dawn could. But trusting a friend and trusting a lover were two different situations. Still. Matthew didn't fuck Jen the way he'd fucked her. The two of them didn't fit together. She couldn't pinpoint why she thought so. She just did. Matthew took off his flannel and tied it around his waist.

"What does that mean?" Dawn said. "Pile."

"The rugs. Luxurious pile, expensive. Feels so nice."

The knotted sleeves rested against his Doors T-shirt, making her so sleepy she wanted to close her eyes, press her cheek against his shirt, and ask how he knew so much when she did not.

She took off her socks and left them near Matthew's boots. A tiny splatter of green hung over one of the toes.

"Why are you covered in paint?" Dawn said.

"Noah," Matthew said, searching for evidence on his clothes. When he found none, he checked his hands. "Big Brothers are doing a Christmas dinner. I made him a collage. You need to meet the kid. He's a cool little dude."

"You have paint in your hair."

"I suck at painting. Truly. It's fun, though."

She motioned so he leaned toward her while she pulled the green flecks from his mop. Matthew had the kind of hair she wanted: waves and loops instead of spirals and more soft than coarse. She cupped the tiny spheres in her palm and showed him. He shrugged. She added them to the top of the garbage bin, sprinkling them like Christmas decorations on a cookie. That kid, Noah, she'd seen his photograph. Matthew took his picture one afternoon when Noah came to his apartment. The kid had brown eyes so dark they seemed black. He sat at Matthew's computer with a hand resting on the mouse. His smile was huge, stretched across his face with top and bottom teeth showing, making it difficult to believe he was underprivileged in the first place. Matthew knew what to do to make people happy. The kid was lucky to have him. Matthew, without buying twenty-seven presents or going overboard, could give that kid the best Christmas he'd ever had. He made you feel like your situation in life was cool no matter what.

"Let's go see that porn," Matthew said, rubbing his hands and blowing into them.

"If you want, you can keep it for your weekend in Savannah."

"Please. We both know the person in this house couldn't hold a candle to what I like."

Matthew stopped at the sight of the wheelchair lift and pointed.

"Not now," Dawn said.

She pushed so he started walking upstairs. He peered at her over his shoulder with astonished delight, still pointing.

"I know, I know. I'll demonstrate later. You can ride it."

"Nothing upstairs is going to beat that," he said.

Behind him, she was giddy with the pleasure of their shared experience and pleased that the McIntyres' home would live up to his expectations. She'd become so accustomed to the nuances of her customers' lives that weeks might pass without her paying attention to any of the good details. The chairlift, of course, topped the list for its strangeness and shock value. Its oldness added to its distinctiveness. Like a valuable antique, it could be the only one left of its kind. Still pristine in ways—like the smooth seat cover of beautifully worn leather—yet its aged on-switch required extra effort to flip due to years of buildup—was it corrosion? Dirt? Dust?—that reminded you the original user was long dead. Houses weren't haunted, Dawn decided. The items inside haunted them.

She thumped up, ready to push Matthew again if necessary. The stitching on the pockets of his jeans swirled like fancy figure eights. It wasn't like Matthew to buy new or stylish apparel. The rivets, instead of regular copper, were gray/black. For once you could see the shape of his butt. She followed him to the doorway of the bedroom, mesmerized by the sudden awareness of new details. The straps of his camera bags crossed his back. One curl had gone rogue, creating its own spiral. The texture appeared softer than moments before. Nearly reaching to confirm it, she remembered herself and clasped her hands together.

Matthew entered the McIntyres' bedroom. Dawn stopped at the threshold.

"There, on the bed," she said. She lifted her hands to her face in anticipation.

Matthew picked up the photograph. He studied it for a few seconds, flipping to read the fine print on the back of the photo paper. "This is sad. That poor animal."

"What should I do with it?"

"You want to take it home? Frame it?"

"I would *not* take that home," she said, clutching her stomach and laughing. "Should I prop it against the lamp on the bedside table?" she said.

"Stick it under his pillow. He'll see you were trying to be discreet."

She snatched it from Matthew's hands and shoved it face down under Robert's pillow.

Matthew slid it out and studied it. He seemed unfazed by the details that had shocked Dawn earlier.

"What is that on her hoochie? Nutella?"

Dawn covered her mouth but she lost it, if not from the word *hoochie* then the idea of Nutella being applied like bikini wax. She collapsed lengthwise on the bed and cackled, kicking the mattress. After a moment, she lifted her head from her crossed arms.

"It has real hazelnuts," Matthew whispered in her face, having snuck around the bed.

She laughed until tears streamed. No one could be a better friend than Matthew. When they got carried away, he seemed to gain strength from her laughter, which only led to more hysterics. He dropped to his knees and laughed with his forehead pressed into the carpet. Stoned, they might be best friends.

"This is nice pile," he said.

Dawn rolled off the edge of the bed and pressed her nose into the shag.

"It smells like old twine. That can't be good."

"I used to work at this carpet shop," Matthew said. "The dude was dealing coke in the back. We'd get high and walk around barefoot on all the rug samples. Sometimes we'd try to swing on the area rugs on display."

Matthew sat up and chewed his thumbnail.

"Do you like cleaning here?" he said.

"Good money. It's never very dirty."

"Who knows what else that guy is into? One dirty picture always leads to more. People progress to bigger and better habits."

"I'll take my chances for $200 a week. I'll dust his dirty pictures. Whatever he wants."

"You've got a lot on your mind as it is," Matthew said.

Dawn pulled her knees in and hugged them. She brought her forehead down. If only Matthew realized. Sure he could tell she got stressed out; she'd survived an accident after all. But for all he knew, Dawn was a worrier before the accident. Robert, he barely mattered compared to the swirl in her mind—Nick's fingers wrapping the brass handle of Terry's coffin; the incredible depth of the scab on her hip; smelling engine exhaust and gravel and the plastic newness of the trailer; Mrs. Folly turning her head away. The swirl had grown—a bundle of moving clouds—until she'd started questioning rocks behind her tires, karma, fate, a wad of chewing gum on her porch, anything.

Wait, he could mean her decision about moving. That had to be it. Jesus, she did have a lot on her mind.

"Don't think. You're stoned," Matthew said. "I didn't mean to make you go to the bad place."

Dawn lifted her head.

"I'm not worried about the guy who lives here."

"Sometimes you're a little naïve. That's all."

"Oh, so you're an expert because you worked for a coke dealer? Please. I can handle myself."

"I'm saying, how do you know he's not nuts? Or dangerous?"

"Everyone is nuts," Dawn said. "People are into all kinds of weird shit. No one murders their cleaning lady."

The revelation pleased and relieved her. Matthew switched hands to chew on his pinky nail, nodding slowly, or it probably just seemed slow.

"Want to take a ride on the lift?" she asked.

Matthew jumped up and galloped out of the room.

She noticed the Buddha had been positioned at an odd angle with its face toward the wall instead of the expanse of the bedroom. Surely she didn't leave it like that. She'd never.

Within the seconds of an inhale and exhale, the Buddha had moved itself, or was moved by ghosts, or simply left amiss by Dawn without her remembering. The truth didn't matter. A mind could create and rationalize anything to solve a problem. She stepped to the dresser and fixed it.

She found Matthew in the hallway.

"Jesus," he said. "Is this safe?"

"Be sure to wear your seatbelt and keep your arms inside the vehicle at all times."

The inside of Hilary McIntyre's walk-in closet smelled like cedar mixed with the individual plastic bags that held her collection of cashmere sweaters. About a hundred pairs of flats filled the built-in shelves against the back wall. Not one pair had a heel higher than an inch, which Hilary could have used because in addition to being stocky she was also short. There was a pair of sneakers, odd white Reebok high-tops with space-age rolls like a mini sumo wrestler.

Hilary's closet made Barb Turner's closet a knockoff. The smooth cedar shimmered under the track lights that illuminated automatically. The brushed-nickel bars and drawer knobs were nicer than anything Dawn owned. Rolling open a drawer required as much effort as tapping the ash off a cigarette.

Matthew had picked out his favorite women's suit, blouse, and shoe combination. He insisted Dawn stuff herself into a pair of Hilary's nude pantyhose, which was why it was taking so damn long for her to get dressed. Her legs had six inches each on Hilary's and despite careful tugging, the cotton crotch of the pantyhose hung somewhere between her knees and the proper place. She unclipped the skirt from the hanger. It surprised her to find it fit around her waist. She slid her arms into the sleeves of the blouse. The cuffs came to her forearms. She tucked in the shirt without bothering to be neat about it. She fought the instinct to flex and bust out of the back seam.

Before she forgot, she opened the top drawer of the accessories cabinet and selected one of Robert's gold cuff links. She dropped it into the pocket of one of Hilary's summer jackets that would go unworn for months. Fucking with the McIntyres took innovation and creativity so as not to be found out. The cuff link mattered just enough to awaken the thrill of satisfaction.

Robert would suspect Dawn, but it wouldn't add up: *That woman has no use for cuff links and if she wanted to pawn them she'd have stolen both.*

A sense of power came with planting the seed of insecurity in someone. People wanted to fuck with her? She could do it, too, in her own way.

Dawn blew a puff of air up into her hair and stepped out of the closet to show Matthew. He extended a strand of pearls the size of gumballs.

"You've got to be kidding," she said, clipping them around her neck. She dropped the black patent leather flats on the carpet and slid her toes into them. Her heels hung over the backs of the shoes so she skated toward the bed.

"I like how her clothes fit you," Matthew said. "Not too tight, but too short. Gives the feeling of being awry despite the obvious high quality of the threads. Like a fish out of water or someone trying to fit in. You know what I mean?"

"Where do you want me?"

"Don't be so negative. Come here, I'll fix you."

"I am not broken."

"You know what I mean. This is supposed to be fun."

He wrapped his arms around her back to smooth the lumps

from the blouse. The scruff on his face smelled like marijuana. She let him twist her hair to the top of her head. The clip snapped and Dawn was surprised to see in the mirror he'd done a decent job making her uppity and conservative. The pearls made her successful.

"It feels late," she said.

"Stop being paranoid."

"These pantyhose feel like a chastity belt."

She lifted a foot to catch the control top and stepped on it to take them off. She wrapped them into a ball and threw it at Matthew's head.

"Ha," he said. "Like you'd know."

She raised her eyebrows, though she hadn't slept with anyone else. She sat on the edge of the bed. Matthew began pacing the room, taking in the scene. Dawn sat taller and stretched her neck to get a glimpse out the window. The lake wasn't in her view so she focused instead on the sky and clouds that rolled past, tumbling toward a warmer and more wondrous location. Her tongue lay thick in her mouth and she realized how stoned she was and how badly she wanted to crack a cold beer and feel the can on her bottom lip, a Key West beer so she'd feel the sun on her face.

Downstairs in the library, Matthew handed her a driver from Robert's bag of antique clubs and reached for the stuffed beaver. Underneath its tail, Matthew had unthreaded a few inches of the seam. Dawn held the driver upright while Matthew jammed the beaver over the metal head.

She stared at the animal with its ridiculous patchwork teeth and golf club shoved up its ass. Despite her best efforts, her mouth twitched and the bubble of hilarity rose to her throat. She met Matthew's gaze, the worst way to maintain composure. He held up a hand to block the sight of her face.

"You're messing with me," Dawn said. "There's no Krindle grant, is there? You invented it, didn't you?"

"I'm not going to use the animal. He's just for inspiration so you can get into character."

Dawn found the animal's beaded eyes through the synthetic fur. "Sorry," she said to it. "Not a beaver shot."

"We shouldn't have gotten stoned," he said. "We're too distracted."

She balanced the beaver-topped club against her shoulder to avoid it.

"Tell me what to do before I start laughing again."

Matthew peered through the lens of the camera and made adjustments. She wondered how her image transformed as he rotated the focus. Too bad a person couldn't fix their problems so simply. Imagine being able to zoom in a little closer; she'd tweak every photograph that had ever been taken of her. Like the family photo with her parents the Christmas she was five, a photo she kept wedged between the pages of the battered copy of *The Great Gatsby* she'd been assigned to read in school. Not because she wanted her parents to be together. More that keeping a picture of the three of them proved they'd been together once.

In the photograph her mother still rode the big hair wave from the early nineties. Her curls were long and full with bangs teased for more height. Her long-sleeved dress buttoned up the front in a weird Quaker style. She wore black tights and shoes. The black eyeliner fully enhanced the edgy expression on her mother's face, as though darkening her mood more. That would be the first tweak: to soften the expression. Dawn remembered her in a constant state of suspicion, irritation, or straight-up anger. She always criticized.

For God's sake, Jack, get the door. Jesus, Jack, tuck in your shirt. Your haircut is terrible. Did you tell her to cut it like that? Dawn, stop goofing around with your father and bring me your plate. Be quiet, you two are giving me a headache.

In the photo, her father needed some sparkle in his eyes. His shoulders slumped in the navy-blue sweater with white snowflakes and a zipper up the front. The pleats on the front of his pants made him look like a member of a boy band. His hands were stuffed into his pockets. Dawn stood up front and to the right in her two-tiered red skirt and white sweater. Her own hair was a shoulder-length combination between an Afro and a poodle; she'd zoom in and fix that immediately. At least one of her parents should have a hand on Dawn's shoulder or an arm around her. She'd bring the three of them closer together and connect them in some way. She reminded herself that photographs—all photos—were false representations. There was always more going on in the background. And, if you were smiling, chances were you hadn't meant it.

"Today is about discovery," Matthew said. "People discover qualities about those they think they know best. The question is, how do they react? Do they react the way we expect them to or in a way that's unexpected?"

Dawn turned her attention back to the McIntyres and Robert's pornographic photo.

"The expected is that she's horrified like we were. Repulsed."

"So, lean over the desk with that in mind. You're seeing the worst for the first time."

Dawn considered the worst.

So many iterations existed. Matthew knew it. His mother kicked him out of the house at age seventeen. He earned money by drawing in chalk on the sidewalks and selling watercolors in the park. But Matthew wouldn't consider that the worst. He was glad to go, he said, because being a homeless kid on the streets far outweighed the sadistic tendencies of his stepfather.

His worst might be farther behind him, like the story he always told about falling off his bike and breaking his arm when he was miles from home. *I dragged my bike down a dirt road, crying. At one point, I lay down and waited to die. I wanted to.*

Dawn's worst discovery, easy.

She wished it hadn't come to mind. Three weeks before the accident, Katelyn confided she'd heard Terry and Nick discussing sex with that girl from the Superstore. Sex with Terry, not Nick. It made Dawn sick to think about, even now.

She'd managed to keep quiet. Not letting on that she knew kept the actuality from reality, which she'd needed at the time. She needed to decide how to respond. With another woman in the picture, breaking up with him would only push him to her. Jealousy, anger, and plain old pride wouldn't allow it. If Terry wanted to dump Dawn for the Superstore woman, he would have already done it. That meant she was still in it.

Humiliating Terry had crossed her mind. Hurting Terry had crossed her mind, like kicking him in the nuts as hard as she possibly could or slicing his penis and leaving him bleeding. Forgiveness was also an option, assuming he didn't want to be caught. They could chalk it up to curiosity or one last fling before they got married. She could cheat, too, and let Terry know so they could call it even.

"Getting anywhere?" Matthew said. "Discovery."

Dawn tried to channel the idea of discovering a disturbing secret about a husband, someone you'd vowed to love forever. Someone who'd vowed to love you. Someone like Robert who'd tolerated the white bedspread with embroidered roses all those years. She wanted Hilary to blow his mind with her reaction, just like Dawn had wanted to shock Terry into capitulation, the kind that comes when you realize you already have exactly what you need.

She set the golf club on the desk and reached for it. She listened to the ticks as Matthew snapped pictures.

She hesitated; no one would want to stare down the obvious. Or would they? She tilted her head—just a little—to get the tiniest glimpse of the shaft disappearing between the split of fabric. Curiosity, after all, must play a part.

"Interesting," Matthew said, from behind the camera.

The best way to tackle a problem is head on, her father liked to say. That's exactly what Dawn had planned to do. Stare the cheating in the face and find a way to make it work to her advantage.

Dawn backed up and sat in the McIntyres' leather chair. What if Hilary liked the picture? What if the picture aroused her a little? Dawn crossed one leg over the other so the skirt slid up her thighs. She paid attention to the tender stretch of her inner thigh brushing against the other. If the picture drew Hilary in instead of pushing her away, the picture became a tool instead of an obstacle.

She verified the lens was watching. The camera clicked and stalled as Matthew tried to shoot faster.

Robert McIntyre would never expect his wife to be aroused. Hadn't crossed his mind. A discovery like this could give the two much-needed common ground.

"Go with it," Matthew said.

Dawn opened her eyes and peeked under the beaver's tail. She slid her hand up the shaft of the club to finger the rim of the hole.

"Do it," Matthew said.

She pushed her finger into the hole and lifted her chest. Because the suit jacket strained across her breasts, Dawn reached down and popped the button. She unbuttoned the top buttons of the blouse and slid her hand into her bra, pausing for a moment to give Matthew time to take it in.

"If she were into it, wouldn't she loosen up?" he said.

"No way," Dawn said. "She's still Hilary. No one will ever guess what she lets Robert do."

"Damn," Matthew said, finally lowering the camera. "I didn't see that coming."

"Think of the newfound freedom it would give her."

Matthew wiped his forehead with his arm.

Dawn sat up in the chair and removed the club from the stuffed animal. Its tail hid the hole so she returned it to the shelf, making sure it sat at the right angle. She straightened the other items on the shelves.

"You think she's really down with it?" Matthew said.

"Doubtful. We all *want* to believe we'd be able to get on board. No way. But how awesome to think she might be. It takes all the power away from Robert and puts it back on Hilary."

Matthew stood with his hands on his hips, nodding at the

impeccable surroundings. He put his camera in the bag and let his fingers graze the leather arm of the couch.

"Are they really going to give a grant to work this explicit?" Dawn said. "This is odd shit we're coming up with."

"The final exhibit will only give a glimpse. What we're feeling here, you'll see it in some way, even if it comes across differently to different people. That's the beauty of art."

Through the window, the willow tree in the yard swished back and forth in the winter wind. Whether Matthew let her see the photos or not, they'd created together. She was sure of it. They'd imagined a scenario no one expected, a human reaction that touched upon a possible, if unlikely, truth.

She'd wanted to do that with Terry only he'd crashed.

Matthew gestured to let her leave the library first. The cool hallway refreshed her like a drink of water. Dawn liked the cold marble beneath her feet. The clean glasses and brushed aluminum sink from the bar smelled like walking into a fancy restaurant.

"How did it go with your dad last night?" Matthew said.

"Think about being somewhere warm with the sun and ocean. All new people. Plus it's a place where everyone is on vacation. None of this uptight bullshit. He thinks I should come today."

"So why don't you?"

The hallway opened into the vast living room.

"We're doing this project, for one thing."

"Come on, Dawn."

Her chest ached and she longed to be able to explain to him the complexity of it all. Mrs. Folly's phone call and invitation. The trailer she hated, it pulled her with a force meant just for her. Matthew nor anyone else were meant to understand. Dawn belonged in it the way a drug grasps an addict and holds on.

"If I leave it will be over," she finally said.

"What will be over?"

"Forget it, it's complicated."

"This accident will haunt you forever if you let it."

"It's not that. That's not what I meant. I don't have the money to move. Not enough for gas."

"You think if you leave, it means your relationship with Terry is over?"

"That's ridiculous. I know that's over."

The bitter sweetness of the lie; she heard her words and realized how untrue they were. Everything had changed since the familiar number illuminated the screen on her phone. Mrs. Folly's voice, it sounded more familiar than her own mother's. Terry was gone, yes, but his mother wasn't. She envisioned them standing shoulder to shoulder in church next week. Dawn knew the church. She'd gone with Terry and his family. Mrs. Folly used to call Dawn her future daughter-in-law. She'd put her arm around Dawn's shoulder when she introduced her that way. *Call me Mom if you want,* she'd told Dawn again and again. *You know you want to.* And Dawn had. Sometimes calling Mrs. Folly Mom came more naturally than her real mom.

Once again, she swallowed the urge to explain it to Matthew. She knew he'd point out that Dawn had rarely mentioned the woman in all the time they'd been friends. He'd see that she'd only revealed part of the story. But that was for self-preservation. She'd had to convince herself that her life with Terry *was* over. It had been over. Except now it wasn't.

"You're too scared because you've lived here your whole life?" Matthew said.

Dawn gave him the finger, grateful he'd moved on to a new theory.

"You're not giving any good reason. You have a job there, right? Waiting tables?"

"More like a partnership. My dad's going to need someone to turn it over to when he retires. I can learn and be ready."

No one had ever said that, but it could be true. Despite her mother's insistence her father cared more about piña coladas and suntan oil, he'd called Dawn and asked her to come. And,

really, how had her father ever let her down? She wasn't sure
he ever had. Instead of picturing herself pressing foreheads
with Mrs. Folly cupping her face, she knew she should picture
herself behind the bar with her dad grinning at her from the
swinging door to the kitchen.

"Who in their right mind would pass that up?" Matthew said.

"You're trying to get rid of me," Dawn said. "Shit, dude, I
can take a hint."

"You know I'd miss you. But as your friend, I'm supposed to
point out when you're making stupid decisions."

"Maybe I'll go. At some point."

Matthew reached into the back pocket of his jeans and extracted a crumpled pack of American Spirits. He pulled one
from the pack and put it between his lips. He shrugged and
motioned to the lake outside.

"I might like a place like this," he said. "You know, a wife and
a kid. A couple dogs. Minus the bestiality."

"Seriously? A kid?"

"Why not? You don't want kids?"

"God no."

"You're unreal, D-tester."

"It's stupid to insult me when I'm holding a golf club."

"Good point," he said.

She returned the club to its leather bag and adjusted the
wood and aluminum bouquet.

"I almost asked Jen to pose for me. We never would have
gotten into this kind of depth."

"Does she know that?"

"I'm not an idiot," Matthew said.

"Sure you are."

"Be that as it may, I am very grateful to you."

He reached forward and set his hand on her shoulder while
he said it. The weight of it could crush her if she let it.

"Call me tomorrow," he said, heading for the door. He
waved the cigarette over his head. "I need to smoke this."

The door slammed when he went out into the cold.

On the way down the stairs to sweep up the laundry tags and remove the evidence, Dawn shivered. The only warm place was where Matthew's hand had landed and she was sorry he'd left her alone with her thoughts. She didn't want to be alone anymore. Finding a Matthew in Key West would be impossible.

The Northeast in December sucked for its short days, leaving little daylight by the time Dawn left the McIntyres'. The boulevard leading away from the lake practically buzzed from the electricity required to illuminate the trio of massive pine trees ahead. The rich people in the neighborhood probably paid someone to figure out a way to siphon electricity from an unsuspecting poorer neighborhood. That would explain why their holiday lights seemed the brightest. Everything became so much more beautiful when the rich got a hold of it.

After Christmas passed, the sunset held off a little longer each day. Another reason to want to get through the holidays.

Dawn smoked the last cigarette in her pack and stopped at the pharmacy on the way home. She walked the aisles in search of God knows what. By covering the entire store, she could think about each collection of products to figure out what she needed, what she didn't need, and why. These days, pharmacies sold just about everything: cards, flip-flops, holiday decorations, wine, nutrition bars, batteries, cleaning products, kits to see whether you were HIV positive. A person could really think about her life in there.

Dawn stood on equal ground with anyone else who happened to be shopping: people who went to college or didn't, women who were married or not, men who drove trucks or worked as lawyers, the rude guy who answered the phone when you called about your insurance claim. They all bought the same mouthwash from the same shelf. Hilary McIntyre might have stood right here in her four-hundred-dollar shoes and selected a package of generic polysporin because what difference did it make compared to the name brand?

Perusing the compact bottles and boxes made the world
seem smaller and more manageable. Like therapy. A purchase
was unlikely for Dawn, as the pharmacy mostly sold the smaller-
sized items. Dawn preferred to buy in bulk and save. There was
no way she'd pay $1.69 for nine ounces of dish soap when she
could pay $7.68 for a fifty-six-ounce refill at the Superstore.

On her way to the front counter, a familiar figure caught her
eye. The woman stood in the Christmas aisle, past the boxes of
cheap bulbs and plastic Santa figurines. She wore an oversized
winter coat and had her hands shoved into the pockets. Her hair
was pulled back into a thin ponytail, her eyes tired and distant.

It was Barb Turner.

Dawn held her breath and kept walking. Barb's psych report
sat on her kitchen table and she hadn't stopped to read it carefully. The words that meant the most had stuck: rape, trauma,
fear. Barb Turner, her family, the silk flowers, and Barb's problems were meant for Mondays. But today was Tuesday. Barb,
for all intents and purposes, didn't exist on Tuesdays. But there
she stood.

Dawn tried not to cringe when she sensed her customer's
approach as she stood at the counter, waiting for the clerk to
get her carton of Marlboro Lights. Buy in bulk and save, only
now Barb would see her purchasing cigarettes in mass quantity.
Funny how Dawn had been perfectly okay with it when nobody
she knew saw her ask for them. She'd been smoking at least a
carton a week. Dawn didn't need someone sniffing in judgment
at her expensive and unhealthy habits. The package clearly stat-
ed that smoking kills.

She considered paying and walking out without showing her
profile. Barb probably wouldn't recognize her from behind. She
seemed too close, though, and when Dawn fixed her eyes on
the floor, her customer's Nike sneakers and anklet socks came
into view with a slice of pale leg and the unmistakable hang of
the Land's End nightgown underneath her coat.

She swiveled and found Barb's eyes, regretting it instantly.
The nightgown had caught her off guard.

Dawn swallowed, then smiled. It didn't take long for the flicker of recognition.

"Oh, wow. Hey," Dawn said.

Her eyes ached from the effort to not drift to the plaid flannel.

"Dawn. What a coincidence," Barb said. Her skin seemed thinner and the hue practically matched the white floor, pounded to a dull gray from the dirty shoes of customers bringing the outside in.

Barb held her gaze steady, which to Dawn seemed like anywhere but down to where the nightgown showed. She sensed Barb's embarrassment as though she—Dawn—were the one out shopping in her pajamas.

"I had to get out," Barb said. "One of those grab-your-coat-and-go moments."

"Out?"

"Of the house. It can be stifling. The kids. All the fighting. I come here and find what I need."

"Yeah, me too," said Dawn. "Which tonight happens to be a lot of cigarettes."

"Well, who am I to judge?"

Barb cradled two large jugs of red wine.

"You're as bad as me," Dawn said.

"You're too young to be as bad as me," Barb said.

Her customer smiled so that her eyes seemed taut against the pull of her ponytail. Circles hung beneath them like ash. Barb looked exhausted, defeated, but nothing like the permanent glaze of pissiness Dawn saw in her own mother, as though every task requiring her to do for another came with a pulse of annoyance. Barb's variety of overwhelm lacked energy and enthusiasm. Dawn paid the cashier, who slid a receipt into the plastic bag and handed it to her.

"Thanks," Dawn said. To Barb, she said, "Hey, nice seeing you. Have a good night."

"You too," Barb said, stepping forward and bending her knees to lower the jugs to the counter. "I think it's possible now."

Her customer nodded toward the bottles and Dawn laughed, the loud, natural laugh she'd been known for in high school. The sound of it startled her. She had nothing to do but walk out the automatic doors to the parking lot.

Fresh night air blew into her face. She sat at the picnic table where employees took cigarette breaks. A sensor caught her movement. Light burst onto the table so Dawn could see the graffiti carved into the wood with car keys and penknives. She and Katelyn Rice did that in high school, scratching their initials on park benches and bathroom walls. *Katelyn + Nick. Dawn + Terry.* Sometimes they got silly and wrote stupid phrases or song lyrics.

Someone slid onto the bench across from her. Dawn nearly screamed.

"This is horribly inappropriate, but can I bum a cigarette?" Barb Turner said.

Dawn fumbled to open the carton, extracted a pack, and removed the cellophane. She pulled the aluminum tab, flicked the bottom of the pack to raise a couple cigarettes and extended it toward Barb.

"I quit smoking twenty years ago," Barb said, taking one.

Dawn dug around her purse for the lighter. She lit Barb's first, then brought the flame to the end of the one she held in her teeth. Dawn didn't mind the company, but sitting there with a housewife made it seem like a lifetime since she'd been friends with Katelyn and had a fiancé. Adulthood had taken hold. Barb had no reference to think of Dawn as anything but a woman. Dawn was starting to realize that no matter how old she got, there was no official moment of transition from kid to grown-up, from girl to woman, from a person needing to be cared for to a person who cared for others. The transition, it seemed, had taken place without her noticing.

"I wouldn't have expected you to be a smoker," Dawn said.

"Sometimes the world crashes in," Barb said.

Dawn nodded.

"I'm an old mom. It's amazing how you lose yourself, how

easy it is to lose yourself. If you keep having babies, the babies are all consuming. You don't have time to deal with any of the real issues. It's all about making sure everyone's fed, no one's crying, no one's flunking."

Dawn nodded and smoked for time to think of a response. She didn't know shit about kids except that Barb's had twenty-seven presents under the Christmas tree. Somehow this didn't seem as much of an overindulgence as it had before.

"Does Fred help?"

"Sure," Barb said, deciding to flick her ashes on the corner of the table. The wind caught the little heap and it rolled like a crooked ball over the edge onto the pavement. "He's a great dad. He's the fun one. I'm the bitch who makes everyone do their chores and go to bed."

"I don't want kids," Dawn said.

She exhaled, noticing how her breath froze so she wasn't sure when the smoke stopped being smoke. She liked that Barb appreciated her husband's help, even if life got more difficult in other ways. Somehow she doubted Barb was the bitch she thought herself to be.

"No? Why not?"

"It's hard enough to take care of yourself."

"What you need to realize," Barb said, "is you get to ignore yourself when you take care of someone else. It's an excellent form of denial."

"Yes, but here you are at the store because you had to get away. You can't always ignore yourself."

"True. But still. If I didn't have them, I'd probably be crazy by now from having overanalyzed what's wrong with my life. Too much idle time is dangerous."

Dawn pictured herself in the dim kitchen of her trailer with only her thoughts and whiskey to pass the time. Sometimes the minutes ticked by so slowly it seemed worse than watching the second hand of the clock limp around and around during the last hour of school.

"Being alone can be dangerous," Dawn said.

"Do you have a boyfriend? Does he know you don't want kids?"

The question stunned her, as though she expected Barb to know her story. Having been written about multiple times after the accident—with her senior picture featured, followed by the one Matthew took—led her to believe most people connected her to the girl who hadn't died. Self-consciousness followed her around the town she'd lived in her entire life—not a huge place, but large enough to have its own newspaper and community center. Dawn had assumed most of her customers hired her because they pitied her. If they didn't know specifics, they must have seen the scars.

"No."

"Why not?" Barb said. Her customer practiced smoke rings by tapping the side of her cheek with her index finger.

"I was engaged."

"Oh shit, you're too young to be engaged. It's for the best it didn't work out," Barb said.

"We got into an accident on his motorcycle. He died. I didn't."

Barb stopped tapping her cheek and smoked some more. Watching her process the information revealed she'd never stopped before to imagine Dawn's personal life.

"When was this? Was this in the papers?"

"A year ago last August."

"I read about that. I remember. What was he like?" Barb said. "Your fiancé."

Dawn thought for a moment. No one had ever asked her the question before. She liked Barb's curiosity about who she'd been with, as though it would reveal who she was as a human being.

"He bought me a pack of cigarettes every time he bought one for himself."

"It's too bad smoking is unhealthy. That's actually a very sweet gesture."

"Whenever I stopped to get gas in my car, he pumped it for

me without me asking. He was handsome, too, really hot, and he liked to work out. And there was his motorcycle."

"I remember. You were hurt. Badly."

"Elbows skinned to the bone. Went off the back going 45 miles an hour."

"Show me," Barb said.

Dawn paused, then pulled an arm from her coat and stuck her elbow under Barb's nose. Barb gently took her bicep and leaned back to get a better view. Dawn watched her expression, but she didn't react.

"That's gotta hurt."

"Not as much as what happened to Terry."

Dawn slid her arm back into the sleeve and zipped her coat. The admission had tumbled out automatically, kicking back a well of emotion—an upward waterfall—through her body. She pressed her lips together to hold in whatever might spill out.

"He died instantly," Barb said. "That part I remember. So, no, what happened to you probably hurt more."

Dawn pulled a fresh cigarette from the pack and lit it from the old one. Barb reached for her bag. She unscrewed one of the jugs, leaned over, and took a swig.

"Come over on this side if you want some. I don't want to get arrested."

Dawn found herself on the bench next to Barb without realizing she'd moved. Barb held her cigarette while Dawn managed to lift the heavy bottle to her lips. She nodded so Dawn lifted it a second time, then a third. Barb set the bottle on the ground and placed a hand on Dawn's arm.

"Don't minimize what happened to you," Barb said. "What happened to you matters. It never stops mattering. If you don't face that now, you'll have to face it sometime."

"I am facing it."

She clenched her cold fingers into fists. Just because Barb remembered a newspaper article didn't mean she had a clue about the experience. How it really transpired. And anyway, people dealt with death in their own, individual ways. Dawn had been facing it since the moment it happened because it faced her. People didn't walk around with their eyes closed.

"What ends up happening," Barb said, "is that you meet someone and get married before you know who you really are. Then you're in the middle of some stranger's life. And God forbid you try to rip off any of the Band-Aids. People don't like it when you suddenly have wounds you never had before. In fact, they hate it. They hate you for it."

Dawn stood up. Her sudden anger confused her, but it had to do with the way Barb had gone from talking about Dawn to talking about herself. And how Barb told her that what happened never stopped mattering when Dawn's own mother never wanted it brought up.

"Where are you going?" Barb said.

"I have to get home."

Barb sighed, as though Dawn had somehow failed.

"How are you facing it?"

"Believe me," Dawn said, louder than before. "I'm facing it every day of my life. Believe me."

"Good. Don't stop. Ever."

Dawn tossed the pack of cigarettes on the table for Barb to keep. Barb pulled it toward her chest and held it like a prize.

"See you later," Dawn said.

Dawn assumed she watched her walk to the car and get inside. She tried to appear casual, not emotional, because Barb, after all, was a customer. The orange tip of the woman's cigarette glowed like a smoky beacon from the picnic table. Dawn could still see it from across the lot when she pulled away and drove toward the dark.

WEDNESDAY: CONTRAST

DON'T BE SURPRISED TO FIND
ALL THE MESS IN ONE ROOM.

Dawn woke to her alarm playing that perky Christmas commercial for the mall. She groaned and tugged the drawstring of her sweatshirt to release her head from the hood. It took a few seconds to un-cinch from when she'd pulled it so tight during the night that only her nose and lips were cold. She'd grown accustomed to sleeping in long underwear, socks, sweatpants, and a hoodie. Chill infiltrated the space behind her earlobes and beneath her chin. Retaining heat in the trailer was impossible without spending a boatload on bullshit that probably wouldn't help much anyway.

Justice had given her advice last March when she moved in. He'd stopped by every day or two—in his official park-manager polo—to see what she needed. Dawn hadn't minded. She liked the way the black edge of an ominous tattoo crept above his collarbone, mostly hidden by his shirt but visible enough to make you wonder about the rest of it.

One morning he arrived with a long comb inserted in his Afro. He leaned into the doorway when Dawn answered his knock. She never asked him inside, but he didn't seem to expect her to. His right eye squinted when he laughed, which was a lot, and he wore the exact right amount of cologne: enough to make your stomach flip without sucking all the oxygen from a room.

"Don't be letting the heat run all the time," he'd said. "You spend all that hard-earned cleaning money on bills. Ain't no way to live."

Dawn reached forward and he'd actually flinched in surprise. She extracted the comb and tossed it over his shoulder onto the sidewalk.

"Hey! What's up with that?"

"The other option is to spend it on insulation and under pinning, whatever the hell that is," Dawn said. "Not to mention I have no idea what to do with it."

"You don't like my 'fro pick?"

"This isn't 1985. Trust me."

"And I thought you might be bitchy."

They were friends after that. She left random items in his mailbox, like a giant pick she found at the pharmacy with long metal teeth and a black fist on the handle, or fake notes from residents complaining about used condoms on the entrance lawn. Dawn stopped by his trailer with questions, or complaints really, about how to stay warm.

"Take your Black ass to Home Depot," Justice said. "I can help you find the right materials."

"I'm white in case you didn't notice."

It wasn't the first time he'd commented on her body, but Dawn was used to it. Her mother said the trace of Greek heritage gave her an exotic aura. Her curly hair and big butt, that was what men seemed to like.

"I won't believe it until I see for myself."

"What would your mother say if you brought home a white woman?"

"My mama don't pay mind to skin color. She colorblind."

"Everyone can see the difference between Black and white, idiot."

Justice had laughed and flipped her off across the card table in his kitchen, where he and Dawn sometimes sat to do shots or smoke weed. Justice dressed in layers, too, so the two of them appeared a cross between skiers in a lodge and homeless people. Justice did the insulation and under pinning work on his trailer, which he lived in rent-free as the manager, so sometimes it warmed enough to remove a layer or two.

She wished now she'd taken Justice's advice and offer of help. Saving a few bucks hardly seemed worth it when she could practically see her breath in the room. She slid a hand from the warm covers. Her phone on the bedside table said 9:20. She closed her eyes and imagined lifting her face to the sun.

All she had to do was call her dad and say yes.

I'll come, Dad, but you have to swear it's not because you feel sorry for me.

I'll come, Dad, but don't think for a minute you can tell me what to do once I get there.

I can't stand it another minute. Of course I'm coming.

Thank you, Dad, thank you, thank you, thank you. I never dreamt it would get this bad.

After the accident, she'd gone home to her mother's house, got into bed, and stayed there for six months. She had no plans, no fiancé, a serious injury. Her elbows wept from movement. She tried to stay still, not giving herself permission to move her toes under the covers. Sometimes she hummed the theme song from their prom, just to remember a time when she and Terry went a whole night without one argument. They rode in a limo and drank champagne with Katelyn and Nick. Terry sat beside her and held her wrist between his middle finger and thumb. He'd always been amazed by the daintiness of her hands and wrists.

Dawn's mother came into her bedroom at the scheduled intervals and changed her bandages or put ointment on the skin grafts. Her mother raised her eyebrows at the humming so Dawn stopped. Dawn took Valium and Vicodin to keep from caring. Sometimes her mother brought her a sandwich or bowl of soup. After a while, she told Dawn to get her butt out of bed and come to the kitchen if she got hungry.

Practical, her mom, and married to Davis for less than a year at that point. She smiled more in his presence and complained less about Dawn's father. The marriage didn't stop her from making isolated comments to Dawn about the unlikely truth of the sewage backup at the bar in Key West the week prior to the accident, making it impossible for her father to come to New York for almost a month after Terry died. Dawn didn't bother arguing that her father told her about the problem before the accident, or that they could just as easily talk on the phone, or that it wasn't like Dawn was in critical condition or at risk of dying.

Sometimes Dawn lay awake the whole night and eaves-dropped on her mother and Davis at the kitchen table. The house was small, a two-bedroom on a block with more of the same, and her bedroom was steps away. Through the crack and spit of beer cans, they talked about everything and nothing. Dawn noted how her mother finally seemed constant, like a radio playing partial static that finally came into tune.

"It's not clearing up," her mother said.

"What's not?" said Davis.

"The dry patch on my arm. Feel it."

"Huh," said Davis. "Have you tried hydrocortisone?"

"That's helpful. I will."

Dawn and Terry would have never become that boring. Such a waste. Davis should have been the one who died, the dud. Nice guy, sure, but never an interesting word to say. Never a criticism either, which pissed off Dawn more. She and Terry fought. They fought hard, to win. She yelled. He yelled. She swung at him. He blocked her and wrestled her arm behind her back. She'd shriek about him being a woman beater. He'd let go.

She doubted her mother and Davis ever needed to have make-up sex. They might not have sex at all. They seemed satisfied by hours of slow-moving conversations about the new credit card reader at the gas station, the ingredients in a bag of Funions, how Davis needed to make an appointment for a haircut, or what the new disclaimer meant on the electric bill.

"It doesn't *mean* anything," Davis said.

"Yes, well, it could mean we pay a higher late fee if we're not on time."

"I don't think so. See this here? It's worded to protect them against fraud."

"I hope you're right."

For as tiring as it was, Dawn couldn't sleep. Her mother and Davis usually went to bed well after midnight. His alarm clock went off at eight-thirty in the morning. Dawn woke up to the sound of her stepfather murmuring and exclaiming to himself. Discoveries were a constant source of surprise as he puttered through the kitchen making coffee.

"Huh! It is easier to open. Arthritis Foundation knows what they're talking about."

Dawn knew she'd never be able to have sex with another man and not think of Terry: his muscular biceps, which she liked to grip when they did it, his smooth hairless chest, chiseled from an hour a day in the gym, the tip of his dick against her the second before he pushed it inside, making her feel whole.

Davis, what a waste of a human body. He reminded her of a dog too absent-minded to think about digging a hole, let alone burying a bone.

"I know it's hard to believe, Dawn," he'd said. "But there will be a day it doesn't hurt like this. Trust me."

Dawn threw off the covers and sat up in bed. Best to handle the cold like ripping off a bandage. She shoved her arms into the sleeves of her terrycloth bathrobe, her feet into old-lady slippers. She scuffed to the bathroom, turned on the shower, and waited for the steam. The cheap plastic toilet seat caved a little when she sat on it. The vanity was so close she rested her cheek against the white semi-gloss countertop. She conjured up a Florida morning with overcast skies and warm air. Living with her father lacked appeal, but she could see herself in a garden apartment over one of the narrow streets of Key West, behind the main drag where vacationers and cruisers came to eat, shop, and drink at her father's bar. She pictured a little stone path leading to the sidewalk. A wrought-iron fence and a weedy patio with a table big enough for two people to have coffee. She'd wait tables or tend bar in the beginning. Soon her father would trust her to do the books and manage the staff. It was Ricki's job now, but Ricki was in her sixties and couldn't work forever. Dawn would leave her apartment in the morning with a leather planner tucked under her arm where she kept a to-do list and calendar. She'd sit at the bar in the morning and work with a glass of juice beside her: orange, mango, grapefruit, pineapple, or guava depending on her mood. When the occasional regular came in to drink before noon, Dawn would lend an ear and offer counsel.

Cleaning houses in Florida would not be an option. She wouldn't have to. This was where her brain got stuck, always. People and their goddamned assumptions, as though moving away for that fresh start were the same as a reset button. Once you saw something you couldn't unsee it. Once you put miles on a car, you couldn't undrive them. As sure as logical people like Matthew said just do it, those people hadn't shredded a pair of jeans skidding onto the pavement, a landing so forceful and abrupt you got stuck there. Of course she wanted to go, but wanting to go and going weren't the same.

I'm not coming, Dad. Go ahead and hire someone. My life is here, with Mom and Davis.

She wouldn't admit the truth, that living in the trailer in the same old town was her penitence. Now that Mrs. Folly had reached out, she experienced new yearnings of hope that she could be forgiven.

With Christmas coming, you've been on my mind. I'm holding a prayer service. Perhaps you could be there.

Mrs. Folly's voice had been strained, with each word clipped from the word before. Terry always said that sentimentality was her most annoying trait. He hated posing for the photos, missing parties for family reunions, the way she saved his baby food jars in a plastic container in the basement. Dawn heard it and wanted to believe Mrs. Folly missed her. Not just Terry. Her.

Dawn peeled off the layers and stepped into the shower stall. The water washed her with a chill until its heat broke through. She pumped shampoo into her palm and worked it through her hair. Standing in the steam, she inhaled the green apple scent. Getting ready had always been one of her least favorite chores. Exhaustion overcame her. She had no idea what was going through Mrs. Folly's mind. Even if she did, Terry would still be dead. She rinsed the shampoo out.

Were it not for Matthew's photography project, she may have wrapped her hair in a towel and crawled back into bed. She was grateful for a reason not to, a reason unrelated to the Follys or the accident or the past. She used twice as much conditioner

as she should. Matthew she could deal with. Matthew kept her
sane. Wednesdays were the Rileys. They could make it fun. She
left the conditioner on an extra minute.
At least allowing Matthew to photograph her prompted
hair-washing three mornings in a row. Certainly a record.

Dawn stood in front of the mirror to apply moisturizer, leaving a thick layer over the patches on her elbows. A car door
squeaked outside as it opened and closed. She pulled on clothes
and hurried. Someone knocked before she could peek through
the blinds, two quick raps of someone's knuckles. Not Justice.
He did a two-pound punch with the butt of his fist. Her heart
beat in her throat. She considered opening the door with the
chain latched, but couldn't get up the nerve. For as many times
as she'd imagined someone finally coming for her—police de-
tectives, Terry's parents, the woman from the Superstore—she
must not have really believed it.
    She heard a key in the lock as the knob began to rattle. In-
stinct kicked in. She held on tightly and leaned with her full
weight toward the inside of the trailer. She willed herself to be
as heavy as cement, heavier if it meant keeping someone out.
The person on the other side tugged. The door opened an inch
and thumped shut. Dawn tightened her grip and held on.
    A whimper escaped her. She lost her handle for a second
and heard the knob rattle when she fumbled to get her hands
around it. She watched a spray of saliva land on her forearm.
The droplets reminded her of being alive—human—and how
the adrenalin firing through her body would help her fight.
    "What on earth?" she heard on the other side.
    Dawn let go in surprise. The door swung open until the
chain latch caught, slamming louder than if it had closed. She
took a moment to steady herself before unhooking the chain.
    Her mother pushed into the trailer wearing her favorite ter-
rycloth tracksuit. The jacket was unzipped far enough to show
off her narrow neck and delicate collarbones.

"It's like Fort Knox in here," she said.

"Jesus, Mom. You scared the shit out of me."

"I didn't think the chain would be latched. Don't you usually leave it undone?"

"The only time it's unlatched is when I'm not here," Dawn said.

"Oh, well, that surprises me. I swear it's never been latched."

"Trust me. It is always latched."

She buried her hands into her damp hair. She twisted it into a knot to keep it off her neck. Taking a breath was always important when her mom came over. Otherwise the conversation went off course so fast you couldn't backpedal your way out.

"Okay, whatever you say. Make your mother feel like a crazy person."

"What are you doing here anyway? You know I'm usually at work by now."

"Your mother can't stop in for a visit to say hello?"

"At least text me. You're lucky I don't own a gun."

"This," she said, swaying and gesturing to the room around her. "This makes me nervous, you being all worked up. That's why I stopped by."

"Mom. I swear to God."

You have to take Susan with a grain of salt, her father said. *She's in a world of her own where everyone's against her.*

Her mother thrived on surface conversations. It always sounded like arguing. Her thoughts went as far forward as tomorrow, as far back as an hour ago, and as deep as a puddle of beer on the kitchen table. Her mother rarely planned. If she had dreams for the future, she was incapable of communicating them. She liked Davis to do the thinking, which he liked too. Delicate, fragile Susan needed taking care of.

"I have a surprise for you in the car," her mother said. "Wait here."

"Why didn't you just bring it in?"

From behind, her mother's figure resembled a prepubescent girl with long, willowy limbs and no curves. She never ate enough and found nourishment in beer and cigarettes. Dawn gratefully accepted her genetic tendencies to like food, her physicality stemming from her father's side of the family. Her mother closed the door on her way out and came back inside a minute later. Dawn tried to glare, but she wouldn't return eye contact. Even if Dawn accused her directly, her mother would never admit coming over during the day while Dawn worked. To what? To snoop, probably, for medical information in case Dawn was keeping secrets. To mess with her in some way.

"Davis wanted them," she said, lifting a box of doughnuts. "I decided to stop by. Want one?"

"No. And you don't need to check up on me."

"But I stopped by. You have to take one."

"This is why you stopped by?" Dawn said, gesturing to the box. "Not this?" She gestured wildly to the room the way her mother had.

Dawn flipped open the box and chose the gross one that looked like a wagon wheel rolled in little pieces of peanuts. She set it on a paper towel on the counter. She knew better than to take a flavor Davis liked. She'd had her hand slapped.

"Thanks," Dawn said. "Thanks a lot."

"Let me see," her mother said, gesturing with her small hands, pretty like Dawn's but older with the beginning of arthritis in her knuckles. Her wedding ring from Davis lacked luster.

Dawn sighed and pulled up the sleeve of her sweatshirt. Her mother set the doughnuts on the counter and dropped to a knee. She scanned one elbow for at least a minute, rotating Dawn's arm. Her mother's hair wasn't as curly as her own and streaked with gray. She always pulled it back into a tight bun. Her face, clean of makeup, was still pretty despite the wrinkles around her eyes and lining her forehead.

"It's awful to see you like this. You're a wreck."

"I thought you were breaking into my house! You know I get to work by ten."

"Did you research that vitamin E oil Davis talked about?"

"I talked to Dad. He said I should move south. He offered me a job at the bar."

Her mother stared at her, her face devoid of expression. The wisps of curls around her face made her look a little crazy, unhinged. Dawn couldn't help feeling satisfied.

"What, forever?"

"He invited me. He asked."

"Is this your way of telling me I'm a terrible mother?"

"Calm down, Mom. A change, that's all."

"I'll have to see what Davis thinks about this."

"Davis won't care," Dawn said.

"He cares more than you think. I don't expect you to believe it. He wants to see you have a happy life. He wants it for you and me."

"See then? He'll be glad to have me out of here. Win win."

Her mother gave her a long stare. For a moment, Dawn thought she'd actually convinced her. After all the years of resentment, her mother would finally let it go. There was no real reason she held such a grudge against Dawn's father. It would probably be a relief for Davis too.

Her mother shook her head and made a sound like a dog's yowl when it yawns. "You're going to have to learn the hard way, I guess. Your father, always making life sound so simple and carefree."

"It's not a bad philosophy, Mom."

Her mother leaned over the kitchen counter and squinted to see through the window blinds. "I have a coffee for Davis in the car. It's probably getting cold."

"I have to get to work anyway," Dawn said.

"We can walk out together," her mother said, companionably taking her arm. Dawn pulled away.

"I'm not ready to go."

Her mother eyed the door. "Try the vitamin E. Have your elbows been hurting?"

"You get used to it."

"I suppose that's mostly true," she said, "even though it's sad to me."

Dawn locked the door behind her mother and sidestepped to watch her through the kitchen window. She paused at Dawn's car and traced the chip on the windshield. She shielded her eyes to peek in the passenger window.

"Christ," Dawn said aloud. "Why?"

Her mother got into her car and drove up the road. How many times had she come in when the chain was unlatched? Dawn wouldn't put it past her; she'd watched her mother remove the lid from the neighbor's trashcan her whole life without flinching when the neighbor complained about the raccoons. Dawn wasn't positive, but she nearly swore on a memory of her mother taking the scissors to her father's paycheck and washing it down the sink. He'd combed the house for it, had even yelled.

Dawn leaned against the door. On the counter, little pieces of peanut decorated the paper towel surrounding the doughnut. One by one, she watched them break away from the surface and tumble down the slope until they dropped. It was like they knew the best escape was to separate from the source of what brought them to her trailer in the first place. Dawn swept the mess across the counter into the garbage can.

She headed to the bathroom to dig the ointment from underneath the sink. At least her mom was right about that. The cool gel eased the burn from bending the joint. She should get in the habit of using the stuff. In a way, though, sometimes the resistance of the skin, pin prickles, and pain that spidered to her arms made her feel better, not worse.

The stairway of the Rileys' townhouse smelled like the caramel popcorn Dawn remembered from the time her parents took her to Chicago before they split. They'd stood in a line that wrapped around the block, waiting for world-famous popcorn that came served up in a paper bag. All three of them dug in at the same time and bumped hands.

Her mother had pulled her hand from the bag, clutching her wrist as though she'd been injured. *Well,* she'd said. *After you two, I suppose.*

Dawn hadn't liked the popcorn. Too sticky. Created a mess. Her father had eaten the entire bag, not happily, but more like he couldn't stop. Finally, he'd found his chance to have an indulgence he craved. Dawn remembered a feeling of divide: her mother seemed pleased Dawn shared her distaste for the situation; her father, glad no one cared to have his treat. Dawn took it as good luck. She'd somehow managed to make both her parents think she was on the right side.

She started her days at the Rileys' with the same sense of hopeful duty; the smell inside the front door was inviting and sweet. It almost tricked you into thinking you'd found the right place, somewhere you wanted to be. Trek up a flight of stairs, though, and it transformed into the shell of a house masquerading as a home.

The building was old, a weathered brownstone, though the front door was new and embedded with modern locks and bolts from a renovation to restore the block of townhomes. Closing the front door left you in stillness. The world disappeared: its sunlight, traffic noises, and sewer smells. She stood in the hushed foyer, a narrow, tall room with a few paces to walk before you hit the stairs going up. An antique hutch hugged the left side of the space. Pulling open the doors revealed two empty hooks. One item sat atop the hutch, a China doll whose tiny legs hung over the edge so you could see she wore bloomers underneath the ivory dress. Aside from the pink circles on the doll's cheeks, she was colorless.

The ground-floor room of the townhouse hid behind French doors, but the Rileys told Dawn not to bother cleaning it. She'd peeked once and understood. The room contained a fully decorated Christmas tree, piles of clothing, wrapping paper, and stacks of books. Old dolls and toys spilled from boxes. A hoarder's dream room. She'd been meaning to poke through the mess to see what she could discover about Bridget and Mitch Riley, best described as hipsters, but a little too dorky for the title.

Dawn gladly passed the hoarding room today and climbed the stairs, clutching the railing and wondering again why they hadn't replaced the threadbare carpet. You'd think the renovation would have included fresh stairs. The heritage must be part of the initial charm. Leave the building face and foyers untouched, demolish and rebuild the rest. The top of the stairs marked the transformation from old to new, from cluttered and sweet to sterile.

The second and third floors of the Riley home boasted expensive contemporary décor in an uninspired color scheme: beige, white, and black with stainless steel accents and appliances.

"Mitch likes neutral colors," Bridget had told Dawn the day she came over to pick up the key and get the tour. "It's simpler this way."

Dawn nodded at the woman, who was probably less than ten years older. She wore tailored black pants and a white blouse. Patent-leather flats. Her brown hair was confined to a low ponytail. Bridget's remark held a tinge of apology, the first hint of dork. To make up for it, she launched into a slew of high-tech phrases about her job, which she must get back to so as not to create any setbacks for her team. Her complexion, flawless if not childlike, made the words seem scripted, part of a role in which she'd been poorly cast.

She'd left Dawn standing alone in the kitchen thinking how Bridget's legs were a little too short and her butt a smidgen too big for her pants. After she was sure her customer was gone, Dawn had tested the echo in the room by calling out words like hello, echo, and weirdo.

People like the Rileys seemed sophisticated on the surface. Most people never earned enough money to afford a townhouse, especially one in the trendy part of town where Adams intersected Vine. A handful of popular restaurants were dispersed among a few blocks. There was even a Starbucks now.

Little shops lined both streets, selling items like antiques, tea, and baby clothes. Some empty shops sat ready for occupancy with wood floors swept and windows washed. Dawn pictured Bridget and Mitch Riley locking their front door and walking down the street to the restaurant with brick oven pizzas and outdoor seating in the summer. They'd leave a 20 percent tip for sure.

After cleaning a couple times, Dawn realized sophistication was the intention, but boring was the truth. She had no visuals to absorb or admire. People in their early thirties might not have a sense of style yet; maybe it took until your forties to figure out what kind of art to buy. But that couldn't be true. Even Dawn had ideas for how she'd fix up a place. She'd at least buy dishes with a pattern and not a pile of expensive white plates and black coffee mugs.

Today Dawn set her mop and bucket on the pale oak floor and relaxed in one of the black leather recliners. The sweet smell was gone, hanging somewhere between the front door and the top of the stairs. Here, two glass side tables held a single stainless reindeer. When it wasn't Christmas, the reindeers were replaced with swirled orbs of black and silver. Not exactly knickknacks. More like accent pieces. All objects intentional for design, no meaning attached. The simplicity of the place made it a breeze to clean. She rarely broke a sweat at the Rileys' even though they paid her $125 a week, an outrageous sum considering the amount of mess.

Dawn closed her eyes and filled her lungs with the dustless, cool air. So quiet, so still, it was easy to imagine being surrounded by an enormous empty warehouse. It always stunned her to open her eyes and see the walnut-stained dining room table nearby, surrounded by high-back chairs with black seat covers. The fabric on the seats did not attract lint, in the event a guest happened to bring some in from the more complicated world outside.

An unfamiliar rumbling from the foyer caused her to leap to her feet. The front door slammed and so did the door on the hutch. Murmurs of conversation accompanied the thump of footsteps. Dawn hadn't known that movement in the stairway caused the mirror on the dining room wall to vibrate. These changes in her perception of the Rileys' townhouse left her unbalanced. People weren't supposed to come. People never came. She could have called out a greeting, words of warning, a question about who was there, but no. She stood there like an idiot with a death wish as the footsteps on the stairs grew closer.

High heels clicked onto the oak as a woman appeared. Clearly not a burglar, or if she was, one Dawn could easily take down with a slide tackle. Definitely not a contractor, as she'd never seen a repair person in a skirt. The woman's forehead appeared longer by the way she styled her bleached hair with one of those plastic inserts to make it taller. Her perfume swept into the room and reminded Dawn of the ladies working behind the makeup counters at the mall.

The woman stepped forward and Mitch Riley followed. Dawn recognized him from the wedding portrait on the wall. He'd lost weight, she noticed, since the tire around his middle had all but disappeared. His eyes were shadowy and undeniable. He had a distinct face, making it impossible to confuse him with someone else. It could have been the sideburns or perhaps the arch of his eyebrows. The weight loss was an improvement, but it hadn't done the trick. The way he stood with his chin forward and head tilted gave him the appearance of trying to see ahead of everyone else despite not being first in line.

He didn't notice her standing there. The woman saw Dawn and stopped.

"Who's this?" the woman said.

Mitch locked eyes with Dawn and brought a fist to his chest with a loud thump.

"Holy shit!" he said.

Dawn reached for her mop handle and churned it in the bucket. She set it on the floor in ready position. The ropes were stiff and dry with no soap or water in sight.

"Hey," Dawn said. "Wednesday. I'm cleaning."

"You scared the hell out of me," Mitch said.

"Sorry."

"She's not here for us?" the woman said.

Her fingers fluttered as she reached back to lay her hand on Mitch's arm.

"This is the cleaning lady," Mitch said.

He stepped out and in front of the woman, shoving his hands into his pants pockets and rattling his keys. Clearing his throat, he extracted them and aimed his car key down the stairs, clicking repeatedly until Dawn heard the distant chirps.

To Dawn, he said, "We're here to pick up some documents from the office. I forgot them."

"Cool," Dawn said, lifting a fresh jug of Magic from her bucket and peering inside for the twine. "Pretend I'm not here."

"Yeah. Thanks," Mitch said.

To the woman, he said, "The office is this way, Victoria."

Victoria followed him to the third-floor stairway. Her black heels were so high her ankles wobbled. Despite the winter weather, she wore no hosiery. Her legs were very thin and so pale Dawn could make out the veins snaking beneath her skin. Her red silk blouse wrapped around her waist and tied in front. She'd gone overboard with the makeup. Dawn always thought it overkill to wear every product at once. It smacked of desperation.

She couldn't imagine how long it took to paint a face like that.

"I thought she was here for us," Victoria said, following Mitch upstairs.

"No. You and I."

"Will it be long? Our meeting."

"A half hour tops."

Before disappearing from sight, Victoria turned and squinted at Dawn, a dirty look if she ever got one.

Dawn's head ached from the confusion. She removed the elastic band holding the mass of her damp hair and shook it out. Her reserves were exhausted from being startled twice in one morning. She almost wished she had eaten the doughnut her mother brought, but she had never liked them. She opened the refrigerator. The Rileys had a loaf of fancy Italian bread so she pulled a slice from the middle and stuffed it in her mouth. She inspected the row of condiments against the door and decided on a lavish raspberry jam. She spooned some in her mouth and tried to mix it around. She helped herself to a bottle of water and chugged. The dizziness subsided. She buried the bottle in the trash.

Dawn sat in the recliner to think it over. What did she care if Mitch brought his secretary home and banged her? The woman had no reason to give her the stink eye, none at all. It wasn't so much the stare as the nature of the stare. She recognized it because she'd given it. It said *fuck you*. It said *don't judge me*. As if a cleaning lady could judge someone with a job in an office that required skirts and heels. Dawn scrubbed toilets, for God's sake.

Perhaps Victoria hated other women, regardless of job classification or pecking order.

Dawn vacuumed first to make it clear she wasn't listening. As she pushed their Miele Complete C3 over the area rug and across the wood floor, she cheered herself with the thought that once Victoria screwed her way to a promotion, money could buy her a little class.

Dawn took a moment to breathe against the glass an inch from her nose. The warmth bounced back to her face. She could almost take a nap there, between the glass of the coffee table and the shelf below. She closed her eyes to enjoy the sensation of being trapped within the glass coffin. She imagined how she might appear from above, like the splayed outline of a drowned woman in a pool with her hair floating around her head. Or like a doll imprisoned in a shadow box.

She listened to the smooth hum of the refrigerator that rose

toward the high ceilings combined with the intermittent ticking
of a crystal clock on the mantel.

When she first started cleaning at the Rileys', she'd fired a
ring of Magic around the perimeter of the glass coffee table
and another on the shelf. Despite the squeaky-clean pane and
gleaming wood, Dawn never walked away satisfied. She'd considered the possibility she'd discovered a surface unresponsive
to Magic.

Then she'd swept her thumb under the glass. It left a greasy
smear. After evaluating the predicament of how to wash the
underside of the expansive tabletop, she'd dropped to her knees
and back-bended to find she could, indeed, fit under there. A
tight fit, yes, but no worries. She'd perfected the process.

She opened her eyes now to Mitch Riley standing over her, a
surprise since he and Victoria had left hours ago. The sight of
his pale blue tie hanging down the front of his shirt gave the
illusion she was about to be impaled. Dawn screamed and lifted
the heavy tabletop with her knees before recognizing her boss
and letting it drop with a rumble and scratch. She sat up, though
not far before clunking her forehead and settling back against
the shelf. Mitch's eyes opened wide and his eyebrows creased.
He brought a thumb and forefinger to his lips.

Dawn gave the glass a couple swipes with the paper towels
in her hand before sliding out. She stood nose to nose with her
employer. He was shorter than she'd realized. She leaned to
wipe the tabletop.

"I'll bet you didn't realize I was so thorough," she said.

She stood taller, making sure to straighten any slouch and
lengthen her neck. She wanted Mitch to know she wasn't naive.
Despite being young, she understood his type and wasn't one
of the weak ones.

"I'd forgotten we have you," Mitch said.

His neck flushed. Sweat appeared on his brow. She could tell
by the way he lifted his arm and let it drop how much he wanted
to wipe it with his sleeve.

Dawn waited for Mitch to take charge, which seemed like

the best move for any domestic employee, especially one who had been forgotten. Speak when spoken to. Mitch dug into his pants pocket and handed her a bank envelope.

"Bridget leaves a check," Dawn said, taking it but keeping her hand out so he could take it back.

"No, no. I know she does."

"What's this?"

"Well, uh, I like having you clean for us. We like it. Bridget and I. What are you, early twenties?"

"Pretty much," Dawn said.

"You in school?"

"No."

"Sorry, I didn't mean it to sound like that. I don't want to imply you should be. I wondered."

"Nope. Not in school. I clean houses for people like you guys."

"That's cool," he said. "Cool that you're in business for yourself. You are, right? You don't work for a service? A cleaning service, I mean."

His face flushed more and he transferred the dampness from his brow onto his right cuff.

"Self-employed."

"That's cool," he said. "This is for you. You know, like a bonus."

She let the envelope fall against her thigh and avoided it. She wished for pockets so she could stuff it away, but she always wore leggings to the Rileys' to keep from scratching the coffee table with the rivets on her jeans.

"Kind of like an apology for startling you earlier," Mitch said. "For bringing work home on the day you're here."

"No big deal. Are you sure?"

She lifted the envelope and knew he saw her do it. Giving someone the opportunity to take their money back wasn't the best way to get ahead in the world, but the unexpected handout warranted confirmation Mitch wasn't going to regret it later and find a way to force her to give it back.

"Yeah. Take it. It's for you. As a thanks."

"Okay. Well, thanks."

"I appreciate your discretion," Mitch said. "You know, not overreacting."

"I wouldn't. I work here, but it's your house."

"Thanks. I appreciate that."

Mitch slid his hands into his pockets and rocked back on his heels.

"Okay then," he said. "I'm going to head back to the office. I don't usually schedule meetings here, you know. I won't anymore."

"Thanks a lot. For the bonus. For your faith in my abilities."

He headed toward the stairs. His shoes, gleaming like toffee, clacked until he thumped onto the stairs and disappeared. Dawn had the envelope open before the front door released him. She slid out the hundred dollar bills and fanned them. Five brand new, crisp notes, still hanging on to the fresh, inky smell from the bank.

Dawn gave the Rileys' guest bedroom a quick once over. No one slept there. Nothing moved. The closet remained empty week after week. Sometimes she vacuumed to rearrange the pattern on the carpet, but usually she dragged a handful of damp paper towels across the dresser, bed frame, side table, and windowsill. She sat on the edge of the white quilt and hugged one of the beige pillows. Its linen ruffle made it slightly less uninteresting than the rest of the townhouse. She considered jumping to grab the leg of the China doll from on top of the hutch. All she wanted was a hug. Not that anything was really the matter, but the money from Mitch changed everything.

Here it was, Wednesday, and she hadn't begun to think—really think—about whether she might move—really move—across the country. Flights to Florida cost less than five hundred dollars. She could buy a ticket and go. She could do it today, right now.

Had she written a list of pros and cons of going versus staying? Had she pulled out the lease on her trailer site to find out how to break it? Had she considered telling a customer or two she might not be around anymore? Of course not. Her dad always said actions spoke louder than words. She tried insisting to herself that her lack of doing a goddamn thing proved she didn't want to go. Or if she did, not badly enough.

But stop right there.

Five hundred dollars meant she'd only have to stay with her dad for a night or two. She could find a cheap room and pay first month's rent. Tips from the bar would keep her afloat until a paycheck. Worrying about money, thanks to Mitch Riley, had become a nonissue for the first time. All she needed to do was pack and get the hell out. Mrs. Folly would hold the prayer vigil regardless of her absence. Robert McIntyre could do his own laundry for a couple weeks. She'd never have to see the guy from the laundromat again. Or drive around the sunken pothole at the entrance to the trailer park. Her mother couldn't come over without calling in advance. Matthew, even Matthew, wanted her to go.

The need to protect the money overcame her. She hurried to the kitchen and snatched the bank envelope off the counter. She sat in the recliner and pushed it under her thigh. When that place warmed, she let herself believe it. People always said money couldn't buy happiness, but it sure as hell could buy choices. Or change. You could use it to run as far away as it would take you.

Holding five one-hundred-dollar bills at once was the most she'd ever had in her presence. How strange to see the bills and own them, how oddly normal to already believe she was that much richer. She could picture having more bills, a bigger stack that kept growing as she added to it her tips from the bar each night. It didn't matter they'd be one-dollar bills and fives, with an occasional twenty mixed in. People with money generated more money and that's how they got ahead.

She couldn't sit there all day with $500 under her leg. Putting it in her purse didn't feel safe enough. If Mitch came home to take it back, that was the first place he'd go. She considered tucking the bills inside her bra, which her grandmother used to do, but Dawn's boobs didn't fill out a bra like her grandma's had. Short of swallowing the bills, she wasn't sure how she could be positive they were safe and in her possession.

She remembered the duct tape in the kitchen drawer.

She got a fingernail underneath enough to unwind as long a piece as her arm allowed. She struggled to maneuver the tape, T-shirt, and envelope until she'd managed to bind the money to her left ribcage with a few passes around her body. To be safe, she taped the top of the envelope closed. Her money. Money she'd earned cleaning houses, for being discreet. For being exactly the kind of person she wanted to be.

I dare you to try to take something away from me, she heard herself say to Mitch Riley.

She found her eyes in the mirror and noticed the inverted arc of pale freckles framing her right eye. Her breath caught in her throat and emotion swelled in her chest with such force her eyes widened. The blacks of her pupils dilated and zoomed before she was able to look away.

Dawn's blessed with a wider range of vision than most people, she remembered her father saying to Terry the day they told him about the engagement. He'd lifted her hand and peered underneath his glasses to examine the ring, nodding. *You can't put anything past her, you know*, he added. *She'll catch you red-handed.*

He dropped her hand and cupped the side of her face, running his thumb along the line of freckles. Terry stepped closer and leaned in.

She won't catch me doing nothing, Terry said, and her father cheerfully slapped him on the back.

That was before her dad moved away, when he lived in the apartment complex across town with the pool. They used to swim together and lay out in the summer. Her dad used Tropicana suntan oil, SPF 4. He liked being tan. She imagined the two of them, a couple of beach bums, strolling around Key West together. His hair had gotten grayer since the last time she'd seen him, but he looked closer to thirty-five than forty-five in the last photo he'd texted with Ricki and the waitstaff serving drinks at a street festival. If he wasn't wearing shorts and flip-flops, it was a pair of frayed khakis rolled at the ankle and a button-down shirt, untucked. And he smiled, Dawn realized. He smiled a lot, whereas her mother did not.

Like her dad, Dawn longed to be free from her mother's negativity and lack of support. Misguided support. Multiple personality disorder. She didn't know what to call it. Davis seemed up for the challenge. He needed her mother's kind of neediness.

Dawn never understood why her mother continued to bad-mouth her dad. He never behaved as badly as Mitch Reilly was treating Bridget. Her dad was nice. He'd been nice to Terry.

Dawn lowered her eyes to the silver bands of tape around her torso. The bottom-third of the envelope stuck out. With the five bills inside, its thickness was indisputable. No one would be able to get the money from her body without tearing it clean in half. "I earned it," she told her reflection. "I earned every goddamned cent."

She pulled her phone from her pocket and called Matthew.

"Come whenever."

"It's early," he said.

"It's not dirty here. It's a waste of my time. I'll take their money, but Jesus. I'm not staying here for hours when I don't have to."

She hadn't intended to be crabby.

"I can come," Matthew said. "Nico didn't have an assignment for me anyway. I'm sitting here bored on Instagram."

"Fine."

"No game today, D-flate?"

"I'll tell you when you get here."

"What happened? You sound serious."

"I am serious, Matthew. I'm as serious as a heart attack."

"That is not true, D-ceit. You aren't serious. As much as

you want to be. As much as you think you are. You're laughing inside."

"So?"

"So, it's funny. Laugh. Don't be a bitch."

"I'm not a bitch."

"Sure you are," Matthew said. "It's part of your charm."

"I didn't used to be."

"Bullshit. I don't believe that for a second."

"You didn't know me."

"Dawn. Shut up. You've always been a bitch and you know it. You want me to think there was some transformation, but I know that's a load. Admit it."

"Fuck you. I don't know why I'm friends with you," she said.

"Fuck *you*," Matthew said. "That's why you're friends with me. That's exactly why you're friends with me."

Dawn wanted to tell Matthew to meet her at the bar. She wanted to crumble and let him wrap his arms around her. She yearned to wail and sob between explanations and proclamations about how fucking unfair it was for Mrs. Folly to be angry with *her*. Mrs. Folly should be angry with herself. Dawn suffered too. My God, how she'd suffered: physically, emotionally, and the guilt—all the goddamned guilt—when she was only trying to help. They were supposed to be her family. They were supposed to *love* her. Matthew would listen and understand. He'd buy her however many rounds of Makers she wanted and wouldn't tell her to stop. She'd told herself, though, she was done with that. Crying to Matthew broke all the rules. Now was not the time to turn back.

"Fine," she said. "Come over whenever."

"I'll pick up a pizza. I'll stop and get some beer."

"Buy me some Makers and I'll owe you for life."

"Done. I'll be there in twenty."

"Okay," she said, choking on the word.

"Think of ideas for the shoot. Like if it's a sexy house or a sexless house. Is it old or young? Negligee or housecoat. Juice box or martini."

"Okay. I will."

Dawn set the phone on the table and lifted her T-shirt.

Shit.

She'd forgotten her body didn't belong to her this week. It seemed ridiculous now. Like any sane woman would tape money to herself. Like Matthew wouldn't be reminded how messed up she was, how young and stupid. A hot mess. She looked like a goddamned suicide bomber. She'd never be able to explain.

She sat on the floor to contemplate, noticing a layer of dust around the baseboards. She crawled to her bucket for the Magic and paper towels. As she wiped it away, she considered the option of tearing the tape off, right here and now. It wouldn't be hard to come up with an explanation if there were marks: Justice taped her up for fun. She and Justice experimented with masochism. He'd believe anything if she mentioned Justice. She'd done a great job confusing Matthew about the nature of their relationship.

The wounds would be too fresh, though. Matthew wasn't dumb. He'd see it wasn't possible injuries had occurred the night before. She considered telling him Mitch Riley came home for a nooner and begged for sex. He might buy that. She could laugh about the five hundred dollars. She took it since he wasn't all that good anyway. She heard the sound of the laugh she'd use to convince Matthew she'd slept with a married man. He'd probably buy it.

"That's your problem," she said, standing up.

She avoided the mirror for fear she'd punch her reflection. She pulled her T-shirt over her head and threw it onto the floor. It landed on the damp place and didn't give her the satisfaction of sliding to the corner.

"Why does everyone have to buy what you're selling? Why can't you tell the truth? He's your friend."

The effort to crane her neck to see the edge of the tape shot a cramp down the length of her spine. Truth might not exist anymore. Dawn might not exist. Even if she did, she didn't because she didn't matter. She clawed at her ribs, the envelope, and tape until she got it. She tore the first pass around her body effortlessly, hardly feeling pressure. The second pass wouldn't come so easily, she knew, so she screamed as she did it because it was better to scream on purpose than by accident.

The crumpled mass of tape settled on the floor as the normal sounds of the townhouse settled around her. The white envelope stuck out of the wad. Her torso burned as though someone held fire against her skin. There was no skin, she knew, thus the heat. Her elbows still burned like that. Somehow her body remembered even if she wanted to forget. Bodies prohibited forgetting what you did, why you did it, the sensations, what you'd wanted to happen, what did happen.

She crawled to the tape to pry the envelope free. Realizing the impossibility, she slit through the bottom with her thumbnail and slid the bills out one by one. She placed the money in a pile and leaned into her elbows, understanding they ached, but not in comparison to the rest of her. Pain came in various forms, in multiple varieties. Like the box of doughnuts. She balanced her forehead on the cool floor to keep from passing out. Pain swelled with each breath. She recognized the tickling around her waist as droplets of blood.

Bridget Riley might never know the money was missing from some bank account or another. Mitch could tell lies forever. Just like her mother told lies about her father. Everybody told lies. Dawn lied all the time, to everyone, to herself. She ached for the wash of honesty or realization, an epiphany. She wanted answers: on where to live, on who to be, on what she could do to move on from the pain.

She controlled her breathing until the burning faded to stinging. The stinging gradually reduced to throbbing.

Terry had to have felt it a hundred times worse before he died.

ॐ

Matthew stood with the pizza box balanced on one hand like a deliveryman, gazing around the room. Dawn wondered where he went during those times he quietly observed. Perhaps he thought of photos he'd taken or photos he wanted to take. Maybe he thought about Jen. Surely it had to be deep thoughts, unlike Dawn's shallow lists of things to clean and how to clean them. Her biggest decision on any given day was whether to drink alone or to stop by to drink with Justice. She and Matthew rarely went out for drinks anymore.

Dawn spread the towel over the coffee table and signaled he was okay to set down the box. She ripped some paper towels from her roll, grabbed a couple glasses, and tried to get comfortable on the floor. Matthew opened the Makers Mark and poured at least three fingers in each glass. She filled her mouth with whiskey and tried not to flinch at the pulsing pain beneath the gauze wrapped around her torso.

Matthew flipped open the box. Half the pie was covered in slices of black and green olives.

"I take back every mean thing I've ever said to you," she said.

She picked off some stray pieces.

"Just keep them away from me," Matthew said, pulling from the side with pepperoni and bacon. He sat down on the floor. "The smell of them makes me want to puke."

Dawn munched the olives and sipped more whiskey. She hated mushrooms as much as Matthew hated olives, but she'd never have ordered a half-mushroom pizza. His thoughtfulness touched her. Plus he'd splurged for the Makers. No one could accuse Matthew of being selfish. Granted, he loved whiskey, too, but the pizza was a gesture of kindness that couldn't be denied.

He dropped a paper towel into his lap for a napkin and selected the biggest slice with the most bacon and a bubble baked into the crust. He widened his eyes like a kid getting the prime piece at a birthday party. Dawn laughed and tried to adjust to a comfortable position. The thought of gauze sticking to the wounds left her queasy. At least lunch was a distraction, plus she had a story to tell.

"The guy who lives here, he gave me a $500 bonus today."

"Are you kidding me?"

Matthew stood, his glass in one hand and the slice of pizza drooping in the other. From her position on the floor, it seemed like he'd grown. Despite herself, Dawn smiled and blamed the whiskey.

"It's locked in the trunk with my purse."

"Was it, like, your cleaning anniversary?"

"There was definitely a reason."

"Tell me, D-bunker!"

"He brought home a woman from work. Forgot I was going to be here."

Matthew pushed the bottom third of his slice into his mouth and nodded for her to continue. She told him about Victoria. By the time she finished, his pizza was back on the table. He'd drank half his whiskey and sat back on his heels. He rose to stand on his knees.

"So he nailed her anyway? She wasn't from work."

"Yes, she was. She was all suited up in her professional attire."

"Dawn. She was a hooker."

She dipped her crust into the whiskey and let it soak for a long second.

"A prostitute," Matthew said.

"I know what a hooker is. Who pays hookers? He's a decent enough guy. He can find women to have sex with for free."

Matthew shook his head and laughed.

"If she were from work, he wouldn't have stayed and fucked her. He stayed because he had to pay her anyway."

Dawn pondered this as she ate the soggy crust. Matthew's clarification caused all the details to make sense: why Victoria wore no hosiery in December, the makeup, the way she'd touched Mitch's arm. Dawn was pretty sure she had never seen a hooker before. Then again, who knew? All those women Dawn assumed were cocktail waitresses or sales associates in high-end stores could have been working girls. Prostitutes weren't just ladies walking up and down streets in the bad parts of town at night. Victoria surely didn't have a pimp. She probably ventured out on her own, just like Dawn had when she started her cleaning business. Victoria probably advertised on Craigslist, too, using code words that the hooker underworld understood. Matthew would undoubtedly know the lingo.

"How do you know so much about prostitutes?"

"I resent the implication," Matthew said.

"Answer the question."

"I used to do some freelance work for the strip clubs. That putting-yourself-through-school stereotype is bullshit."

"How much do you think he paid her?" Dawn said.

"It varies. Those girls would blow a dude for fifty bucks."

"Victoria was high end."

She realized now why she'd gotten the glare and her stupidity for not figuring it out. Office worker trumped cleaning lady, but cleaning lady trumped hooker. No question. She folded and refolded her paper-towel napkin. Matthew nibbled a burnt bit of bacon with his front teeth, cheerfully. He loved bacon, or maybe he loved the notion of discussions about the lewd behavior of her customers, or it could be that he found amusement in her inability to interpret mature situations.

"This money could change my prospects," Dawn said.

"The guy is a sex addict so he brings home hookers on the side?"

Dawn nodded into her glass.

"He can't get his wife off?" Matthew said. "He tries and tries, but he can't do it. So he brings home someone he can get off."

"Hookers don't get off. Don't they fake it? I mean, how can they really feel all that sex? Aren't they actresses?"

"Your boy will accept a good faker, as long as he gets a blow job and cums in her face. That's why guys pay hookers."

"Maybe Bridget is the one who's insatiable. Mitch needs to bring home the professionals to practice and improve his game."

"No," Matthew said, reaching for the bottle and splashing

into both glasses. "It's always the guy who wants it more. Always."

"Bullshit. I know lots of women who like sex and want it."

She heard the way it sounded like a taunt.

"Well. Life isn't kosher if the guy's bringing home hookers. He paid you off."

"Lucky for me," Dawn said, shifting. "It could change everything."

"Gas money."

Matthew tilted his head as he sometimes did. He rested his chin in the palm of his hand and used his middle finger to grace the eyelashes of his right eye, like a child might rub a baby blanket. A strange habit for sure, but absolutely original to Matthew so it was okay. He lifted his glass with the other hand and took a sip. He regarded her over the top of it.

She broke eye contact. When Matthew remained silent, she leaned over the box and picked a couple olive rings from the pizza.

"What's the matter?" he said.

Giving him a dirty look seemed logical.

"It's almost like this money's upset you. It's five hundred bucks. Enjoy it. Save it. Spend it. Whatever you want."

"What would you do with it?"

"Me?" He inspected his fingernails before deciding upon his thumbnail. "I don't know, oil paint, new brushes."

She didn't like his answer, not that she knew what she wanted him to say.

"No airplane tickets for a trip to Savannah?"

"Oh yeah. That. I'd do that. Good idea."

She reached for her glass. She wanted to yell, to shriek, and shout that he should move there permanently. Everyone knew that moving away was the solution to the world's problems. The gauze shifted and she caught her breath as she slid the glass toward her.

"You keep flinching," Matthew said. "Are you hurt? Did that asshole hurt you?"

"Why would you say that?"

"The way you're moving."

"What asshole?" she said.

"The one who lives here and gave you $500!"

Dawn sighed.

"You're such a moron."

"Am I? I hope I am," Matthew said.

She finished her whiskey and held her glass across the table. After a pause, Matthew uncapped the bottle and poured a splash. Dawn set the glass on the table and adjusted her T-shirt.

"You're not entirely wrong. But it's unrelated to Mitch. And sex."

"Do you need to go to a hospital?"

"Now you're overreacting."

"What about the photo shoot? Want to skip it?"

"No! We didn't get conceptual yet," Dawn said.

Matthew slowly scanned the room as though Mitch were hiding behind a piece of furniture.

"I'm going to trust you'd ask for help right now if you needed it."

"You're so off base."

Matthew sat back on his heels and pulled a cigarette from his pack. He tucked it behind his ear. He looked her over for a while without speaking. Her insides softened at the idea he was worried about her. He cared about her. He wanted her to be okay and needed a few seconds longer to verify.

Finally, he smiled and raised an eyebrow.

"Why are we binge drinking?" he said. "I'm already loaded."

She was glad he said it. She'd heard the slow and lazy drag of her tongue when she'd said *conceptual*. Alcohol went down faster when there was more to think about and, ever since Victoria had appeared at the top of the stairway, Dawn's mind hadn't stopped. Five one-hundred-dollar bills, like Magic, set the groundwork for serious cleaning with little effort. And Matthew was right: the money had upset her.

"You brought the Makers. It's your fault we're drunk."

"Oh, for Christ's sake," Matthew said. "You're the only person I know who bitches me out for doing exactly what she says."

ॐ

"I have an idea," Dawn said.

"Tell me, D-ceit."

"You already used that one today."

She stood stiffly, but the Makers had done an excellent job with pain reduction. She relaxed and wiggled a little to see where it hurt the most.

Matthew followed her toward the stairway.

"You know how this place is so stark?" Dawn said.

"Stark. What does that mean? Stark."

"You know," Dawn said, leaning against the bannister when heat broke through and sent ribbons of pain around her middle. "It's sterile. Boring. Beige. And I know Bridget doesn't like that. She said. I mean, check out the doll."

Dawn pointed to the top of the hutch.

"It smells like my doctor's office in here."

The idea of Matthew at the doctor made her laugh. She'd never thought about him sitting on the exam table in a gown while some guy in a white coat listened to his heartbeat. The world grew larger, as it does when you imagine. A bigger world cheered her. More to do. More to see. More room to spread the possibilities.

"Can you reach the doll?" Dawn said. "Give her to me."

"Her?" Matthew said, reaching up and pulling it down by a leg.

"Be careful. She's a China doll. Don't break her face."

"A doll is an it," Matthew said, handing it to Dawn.

She balanced her in the crook of her arm and straightened the dress.

"Not to Bridget. She's the only sentimental possession of Bridget's in the whole place. Except for this."

She stepped to the French doors and pushed them open for the big reveal.

"Wow. That's a gorgeous mess," Matthew said. "Do you know how beautiful photographs can be of messes like this? Are those Cabbage Patch dolls? Do you think she sewed all those quilts?"

He turned to Dawn.

"It's a great room, but you'll get lost in the shots. The stuff will take over."

"I thought we could pluck some of the best pieces, like the China doll, to take upstairs. You know, kind of display it somewhere for contrast."

Matthew turned back to the hoarding room.

Dawn waited, wishing she'd brought her glass with her. She stroked the smooth side of the doll's face.

He walked through the door and began digging. Dawn thought to tell him to stop, but doubted Bridget would be able to notice if anything were moved or missing. Plus Matthew straightened a pile of magazines he nearly tripped over. *Cat Fancy*, which was strange since they had no pets. Perhaps Mitch was allergic or didn't like pet hair on his leather seats. Matthew moved on to a heap of clothes with tags still attached. He cleared a space on the table with his elbow and began moving one pile to the other. He shook out each T-shirt, sweatshirt, skirt, or dress and held it up to the light before wadding it back into a ball and tossing it away. He must have liked one, a purple sweatshirt with pastel letters spelling Los Angeles, because he hurled it out the door into the foyer.

Matthew removed his flannel and tied it around his waist. His cheeks had started to pinken. He stepped over to a box overflowing with Christmas lights and peered inside.

"They don't have any decorations out, do they?" he said.

"Not really."

"Two weeks to go. Kind of unusual."

"He's Jewish?"

"Or he won't let her put them out," Matthew said. "Barbies!"

Dawn stepped into the room. A huge storage tub sat on the floor with a tangle of naked Barbie dolls, legs and arms and hair, almost to the top. Matthew took one out by the hair and swung her around. He sent her sailing out the door with the sweatshirt. Dawn lifted the top of the smaller tub next to the dolls to find it full of miniature dresses, nurse uniforms, plaid pants, and bandanas. She reached to the bottom and scooped a handful of tiny plastic shoes: high heels, cowgirl boots, and slippers in all colors.

An old popcorn tin caught her eye so she pried off the lid to an overflow of folded papers that had been shoved down and held with the lid. Dawn unfolded one. She peered over her shoulder to see Matthew lifting the dress of a Cabbage Patch doll.

Amid fat hearts and flower doodles was a message, scrawled in pencil, probably by some sixth grader during class:

Dear Bridget,

You are my best friend, but Sara says you are her best friend. Do you have a best friend or are we both?

Love,

Tina

Dawn reached into the tin and stirred the papers with her arm to lift some from the bottom. She chose a folded piece of stationery, pale yellow, that showed the imprint of small neat cursive on the other side.

Dear Bridget:

I'm sorry I missed your birthday dinner. Spain was productive and worth the trip. I hope we can get together sometime soon or when you come home for Christmas.

Love,

Father

"She calls her dad 'Father'," Dawn called to Matthew.

"So what? He's her father. What do you want her to call him?"

Dawn shrugged. She wanted to dump the entire tin onto the floor and read until she'd decoded every one. She pushed the notes back into the mix and jammed the lid closed again. Maybe Bridget was the kind of woman who picked someone like her dad to marry, someone who didn't bother to adjust his schedule around her birthday. She wondered if Bridget had saved the letter because of the significance that her dad had written, or because it reminded her she couldn't count on him. All those messages saved. Dawn and Katelyn had written a couple thousand notes during high school and passed them between classes, but she hadn't saved a single one. Katelyn had been her best friend yet, except for a few old photos, there was no record. Her father never wrote to her, not even birthday cards. He always called, though. The first phone call on any birthday or holiday was her dad.

She wanted her drink. Badly. The sudden heat behind her eyes threatened tears. Placing her hands on her hips, she stood there pretending to browse a loaded bookshelf until the burning pressure left her skull and drained down her throat, taking the lump with it.

"I've got a good pile going," Matthew said. "We should decide which says the most."

"This room screams homesickness. Between sentimental value and actual prices, there's a million dollars worth of stuff in here." She picked up the China doll and wiped a smudge from her forehead.

"We'll need the money he gave you."

Dawn let the doll fall to her side. The tiny porcelain fingers touched her wrist. "I could buy a plane ticket, you know. I could be there tonight."

"You could," Matthew said. "But I hope you'll wait at least two more days."

She set the doll on the stairs and pulled her car keys from the hook. "The money's in my trunk."

"D-lite."

She caught the keys he'd tossed before they hit her in the stomach. "You're running out of D-words, Matt."

Matthew's eyes were rimmed in red, drunken and heavy.

"Grab my camera bag while you're out there. I'll get this organized."

Stepping onto the front porch, Dawn pushed the door closed
and waited a moment for her eyes to adjust. She pictured Matthew inside, rifling around the piles of color and texture. The
day was bustling and cold, in glaring contrast to the near-silent
innards of the Rileys' townhouse. Observing the street through
her drunken lens, she hurried down the porch steps to get the
stuff so she could get back inside, back to her friend and their
bottle, and the creativity of their project. The other decisions
could wait.

≈

"Five hundred dollars," Matthew said, adjusting the camera.
"Damn."

Dawn sat on the oak floor at the center point between the
kitchen, dining room, and family room. Matthew pulled the
rugs away and moved some chairs closer. Their black legs, he
said, had an ominous feel. The stainless-steel refrigerator stood
behind that.

Thankfully he'd selected an oversized T-shirt for her to wear.
It was pink, depicting side-by-side kittens. Dawn sat cross-
legged. Matthew had surrounded her with a Holly Hobby quilt,
the China doll, a couple bouquets of dusty silk flowers, a handful of lace doilies from the basket.

"I wonder how much he paid the hooker," Matthew said.
"Did he pay you more? What percentage of his income is he
willing to spend on hookers and cover up? How far would he
go to protect his life?"

"Their life feels rickety. Like you could light a match and set
fire to the place. It would be gone in a flash, but they wouldn't
have lost much."

"Right," Matthew said. "Except for that room downstairs, it
completely lacks personality. It's usually a person's belongings
that makes a house a home, but not for these people."

"So what? Mitch is controlling? Bridget has given in to plain-
ness? Bridget is trying to be someone she's not?"

"Think about what a person will see here," Matthew said. "A
woman surrounded by trinkets that don't match the room she's

in. They'll see contradiction. Sometimes it's best to let people interpret the art."

"Can you hand me my drink? Do you think the drink should be in it?"

"No," Matthew said, reaching for Dawn's glass. "A drink implies she's trying to not feel the contradiction. Not having a drink implies she's feeling every bit of it."

"Her loss, not mine," Dawn said, taking a sip and giving the glass back to Matthew.

The essential difference between her and Bridget. Feeling the contradiction might be considered a gain to Bridget. Not to Dawn. She didn't want to feel shit.

"And the money," Matthew said. "It makes it. Don't you think?"

"The money adds a layer. All this stuff. And a bunch of money. But money hasn't bought happiness in this instance."

"There's a doll, a quilt, and stuff with more emotional value. Money hasn't bought status. Money has bought secrets. The stuff she cares about can't be kept in the main rooms of the house. It's stashed away."

He held up the camera and snapped a couple test shots.

"This woman is expressionless. She's empty. She's pleading with me, lost," he said.

The idea of his words filled Dawn with such a sadness she forgot about the camera. Her mind overflowed with sorrow, a pain that swelled and released like her throbbing sores. She thought about Bridget on the constant verge of cracking open, her pale skin and neutral clothing falling away to expose a colorful jumble of organs and blood, messy and chaotic.

She imagined Bridget reaching over and handing the money to her husband so she extended it toward Matthew and the camera. She wanted him to take it away from her. Life could be simpler without choices.

Thursday: Distortion

WHAT STINKS MIGHT NOT
ALWAYS BE WHAT IS DIRTY.

Wei Chen smoked so much that a dirty haze hung near the living room ceiling. Dawn never understood how the carpet stayed so white. Wei must have been careful to keep the ashes from her cigarettes inside the heavy ashtray on the coffee table, which was the same reddish-brown Dawn expected to see if Wei coughed up a lung.

"You only one talk to me," Wei said. "Chinese like disease."

"I don't think that's true," Dawn said. "Have you tried getting to know your neighbors?"

"Neighbor sock!"

Dawn nodded, hoping she came off as sympathetic.

Wei couldn't have been more than thirty, with shoulder-length black hair that didn't shine as much as she expected on an Asian person. Her broad forehead wrinkled and she took a drag, leaned forward, and tapped the ash into the tray.

"Nobody understand I say what. Stupid. Asshole."

"People always try to put others in a different category. It's never about similarities, it's all about differences."

Wei nodded, but Dawn was certain she hadn't understood.

"So what do you have going on today?" Dawn said.

"Huh?" Wei stared at her as smoke poured from both her nostrils.

"What are you doing today?" Dawn said, slower.

"I stay here. Car in the shop. Meng take the Toyota. Dickhead."

"You have no car?"

Wei nodded, pulling a fresh cigarette from the pack and lighting it from the one already lit. Normally, she ran errands most of the morning, sometimes not returning at all before Dawn left. Wei crossed a bony leg over the other so Dawn could see her square kneecaps through the gray sweatpants. Wei sat back against the couch and propped her feet on the coffee table.

Her socks were the short ankle variety depicting tiny black and white cats wearing red bow ties. Between the socks and the cinched pant legs were a couple inches of hard evidence Wei had given up shaving.

"I play Candy Crush. Free life in America? My ass."

Dawn turned to the mantel and shook some Magic on a paper towel. She wracked her brain for activities Wei might enjoy were she to leave the house. She picked up each ornament on the mantel and wiped it with what she hoped hinted at tenderness. She used a different container at the Chens', a ceramic bottle she'd picked up at the world imports store with the typical blue and white pictures of houseboats, palaces, and diving birds. The unfortunate part of the relic was the fat cork that plugged the top. Not as user friendly as the regular bottle, and not being able to shoot streams took a lot of the fun out of it.

Wei had the new cigarette pressed between her lips and squinted through the smoke at her fingernails. She picked at some chipped polish and threw her head back, away from the smoke, in disgust.

"My nail look awful. I don't care."

"You should pamper yourself," Dawn said, moving to dust the painting on the wall. "Just because you don't like it here doesn't mean you can't find enjoyment. There's no sense in being pissed off all the time if you don't have to be."

She dampened a paper towel and dragged it along the top of the gold frame. The dragon was her least favorite piece of art in the Chens' house. Almost cartoonish, the shape of the beast's talons and chicken-like legs reminded her of the roadrunner sprinting through the desert. Its body resembled a snake curved into a double S, giving it a proud, chesty boldness. The yellow tongue hung out of the dragon's mouth like a long, flapping ribbon.

Tacky Chinese art. She wondered if Wei had been Chinese trailer trash before she married Meng. They lived well enough now, but Dawn sensed familiarity in her customer, a jagged edge that made her more human than people like Barb Turner or Bridget Riley with their stainless-steel appliances and neatly folded hand towels.

"What is pamper?"

"I could drive you somewhere. Like if you want to see a movie. I'll be your driver. You can go anywhere you want."

"American movie have too many explosion."

"What about the salon? You could use a manicure. My mother always used to tell me, 'Go and get your nails painted, Dawn, and you'll feel better.'" She actually liked Wei Chen and this lie came with a twinge of betrayal.

"My toenail look worse," Wei said.

"Call for an appointment. There's that nice little place on Liberty. You can call me when you're ready to come home and I'll pick you up. I hate the thought of you being stuck."

"You want money?"

"No, really. I know what it's like to have no car. It sucks."

"I shower. Leave in one hour."

"Whenever you're ready. I'll be here cleaning away. It will be a nice little break for me too."

"You come?" Wei said, brightening.

"Oh, no thanks. I'm allergic to nail polish. The smell makes me nauseous."

She fluttered her unpainted fingernails toward Wei as though performing a magic trick.

Wei regarded her through the haze of smoke, unsmiling. Dawn uncorked the bottle and poured more Magic on the paper towels. She set the bottle next to the ashtray and carefully cleaned the glass over the dragon until it squeaked with each circular wipe. She stood back to admire it.

"Doesn't the dragon represent power over weather?" Dawn said.

"Yang. Dragon is yang."

"Ah," Dawn said, making sure the frame hung straight on the wall before stepping away. She wished she knew more about Wei's culture and what was good about it. "I'll bet this reminds you of home."

The woman was inspecting her fingernails again.

"You smoke?" Wei said.

"I have my own. I'll get them from my purse."

"You come?"

"I'm allergic, remember? Do you know what a barf bag is?"

Wei exploded into a trill of laughter so loud Dawn realized she'd never heard her laugh before.

"Bag on airplane?" she said.

"Exactly."

"Meng want to barf in the bag. He held bag in his lap."

"Men. Jerks."

"Yeah," Wei said, ashing her cigarette and pointing it in Dawn's direction. She stood up and padded toward the stairs, slipping into her native language. She pulled herself up the stairs, wagging her head, and jabbering in unmistakable mockery. As her foot hit the first landing, she clasped her stomach, folded over, and retched loudly, a perfect faux puke in any language.

"Meng is jerk off," Wei called, not looking down at Dawn before going into her bedroom and closing the door.

She drove away from Wei and the shopping plaza too fast and forced herself to ease up on the gas.

"Matthew," Dawn said, pressing the phone to her ear.

"Dawn."

"I'm serious, Matt. This may not work. Not today. Too many uncertainties."

"What are they?"

Dawn explained, but Matthew seemed unfazed.

"The good part is she'll call you," he said. "We'll wrap it up and get out."

"You have to come immediately. Like five minutes ago."

"Jen and I met for an early lunch at Jink's. We can come right now."

Dawn wanted to sigh, but held it. She and Matthew had hit their stride. She hadn't seen a single photo, but could tell

Matthew was pleased. His artistry had flourished since Monday, when they weren't sure what to do. By yesterday, his handling of the shoot displayed confidence and self-assurance: how he wrapped his hand around her wrist to move her hand, his thumb against her cheek to confirm the angle of her face, how Dawn modeled as instructed without talking back or giving him a hard time. It was easy to concentrate with the two of them, but, with Wei out of the house only temporarily and Matthew with Jen, what choice did they have?

"If it's not now, it's not going to happen. I don't know how long she's going to be. It could be a half hour."

"No worries, D-presser. We'll come. Don't panic."

"Is Jen okay with it? Like, will it be weird?"

"It will be fine, D-bacle. I'll give her the scoop on the way over. Missing a day would blow our momentum. Which people are these?"

"The Chinese."

"You say that like we're going to invade China," Matthew said, laughing.

"Shut up!"

"Dawn. Relax. Sometimes the artist has to work with the moment. We'll be there in five minutes."

"Success hinges on this, Matthew. You know that, right? It won't be cool if this breaks our stride. Another person being here, I mean. Nothing against Jen personally."

"I appreciate how much you care but it's going to be fine. I'll talk to Jen. She knows what we're trying to do."

"Hurry up."

"We're getting in the car now."

Dawn heard the car door slam and Matthew and Jen laughing, the sound of two people sharing a joke that no one else understood. She gripped the steering wheel and sped past the Chinese food buffet she and Terry used to hit on Saturdays. Remembering the syrupy pink sweet and sour sauce, she suspected it was the kind of Chinese food Wei and Meng wouldn't go near. They'd laugh if they knew she'd thought herself exotic just for tasting egg rolls. She'd only eaten the fried options, sticking to familiar items and avoiding the brothy dishes with noodles and chunks of vegetables. Terry slurped gallons of egg drop soup; egg whites, he said, were great protein before the gym.

Dawn got caught at the light crossing Plant and noticed the wispy clouds crisscrossing the blue morning sky. Did Jen pay attention to such things? Why had Dawn forgotten to see, until now, beyond the road construction barrels and crumbling curbs at the entrances to strip malls and fast food restaurants? When the light changed, she accelerated fast enough to beat the two other lanes of traffic. She wanted to believe Matthew that Jen knew what they were trying to do, but she didn't. Their project seemed like an important secret only they got. Creativity was personal. She doubted Jen considered herself a creative person.

She was positive Jen had ordered the new kale salad on the menu at Jinx. And she'd liked it.

Dawn pulled into the Chens' driveway and killed the engine. She wouldn't forgive Matthew if Jen messed this up. Jen might have stupid ideas. Matthew might not tell her no. Dawn wanted to believe Matthew's artistic process came before his wanting to please his girlfriend, but you never knew.

Dawn let herself in the front door with the Chens' house key and planted herself on the couch. Matthew could make decisions today. She refused to brainstorm for ideas.

"This place reeks," Jen said, stepping into the house and making a face.

The screen door closed behind her, separating the women from Matthew, who stood with his arms full of equipment on the other side. "Hey, thanks for the help," he said.

"Sorry!"

Jen opened the door, leaning out to hold it open so Matthew could squeeze inside. She wore a black wool trench coat Dawn had never seen but, then again, she didn't see Jen much during the week. Through the split at the bottom, Jen wore wide black pants and tired boots with scratches and worn toes. Dawn recognized the perfume as the same her mother wore.

"You look fancy," Dawn said.

Dawn shrugged at Matthew and laughed. She motioned for him to move faster.

"Fancy how?" Jen said.

"It's odd to see people in slacks," Dawn said.

"Slacks?" Matthew said, leaning from side to side to unload the various camera bags. "Who says that? Slacks."

"Trousers," Jen said.

"How about pants?" Matthew said.

"What am I wearing the other times she sees me?" Jen said.

"Jeans," said Matthew.

"You look nice," Dawn said. "That's what I was trying to say. Professional. Different than normal."

"Thanks," Jen said. "You look...pretty much the same as always."

Dawn wore her softest pair of sweats, the ones so thin and flowing they could be mistaken for pants of a nicer quality. Considering she had paired them with an oversized hoodie, today she dressed pretty much like a scrub, which didn't matter because a.) she didn't care and b.) neither did Wei. Her priority was making sure her clothes didn't rub against the sores around her middle, not that Jen wanted or needed to know about that. Now that they were in a hurry she appreciated the soft pants more.

"The benefit of being self-employed," Dawn said, "is no second wardrobe."

"I dress better when I'm not working," Matthew said, unzipping one of the bags.

Jen scanned his outfit. Dawn enjoyed knowing about the worn-out wallet impression on his back pocket and the holes where the bottom corners had worn through, which Jen couldn't see from her vantage point. He wore a lime-green Mountain Dew T-shirt underneath his flannel.

"I think you're right," she said. "I'd get sent home if I came into the office wearing jeans that old. You're like a vagrant."

Dawn laughed that Jen came up with such a cutting remark off the cuff. Matthew flipped them both off, aiming a finger in each of their directions.

"Any ideas for today?" Matthew said. He stepped further into the room and perused it.

"My job was getting her out of the house," Dawn said. "You should think fast, though, before she calls her limo service."

"That's the ugliest limo I've ever seen," Matthew said, squinting out the window at Dawn's ancient sedan, which had a couple dents in the doors and rust spreading up from the undercarriage like a rash.

"More like a cab," Jen said.

"My point is that the cab will soon be in demand," Dawn said. "So move faster."

"Can we stay on topic?" Matthew said. "Let's focus."

"I'm like binoculars I'm so focused," Dawn said. "I'm in it to win it."

She pointed peace fingers at her eyes and then toward Matthew's, deciding to leave Jen out of it.

"What's up with these people again?" Matthew said.

Jen walked into the living room and took off her coat. She draped it over the edge of the chair and began a slow inspection of the place, starting with a peach-colored vase stuffed with the plastic stems of fake tiger lilies. She picked up the vase and shook it upside down as though confirming how many Wei had managed to jam in there. She had sense enough to put it back where she'd found it.

"They're a couple from China," Dawn said. "Wei and Meng. She hates it here. She thinks Americans are jerks who won't bother trying to understand her. She's given up hope."

"What, like she's suicidal?" Matthew said.

"She'd never say so to me," Dawn said. "I see the evidence. She doesn't eat. She smokes constantly. She's usually wearing the same clothes. Loathes her husband."

"How do you know that?" Jen said.

"Today she called him a dickhead and an asshole. As bad as she speaks English, she's got the curses down."

"It stinks in here. I don't know how people can live like this. Why bother to have someone clean your house?" Jen said.

"Smelling like smoke and being dirty are different," Dawn said, picking up the ceramic jug of Magic and missing the power of knowing she could squirt someone whenever she wanted. She tucked it in the crook of her arm and stroked its smooth surface.

"Why bother keeping the rest neat when you're living in an ashtray?"

Dawn threw a glance to Matthew to see what he thought about his girlfriend's opinions. It wasn't the first time Jen dogged their lifestyle choices, as though she'd forgotten her boyfriend and the woman standing in front of her lit up at least ten times a day. Matthew watched her, listening, as if she were talking about any number of benign topics. "You realize that people who smoke don't smell it, right?" Dawn said.

"Oh, come on," Jen said.

She waited for Matthew.

"That is a true statement."

"You don't think this place smells terrible?" Jen said.

Matthew shrugged. He motioned toward the stairs and started up.

"Doesn't bother me a bit," Dawn said. "In fact, I think I'll have a smoke right now. One of the best parts of cleaning here." She leaned for her purse and lighter, pulled a cigarette, and lit it. "Want one?" she asked Matthew.

"No thanks. Can't very well shoot and smoke now, can I?"

"You did a pretty good job the other day."

She let Jen pass and followed them both into Wei and Meng's bedroom. Matthew inspected his camera, rotating the lens to his face. He wiped it with the corner of his flannel shirt.

"So, a Chinese woman who hates America and her husband for bringing her. She's full of anger," Matthew said.

"Right," said Dawn, taking a drag. "But she's not a typical submissive Chinese woman."

"Isn't that just a stereotype?" Jen said. "Quality art has to be above stereotypes."

"This woman has grit. She might be the boss."

Relief eased a small amount of her stress when Matthew spotted a straw mat and spread it onto the floor. He met Dawn's gaze and nodded for her to continue.

"Someone is usually dominant in any relationship. You know, the women who practically guide their guy around by his dick. And then there are guys who won't let their girlfriends walk out of the house if her bra is showing through her T-shirt. There are women desperate for attention and men who refuse to give it to them. Or women who are so mean to their husbands in public it's a wonder he doesn't grab her by the throat and choke her."

"Huh," Jen said.

Dawn realized the last person was her mother.

Oh my God, Jack, you're eating like a pig. Can't we find a better restaurant than this one? Another half-baked shopping trip for the guy who thinks he can fix it.

She'd have left the bitch too. That her father rarely raised his voice and never took the bait seemed miraculous. Even now, for as hard as her mother tried to paint him as an untrustworthy, uncaring person, he opted to be chill. Her mother didn't treat Davis like that; Dawn wanted to believe she'd learned her lesson.

"What about the sex? Kinky?"

Jen stopped browsing long enough to stare at him and shake her head.

"Matthew!"

He lifted a hand and closed one eye—as though taking Jen out of his line of vision—and continued.

"No. This is what we do. We talk about the people. What about the sex, Dawn? Can you tell?"

"Not really," Dawn said. "Possibly none at all."

Jen moved about the room with her arms crossed and hands tucked under her armpits like a kid trying not to touch breakables. "How on earth could you tell about a couple's sex life? What, do people leave videos around?"

"You'd be surprised," Dawn said. "You can tell a lot by how a person lives. The clothes they wear. What's in the piles. What's in the trash."

"You search through the trash?"

"Not on purpose. It's not like I sort through it. But if you're going to dump it, you may as well see."

"See what?"

"The junk people try to hide."

"From you?"

"People hide things from each other all the time," Dawn said. "Packages are wrapped in tissue. Bottles are shoved to the bottom. Notes torn into pieces. It's also important to watch the back of the cabinets, shelves, and drawers. That's where they put the good stuff."

"So what have you found here? In this house?" Matthew said. He sorted through a little basket of elastic bands and barrettes, extracting chopsticks with butterflies on the end.

Dawn paused to think, bringing the cigarette to her lips and leaving it there while she rubbed her eyes. "She's going to call any minute."

"Come on, D-mystifier. We're here for Christ's sake. Think."

"The guy. Meng. He has an inordinate amount of laxatives in his bedside table."

Matthew laughed.

"Anal penetration can be very stimulating and not only for people who happen to be homosexual," Matthew said.

"Good lord," Jen said. "I have no idea how you come up with this stuff."

❧

Matthew decided on captivity. He collected whatever artifacts he could find to represent Wei's life outside her prison walls: a delicate fan, some kind of bizarre ornamental headdress, silk shirts from Wei's closet with delicate patterns, a bronze statue of two fish with sizeable scales, and the butterfly chopsticks. Dawn watched him place the props, change his mind, and rearrange from where she sat on the vanity bench, while Jen worked to make half her face Geisha with whatever makeup they found in Wei's drawer.

"I'm telling you, too stereotypical," Jen said. "Aren't Geishas in Japan anyway?"

"The internet says they originated in China. Make the left side paler," Dawn said. "White, if possible."

She flipped her phone around so Jen could see the image she'd found on Google.

"Where are you going, Matthew?" Dawn called as he retreated out the bedroom door. "You better hurry up. I mean it."

"Be right back."

Dawn closed her eyes so she wouldn't have to make decisions about where to look as Jen patted her cheek with a powder puff. Dawn had already spent far too much time staring at the crease between Jen's lower lip and chin, which gave her the same neat and tidy appearance one might accomplish with pleated pants or a shirt with a pressed collar. If she and Matthew got married and lived on Bird Lake, chances were he would morph into a man in designer dress shirts and wayfarer sunglasses that cost two hundred dollars. It was always interesting to imagine how a person might change with money. She liked to think Matthew would drive a cool car, like a tricked-out Jeep with the top off when weather permitted. Yet, somehow, she pictured him in one of those giant SUVs with three rows of seats and movie screens for the entire family. She opened her eyes when she heard Matthew come back into the room. Wistfulness washed over her at the sight of his old T-shirt and jeans. She liked Matthew this way. He carried the dragon painting from the living room and leaned it against the corner of the wall.

"There needed to be more visual interest in the backdrop. You're not necessarily the focal point. Well, you are, but only because you're relatively plain compared to what's around you."

"Oh, thanks."

Matthew had picked out a simple white tank for Dawn to wear along with her sweatpants. Jen had ceremoniously ushered Matthew out of the room to let Dawn change.

"I want the edge of this dragon tail to be a focal point, the place the Chinese eye connects with what's around her."

"How's this?" Jen said.

She stepped aside and Matthew spent a good minute inspecting Dawn's face from across the room. She bounced on her knees to show her impatience.

"Nice!"

"Where do you want me?" Dawn said.

He'd only snapped a few shots of Dawn kneeling on the mat when she noticed a humming outside. She sat back on her heels to listen. It could be the neighbors.

"Sit taller," Matthew said. "Straight up and regal, like your spine is a metal rod. Relax your hands a little. Turn your face a touch to the right. Good."

Dawn watched Matthew aim the camera. It seemed impossible her whole body could fit into the frame, but maybe he was emphasizing the painting or fan. It didn't seem like he was taking her picture at all, not at that angle. She jumped a little when she heard a car door open and close so clearly it could only be from the Chens' driveway. Jen heard it, too, and stepped to the window.

"What do you see?"

"A cab," Jen said.

"Mother fuck!"

Dawn jumped up and pushed past Matthew. She pulled on her sweatshirt to cover Wei's shirt and grabbed her socks.

"Put the makeup in the drawer. Wipe the vanity," Dawn said. "Right now!"

"We'll never be able to hide all this," Jen said. "Just explain what we're doing."

Everyone faced the bedroom door when Wei entered the house.

Matthew shoved his camera in the bag and zipped it. He crossed each bag over his head, ready to run.

"What are you doing?" Jen whispered.

Her face drained of color, making her hazel eyes huge and terrified.

"Should we hide?" Matthew said. "Closet?"

"No!" Jen said. "Don't be ridiculous. We're not hiding."

"The hell you're not," Dawn said.

She scooped all the items from the floor that belonged in the bedroom and scrambled to put them in their places. Still, a lot remained, including the painting. They were screwed. Dawn rolled up the mat and tossed it back in the corner.

"Dawn! I took taxi back. Korean bitch no better."

Matthew drew his hands over his mouth somewhat gleefully upon hearing the real Wei. Dawn glared.

"Closet?" he whispered. "If you can get her in the kitchen, we'll go down the stairs and out the front door."

Dawn nodded. It seemed like a reasonable plan and one they might be able to pull off.

"Hi, Wei," Dawn called. "I'll be down in a second. Want to finish this up."

"We are not hiding and sneaking," Jen said. "You're making me feel like we're going to get arrested. We'll have to explain."

"This is not your house," Dawn said. "Technically, you could be arrested."

Perspiration gleamed on Jen's forehead. Her eyes pleaded with Matthew.

"I'm going down. I'll excuse myself, grab my coat, and leave. I'll be polite."

"No!" Dawn said. "Wait a minute and be cool."

"I have to get back to the office. This was a bad idea. I'm going to go."

Dawn watched, helpless, as she left the room. She stood still and listened to Jen's footsteps thumpity-thump down the stairs.

"Excuse me, please," she heard Jen say. "I'm sorry. I was dropping something off to Dawn. My coat."

A few seconds of silence followed, then the sound of the front door. Dawn wanted to punch Matthew and claw at his eyes.

"Dawn? You know that lady?" Wei said.

"Yes. I'll come down and explain."

She gestured to Matthew to stay put. She could distract Wei long enough for Matthew to slip out of the house undetected.

"I show you my nail. They are blue," Wei said.

Matthew slipped into the closet and stepped out of sight. Wei walked into the room with her fingers extended like a zombie. Her hands dropped to her sides when she noticed the pile on the floor. "Huh?"

Dawn tried to think of a reason the dragon painting would be upstairs.

"You stealing my shit?"

"No, Wei."

"Huh?"

"I'm sorry. I told my friend about all the authentic Chinese artifacts you have and she wanted to come over to see them. She's interested in Asian culture. I'll put them back now."

"You make fun of me." Wei threw her hands into the air. Her face grew purple and she spat when she spoke again. "What's on your face? You want to be a Geisha? I smack you!"

"No, Wei. Really. I wasn't. God. Shit."

Tears rolled down Wei's face. "Get out my house!"

"No, let me put these away. Here, I'll put this back."

Dawn lifted the heavy painting of the dragon and stumbled into the hallway. She sat and slid down the stairs, holding tightly to keep it upright. The wounds around her middle seemed to split with each blow.

"Get out of here!" Wei said.

Dawn stood when she reached the bottom of the stairs and hoisted the painting. "I'm going to put it where it belongs. I can't leave your house like this. You don't deserve this. I wasn't making fun. I'd never do that."

She placed the piece on the wall and stood back to make sure it was straight. Wei sat on the stairs clutching her hair. Tears dropped onto the woman's dress. The white carpet felt too soft underneath her feet, as though the ground needed to be firmer in order to hold the house steady. She thought of Katelyn and the way their eyes had locked when Dawn understood Katelyn was siding with Nick, the moment she learned friendship was fragile and theirs had broken. Dawn diverted her gaze from Wei's face in case. She hadn't paid attention before that Wei had changed after her shower, nor had she noticed her transformation to pretty in the cream-colored sweater, belted in brown, with tall brown boots. "Wei."

"Huh?" the woman shrieked, lifting her head and sobbing. It startled Dawn to remember Wei was older than her, married, and possessed a continent's worth of life experience in comparison to her.

Dawn had no words.

"Get out!"

"Matthew," Dawn called up the stairs.

Wei stared.

"Matthew, come down and go out," Dawn said.

"What the fuck?" Wei screamed when Matthew came out of the bedroom with his bags and tried to squeeze past her on his way down. Wei got it together long enough to lean back and kick him in the butt. If it hurt, Matthew didn't stop or say a word. He kept going, opening the front door and pulling it shut behind him in one smooth motion.

"Please let me explain."

"Get out."

"Wei, I want to tell you what we were doing."

"Leave, Dawn. Give my key."

She stood and walked down the stairs, extending her hand.

"Jesus," Dawn said.

She grabbed her purse and removed the Chens' key with shaking hands. Wei took the key in her fist. "Blue fucking mess!" She flipped her fist so Dawn could see the smeared and dented blue polish.

Dawn put her purse over her shoulder and walked out, leaving her supplies—the buckets and mop, the paper towels, and the ceramic bottle of Magic—behind. She hurried to her car, got inside, and drove away as fast as she could. Matthew's car idled at the curb when she rounded the corner, but she didn't bother stopping to talk to him or to see whether Jen was inside.

Dawn shut herself in the trailer and locked the door. She faced the room and strained to listen beyond the roaring in her ears. She tried to quiet her breathing, which came hard and fast.

She lobbed the coffee cup from the kitchen table into the sink so it cracked into pieces. It crossed her mind to check for her mother's lipstick. She didn't bother. She didn't care. Suppose her mother spent the morning sifting through her insurance papers with Davis peering over her. Her mother couldn't hurt her. Neither could Mrs. Folly. Terry couldn't.

It struck Dawn that they'd been pouring over Wei Chen's belongings just moments ago. Remembering the sadness on her customer's face was far more than Dawn could handle without a drink.

She slammed the cupboards and allowed the glass and bottle to hit the kitchen table with more than a thud. The Williams was three-quarters gone, which pissed her off though she longed for the slow smoothness of the Makers Mark she and Matthew drank the day before. In its bottle, the Evan Williams appeared more like orange cool-aid than whiskey. Its stupid label ripped off Jack Daniels with its black and white design. The words on the bottle made it seem elementary, with Kentucky and Bourbon written in cursive, but STRAIGHT and WHISKEY in print for the dumbass people who couldn't read script. Straight whiskey is all they needed to know. The bottle itself lacked the squared edges a drunk needed to get a good grip. The Evan Williams bottle, curved and smooth, could slip right out of your hands if you'd had too much to drink and weren't careful.

She wanted a substantial meal, like a steak and baked potato, to go with her drink, but all she had was a can of chicken and rice soup. It slopped into the bowl. Some of the liquid spilled over onto the glass plate in the microwave, which she'd clean up later because nothing was more disgusting than a microwave full of crusted-over old food. Another one of her cleaning trademarks: leave the microwave and oven range as clean and new as the day they were purchased.

Her cleaning supplies, gone. For all the anguish she'd caused Wei, at least she left her Magic behind. She wanted to believe it might comfort Wei in some way, but could only picture her customer on hands and knees scrubbing the floor with that expression on her face, any hope draining away to hopelessness.

The Williams went down easy as she waited for the soup to heat.

Stupid Matthew and stupid fucking Jen. They'd ruined the project and her business.

She threw a spoon across the room and it nearly hit the window above the kitchen sink. It nicked the wall instead and landed on the counter. The second spoon she threw landed horizontally across the top of her toaster. What were the chances? If only it had fallen inside, sparked, started a fire that burned the whole place down. Now that would be a way to unload the trailer. Most of her stuff was replaceable anyway. The furniture was either from her mother's basement or purchased secondhand. Her clothes were mostly jeans and blouses her mom bought for her when she was still in school. The nicer ones, at least. It's not like she needed nice outfits now so most of them hadn't been worn in a long time and were probably housing moths.

The third spoon she held onto, but then ended up abandoning it to lift the lukewarm bowl and slurp her dinner. When she finished the soup, she took her glass and went to her room. She opened the underwear drawer with some difficulty. No smooth tracks like the McIntyres'. The drawer required coaxing, one side then the other, and enough patience to not yank it onto the floor.

How pathetic, and not just the secondhand dresser. The

faded cotton panties with sprung elastic. The old bras with pills all over the cups and missing hooks on the clasps. She dug for the silk panties from a time she went shopping with her mom at the mall. She must have been about sixteen and her mom let Dawn choose pretty much what she wanted, within reason. She picked up the cream-colored pair with little pink roses. They exhibited no noticeable wear and tear, no torn lace like so much of her stuff. The pink still popped off the ivory with perky freshness. There were other pairs like this: pale blue with white polka dots, plain white, black, orange with yellow stripes. The problem was that Dawn had been thinner then, with a girl's hips and not much of an ass. She didn't bother trying them on since they'd most certainly end up in her butt within a matter of seconds. Tossing them back into the drawer, she removed her prom lingerie and put it on her bed. The only decent stuff she owned, even if it gave off a cheesy, slutty vibe.

She began to undress, but her phone rang so she ran back to the kitchen in her underwear and Wei Chen's white tank top. Expecting to see Matthew's number on the screen, she sat down with her glass and took a deep breath. Her heart pounded in anticipation of bitching him out, of not knowing whether they'd still be friends. But when she went to answer the call, an unfamiliar number illuminated.

"Hello?"

"Hello, is this Dawn?"

"Who is this?"

"This is Barb Turner. I'm sorry to bother you at home. I hate having these kinds of conversations over the phone."

Dawn couldn't imagine what conversation Barb wanted to have that she'd already had before with someone else. The glimmer of friendship she'd envisioned Tuesday night at the pharmacy faded with her customer's formal-sounding words. You didn't say shit like that to friends—stuff about conversations over the phone; you said whatever you wanted whenever. With friends you didn't calculate the best way for a discussion to have the appropriate outcome.

At least she'd apologized for calling at home. That gave Dawn reassurance that Barb planned a work discussion that could have waited until next week. Like an upcoming vacation or needing to change days of the week. Something regular or a routine break of routine. She might want Dawn to clean with Windex.

"That's okay. I'm home. Just finished dinner."

"Uh, this is hard," Barb said.

Dawn remembered the random distribution of the Turners' Christmas packages. The silk flowers. And the worst: the red thong, the missing psych report. Shit. Shit. Shit.

"I know we don't know each other very well," Barb said. "But I feel like I know you. I feel like I see myself in you."

"I'm not sure what you mean."

But her anger, for some reason, reignited.

"It's that you're so young," Barb said. "You probably don't realize the mistakes you're making. It probably doesn't seem like that big of a deal."

"Listen," Dawn said. "You can say it."

"Your fiancé. His death. I'm sure that's been hard."

Dawn swallowed. Terry was not the topic she expected.

"Dawn? Are you still there?"

"Of course it's been hard. My whole life. It's my business, not yours."

"I know. But I'm afraid for you. I see myself. I can help you not make the mistakes I made."

"What mistakes? I'm not married. I don't have kids."

"Not facing the trauma," Barb said. "Don't be like me and hold it inside. You'll regret it, I promise you, because it will catch up with you. It caught up with me. Big time."

"You don't know me."

She tried to guess what Barb might think her life was like, as though she envisioned Dawn in some smoky shithole staring at a black-and-white TV. As though Dawn would consider smoking inside her brand-new trailer and watch reality shows. Her trailer was customized the way she'd wanted it. Yes, it was

a mobile home, but it was nicer than most apartments and half
the houses she'd been in. Her life was getting back on track. She
owned a business. She did quality work. "You must be hurting so much," Barb said. "Don't you want
someone to tell you they understand how you feel? That's all I
wanted. I want to do that for you."

"Trust me, I have plenty of people."

She heard the raised inflection in her voice and recognized
her mother. This defensiveness, she hadn't considered it in the
past to be a sign her mother was lying. Dawn was. She'd never been more aware of her own dishonesty, probably because
she'd spent the last days wading through other people's bullshit,
including hers. Who did she have? What people?

Matthew came to mind first, whose photography project
she'd fully invested herself in, both creatively and at the risk of
the money she used to pay rent. She'd lost Matthew today just
like she'd lost Katelyn.

And her mother? Sure, her mother supported her, but only
so Dawn imagined a sense of allegiance with her that kept them
on the same side. Why had she never considered that her mother used her as a pawn, or that her mother had somehow lost
her ability to be honest about Dawn's father? Could the man be
trusted? Was he a good father? She'd never tested the possibility
for the sake of somehow taking her mother's word as truth.

On the other end of the line, Barb Turner said, "You
seemed, I don't know, so closed off the other night. I can't stop
thinking about you."

And Mrs. Folly. Dawn lost Mrs. Folly too. Loss seemed to
spread out before her, like blood from a wound, and the wound
was Terry dying. She couldn't go there; she just couldn't. The
bleeding had to stop. "I'm going to hang up."

She found herself standing in the middle of the kitchen, her
bare feet cold on the ugly laminate, the glass of whiskey in her
hand. She pulled it up and drank. Barb Turner wasn't what she
needed. She needed to get out of there. Her life needed to be
different.

"Oh," Barb said, and Dawn could hear her starting to sniffle.
"I thought—"

"Don't think about me. Goodbye."

She hung up and set the phone on the table. On her way
back to her room, she removed Wei's shirt and stuffed it in the
bathroom garbage can. She stripped off her old underwear and
put on the black and purple lace. Her jeans didn't feel adequate
over the expensive lingerie, but that must be part of the thrill.
She pulled on her Yankee's T-shirt because it showed a little
cleavage.

Her mind swirled like water circling a drain. She wanted it
all gone: her mother's bullshit spying, Matthew and Jen, and, oh
God, Wei's face, she wanted to forget Wei's face and the fact
she'd caused it. And Barb, had she really called and tried to be
a mother? Who was she to make assumptions? She didn't know
shit. Like Dawn wanted to be her friend. Like Dawn needed
some older lady's company and comfort. No wonder she always
left the Turners' feeling beaten down, as though any effort to
create a nice family and future life would have little payoff and
couldn't possibly be worth the work. Barb's house, Barb herself,
they were ruined.

Dawn's face in the mirror reminded her of Matthew's: pink
and hot. She rubbed gloss on her lips and patted a powder puff
on her cheeks and forehead. She squinted at her reflection to
see if it enhanced her maturity, like Jen in her work clothes. Jen
probably viewed her as Matthew's stupid little friend, the one
dumb enough to agree to his ridiculous creative endeavors and
end up without a job. Matthew and Jen were probably back at
his place, in bed, not thinking about Dawn, her job, or the fact
she'd saddled herself to a trailer and town she hated.

To think that she—Dawn—actually believed Matthew cared
about her more than Jen. And why would he? Why did she
want him to? She allowed her reflection to come into focus in
the mirror. Wearing makeup helped. She almost looked pretty.
Justice would think so.

ॐ

"So the man let his girlfriend blow it wide open?" Justice said.
Dawn drank the shot he poured her. Some cheap vodka, but
she didn't care. The day she'd had, she'd drink rubbing alcohol.
Her throat burned and her eyes watered from the booze.
"We were busted. What could we do?"
"She shoulda been cool. If her man has a friend, she should
be cool. I mean, really."
"She couldn't handle the situation. She froze. Didn't know
what to do except wave her white flag. Clearly a rule follower."
"Forget that shit!"
"I know, right? This is my job. I'm doing this for her boy-
friend. Trying to help his career. Trying to help him find his
inner artist."
"It ain't right," Justice said. "You were being a friend."
"Trying to. I don't think I know what that means anymore.
What's a friend? An enemy. All my friends have become ene-
mies. Why should Matthew be any different? I'm sure he'll take
her side."
She tapped the shot glass on the table so Justice filled it
again. The thought of forcing it down constricted her throat,
but she did it anyway. Lumping Matthew with the friends she'd
had in high school made zero sense, but this was Justice, someone who didn't have the background to call her out on bullshit.
He filled his glass, too, and tipped it into his mouth.
"Dawn. You gotta calm down. I'm sure Matts-his-name will
smack sense into her. Maybe it's for the best. You don't need a
friend like that."
"His name is Matthew. He's not the violent type."
"I was speaking figuratively, not literally. There's a difference,
you know."
Dawn reached for her cigarettes. She packed them—*smack*,
smack, smack—against her hand. She stared at him across the
table until he lifted his hands in question.
"Your inner gangster has left the room."
Justice reached for his own cigarettes, slapping the table a
few times before his palm landed in the right place. He swatted

the pack off the table. Dawn, fully intending to get a rise out of him, hadn't expected such annoyance.

"Well? The fuck, Justice? One minute you're all ghetto and the next you're as articulate as Barack Obama. Which one is it?"

Justice picked up the saltshaker on his kitchen table and polished it with his shirt. He set the orb on the table and scowled toward the ceiling. Dawn checked, too, and noticed his ceiling tiles were better than hers, not bumpy at all, and not one of them had a water stain.

"I'm a Black man. I came from shit. I go to college now. I'm going to graduate. I'll have management experience from this place. Yes, I know how to talk like a white person. Any sensible Black man knows if he wants to get ahead, you can't talk like a nigga."

"Isn't that supposed to be a bad word?" Dawn said.

He sat back in his chair and laced his fingers behind his head. He sighed loudly. "What about you? Isn't that the question we should be asking? One minute you're dissing Matts-his-name and next you're defending him. Pick a side, lady."

Justice bore his stare so deep into hers Dawn forced herself to maintain eye contact. She crossed her arms. Leave it to Justice to turn the tables. "I'm waiting," he said.

"What do you want me to say? I've tried to explain. I don't know how to move forward. I can't."

"You're not trying from what I can see. What are you doing to get ahead?"

"Nothing. And fuck you for assuming everyone has goals. Trailer trash goals to be successful. Nigga goals to break free from the man."

Justice stood, pushing his chair so far back it bumped into the wall. Dawn, startled, jumped to her feet. He rounded the table and took her by the shoulders so her breath was already gone by the time her back hit the wall. She didn't care. His mouth was inches from hers when he spoke. "You calling me names, Dawn?"

"No."

"You sure about that? I'm getting mixed signals."

"Words come out that I don't mean. I don't know who I'm mad at. I don't know what I say."

"You mean what you say more than anyone I know," Justice said.

"Your body is warm," Dawn said, a choked whisper. "I hate being attracted to you or anyone else."

He stepped back and threw up his hands. "If that's how you feel, why are we in here fussing at each other?"

"I don't know what I'm doing. I don't know who to be mad at."

Justice cupped the side of her face. He leaned so hard against her she worried the cheap boards behind her back would crumble away. She imagined that she and Justice would fall into the pile of disorder on which their trailers sat, this park full of poor people, some who tried harder than others. They'd become remnants of the soil, wedged underneath a ceramic gnome, a plastic Jesus, or any of the godforsaken symbols poor people bought at Wal-Mart and resurrected in front of their trailers. No doubt they'd fall in different directions. Justice would be half-stuck underneath a block of concrete steps leading to someone's door. They'd connect eyes, with Dawn knowing she wasn't deserving of someone working through college, a Black person with roadblocks she'd never understand.

His lips were warm and full against hers. His body, hard like Terry's only different because Justice was taller and leaner. She suspected he didn't need to work so hard to be in the shape he was in. He wrapped his arms around her waist. She almost liked the pain. She heard the desire in her breath and wanted to.

His mouth was on her neck when they heard the knock on the door. Justice froze and listened while they waited to see if the person would leave. The knocking became more persistent so Justice backed away.

"Right now?" he said. "This very minute?"

"You should answer. It could be important."

"The old lady in seventy-six better not ask me to snake her

toilet again." He walked to the door and opened it. The voice filled the room and swirled through Dawn's mind—in and out—and then circled through her body like a battering ram.

"I'm trying to find Dawn. I know you're…involved. Friends. I need to make sure she's okay."

"She's right here, man."

He pointed across the room so Matthew stepped into the trailer and saw her, still against the wall behind the kitchen table. His presence filled the small space to capacity. Justice, on his own, was more than enough. The sight of them side by side—Justice an inch shorter, but somehow more solid and fitting in his own kitchen, and Matthew with cheeks flushed from the cold and windswept hair. Dawn couldn't begin to define Matthew in the same way, piece by piece, that she could Justice. Matthew was one entity, all parts combined, as though removing an arm or leg from your imagination made him disappear. He was all or nothing.

Dawn's chin dropped to her chest and Matthew's hand—soft—gripped her forearm.

"D-coy. You okay? I'm sorry. God, I'm sorry."

"Why not take that up with your girlfriend?" Justice said, standing with his hand on the open door.

Dawn, surprised, thought Justice was referring to her as Matthew's girlfriend. She couldn't remember what she might have said to make him think that. Having been making out with Justice minutes earlier, her mind scrambled to reset the facts of what was occurring. Justice kissed her; now her boyfriend was here.

Matthew stared at Justice long enough to give Dawn time to remember Jen. That's who they were talking about. She watched Matthew process: Justice knew the whole story about Jen and the Chens. Dawn told him the gory details. Matthew was probably connecting the dots that Dawn and Justice were, in fact, a couple.

"She's upset too. You think she's not upset about what happened?" Matthew said.

"She fucked over your friend is what she did."

"Not on purpose," Matthew said. "She fucked up, yes. Her heart's in the right place."

"What does that mean, bro? She gets a pass?"

"My name is Matthew."

"I know your damn name."

"Then you don't need to call me bro."

"Hey," Justice said. "My girl's upset. That's all I know. On account of you and your girl. Shouldn't you be with her?"

"My friendship with Dawn comes first. You know that, right, Dawn?"

She remembered Jen's long coat and the way it split when she walked, revealing the work slacks—or trousers or whatever they were called—and how the slacks were pressed to crease along the length of her calf. When Jen folded her coat over the Chens' chair, Dawn noticed the little pills that had formed; the coat was not new. Perhaps Jen couldn't afford a new one or she didn't care. The slacks seemed to hug her butt as she leaned to place the coat. A perfect fit, actually. Jen had a nice figure with balanced proportions. Were Dawn to shop for slacks, she'd have to search for the kind with room for hips, not that she had any reason for pants like that.

"My job is all I've got. You brought her along and now I've lost a client. Just when I was getting close to being able to leave here."

"Ha," Matthew said, but it wasn't close to a laugh. "I should have seen that one coming."

"Don't you say that to me!"

Her shriek echoed and fell to silence as they stared at each other.

"Listen, man," Justice said. "Y'all are upset. I think you should go and sleep on it. Talk about it later."

Matthew raised his hands.

"I'm going," he shouted toward the open door.

He wore those new jeans again and the sight of the stitched pockets combined with the way the left side of his hair curled pissed her off more than anything Matthew had ever done. She pushed past the table and managed to catch up and swat the back of his head before he crossed the threshold. Dawn pulled her hand to her chest and was grateful his hair was so soft because she'd whapped him hard enough to sting her palm.

"You're hitting me now? All that does is make me want to ask you again. Do you remember it, Dawn? Do you remember that night? Is that what this is about?"

"No."

"Things are never going to get better for you," Matthew said.

"Thanks, Matt. You're a great friend."

He stepped to the doorframe.

"I'll ask one more time."

"Go ahead. You already know the answer."

"Do you remember?"

The word *no* nearly fluttered off her tongue, as small and easy to say as ever. This time Matthew didn't wait for her answer. He stormed out so she grabbed his arm, wrapping her fingers around the flannel shirtsleeve. All of Matthew met her gaze. The truth, held in for so long, came so easily she wondered why it had seemed important to lie. She'd never been a liar. Honesty was crucial. She told Terry that all the time.

"What if I do remember?" Dawn said. "What does it matter anymore?"

She swore by his face and the way his eyelashes seemed so dark that he could cry and would if she pushed hard enough.

"It matters," he said.

Matthew retreated, shoving his fingers into his hair as he descended the steps. She hadn't expected him to walk away. She closed the door behind him so she wouldn't see his face. Ignoring Justice, she headed down the narrow hallway to the bathroom and shut herself inside where she leaned against the sink to breathe and count to sixty.

Need overcame her and a longing so strong she found it impossible that she didn't know for what.

Justice sat at the kitchen table when she came out, an empty shot glass in front of him and a full glass in front of Dawn's place. He watched her approach. She stood beside the table and drank the shot.

"That fight was about more than today."

"No, it wasn't," Dawn said. "Today told me all I need to know."

"I get it if you have to go."

"No. I'm staying and you're going to fuck me."

"Dawn."

She could tell by Justice's face that he now considered the idea preposterous, that whatever had just transpired between Dawn and Matthew had enlightened him in some way to a conclusion Dawn hadn't yet figured out.

"Okay, fine."

Justice raised a hand to cover the amusement on his face.

"You're one of those women who takes a mess and makes it worse. Don't drag me into your business."

Flipping him off seemed natural.

"You don't mean that. I'm on a path. You know."

"Yeah, you're paying your way through college and getting ahead."

"I don't say this much, but my brother James got shot dead. Whatever I do from here has to make that fear in my mom's eyes go away. I gotta have my shit together for her sake and my sake. You're still working that out."

"Yeah," she said, standing to go. "I guess I am."

He took hold of her arm as she passed.

"We're better as friends. You'd be bad for me."

"I know."

She stepped onto his cold concrete porch and down to the earth.

"Night," she heard him call behind her.

She raised a hand and kept walking. His door closed, leaving her alone amidst the narrow streets and pathways between trailers. Enough people were still awake to cast ample light. Through kitchen windows and front door panes, she observed colored holiday lights and Christmas trees tucked into corners.

One resident had a snow shovel and bag of rock salt next to the front door. A kid had built a snowman with giant Oreo-cookie eyes and buttons. In high school, she and Katelyn might have tipped it over, not stopping to think about how some kid would see it in the morning and cry.

Ahead, the warm light from her trailer flooded her with relief that she'd had the foresight to keep it on. Her key in the lock felt like home as she pushed her way in. She passed through the kitchen and the mostly empty whiskey bottle, past the orange couch and old pictures, to her bedroom where she shed the prom lingerie, crawled into her sweats, and fell into bed.

FRIDAY: RETOUCHING

YOU CAN ALWAYS COME BACK LATER
TO CHECK YOUR WORK.

Dawn stood in the cleaning aisle of the Superstore, scanning the glimmering bottles of cleaners, disinfectants, and scrubs. At eye level were the medium-sized bottles of Dawn dish soap in an overabundance of colors and varieties, from the traditional green and blue she remembered from childhood to the more modern purples and pinks. She couldn't believe the choices these days: Dawn with Olay Beauty, Dawn with OXI power, Dawn with bleach alternative. Her favorite had always been the straight-up orange, the antibacterial/hand soap combination. Down the line were a selection of mops and buckets. She squinted beneath the florescent lights and wondered how anyone could work in a place like this for an eight-hour stretch. She hated coming here and hated more that she had to fork out cash to replace the supplies she'd left at the Chens'.

At least she'd gotten drunk on Justice's dime last night. She was too tired to be sufficiently mortified about being rejected, but partially grateful for his morality. They'd most likely laugh about it when they saw each other next, whereas if they'd slept together she'd have probably lost a friend. At a time she hadn't any left to lose.

She tossed the orange Dawn into the cart.

Dawn chose a traditional broom, the kind with the straw-colored bristles, though it cost twice as much as the one with the blue plastic stick and red bristles. A good broom was worth it. The ends on her old broom had split so she didn't mind having to buy a new one. The bucket and other stuff irritated her as she calculated prices. Money wasted, all thanks to Matthew and Jen.

Matthew and Jen, such a pair, except she couldn't stop thinking about Matthew's face when she admitted she remembered. Justice had seen it too. One night together, ages ago, before they really knew each other. She'd been even more fucked up then, confused and out of control. She'd run into the photographer from the hospital at the liquor store. His name was Matthew, he'd said. She should come over tonight, he was having people over. Come on, she could follow him there. Dawn had paid for her bottle of whiskey and walked beneath his arm when he held open the door.

Hours later, Dawn lifted her gaze from Matthew's portfolio. Everyone else had left. She'd been flipping pages for at least an hour. She had never lost her sense of the outside world before. The empty apartment stunned her, but more than that, she experienced a pull back to the dreamlike place she'd found in his photographs. Matthew sat on the couch.

"I'm not leaving until I'm done," she said. "It's like an open beer. You have to finish."

"Take all the time you want. I have my whiskey and this magazine."

So she'd continued flipping the pages, photograph after photograph, until her throat swelled and she wanted to cry. She sat without moving for a long time, listening to the swish of Matthew's pages. Every so often, his glass clicked on the table. It sounded so peaceful. She'd blended into the scenery, had become invisible in this photographer's apartment. He'd said he'd gone to art school. He said he believed he had talent, but wondered if all artists thought they were extraordinary. He said he'd keep at it until there was proof he was no better than anyone else. Dawn had stopped on a photograph of a pregnant woman, naked on a white blanket. Her body curved around the swell of her stomach and breasts. The shadows made her incredibly beautiful and sexy. Maybe it was how her fingers brushed her breastbone.

Behind her, Matthew laughed. "What has two legs and bleeds?"

"What?" Dawn managed to say, shifting in the chair.

"Half a dog."

Dawn started laughing, but it burst out like a shudder. She couldn't even laugh without coming off like an insane person.

She never got a peaceful moment, like Matthew reading his magazine or the pregnant woman in the picture. Everything she did was crazy. Wrong. Led to disaster. Death. Matthew must have realized her distress because his hand landed on her forearm.

"Are you okay? What is it?"

Dawn couldn't speak.

"What a stupid question. We know what it is. Come here. Have a whiskey."

She let him lead her to the couch, where she sat and watched him get another glass from the kitchen cupboard. He poured some and took it to her.

"Is it physical pain?" he said. "Or emotional? Or both?"

She sipped whiskey and couldn't think of an answer before he spoke again.

"Have you ever noticed how people usually know the answer before they ask the question? What a mind fuck."

"My elbows hurt," she whispered.

They hurt so much she could barely breathe sometimes and God forbid a wave of grief hit at the same time. She sipped more whiskey. It was the good kind, the kind that went down smooth. If she could feel nothing, just for a while, she could survive it. When she set the glass on the table, Matthew took her wrist and twisted it to see her right elbow. He brushed his lips over the wound, still a scab at that point, and pressed the top of his head against her arm.

"You shouldn't have to hurt like this," he said. The warmth of his breath traveled the length of her arm, like it could heal.

"It's not fair."

"It's worse than you think."

"What do you mean? Are the grafts not taking?"

The apartment grew so still. She heard the ticking of a clock she didn't see and the hum of a furnace. Somehow the silence seemed the loudest noise in the room.

Deciding to tell a stranger the worst didn't seem like a decision at all. What else would she say at that moment? She'd watched him all night in easy conversation with others. He laughed with the older guy in the army fatigues as they threw darts with cigarettes between their lips. The cigarettes moved to their hands when they talked, and back to their mouths to aim and throw. Later he relocated to the kitchen area to slice lime wedges for two women in yoga pants. One had a small flower tattoo on her wrist, which Dawn noticed when Matthew passed her a lime. He seemed comfortable with everyone, which she guessed he would be since it was a party at his apartment, but still. She'd never known anyone to be equally interested in everyone, including her. She wanted to talk to him like the others had in the calm, relaxed way of an adult social gathering.

Her words came in a rush. He'd never moved from his position with his head against her arm so she never had to see his reaction. She knew he listened because, at an important point, he put his hand over her hand. She badmouthed Terry, his inconsiderate actions, and confessed things he'd said leading up to the accident. It didn't seem necessary to try to make it sound less awful. The photographer had an edge to him, she could see that now: by his worn-out jeans, the way his apartment smelled like smoke and incense, how his curly hair was just long enough to be a mess. She could tell by the photos he took that he wasn't the type to judge her.

"That doesn't mean it wasn't an accident," Matthew finally said. "I mean, no offense, but it sounds like the guy was being a prick. The day went wrong."

Dawn grasped his arm and squeezed it until he sat up and winced. He yanked free and inspected the fingernail marks. He seemed to understand Dawn wasn't mad at him, just at the situation, and unfazed she'd taken it out on his arm. She hadn't drawn blood, but he raised his forearm to show her the deep red welts and raised his eyebrows as if impressed by how close she'd come.

"God*damn* that hurts. It's good to be alive," he said.

"He *was* being a prick. A giant prick. A total asshole. A goddamned fuck."

She drained her glass and set it down sloppily. It crossed her mind to say sorry for pinching him, but what the fuck did she care? The photographer—Matthew—didn't care. He almost seemed to like it. Not having to make excuses was such a relief. Someone was listening to her. She'd talk forever as long as he didn't give any indication it was time for her to get lost.

"So there. Now I'm hammered and I blamed my boyfriend for killing himself when I started it. I feel much better. Pour me another, why don't you?"

Matthew did, and added a splash to his own glass. That he didn't tell her she'd had enough to drink or needed to go home motivated her to stay. They sat in silence for a long time, but not an uncomfortable one. Somehow, she'd run out of conversation. He shifted in his seat. She wondered if the electricity crackling around her affected him too.

"Maybe you'd let me photograph you some time. You're sexy. I don't think you see it. Or maybe you do. It's your hair, I think." He reached forward and twirled it. "And your ass. But you know that."

"You're not my type," Dawn said.

But the way he talked about her ass without breaking eye contact wasn't what she expected from someone she'd predicted to be more wholesome. She could see he was different—way different—than anyone she'd known: artistic, mysterious, fascinated by the length of her hair when he stretched the lock. He gathered more in his hand, sending shivers through her body when his fingers brushed against her scalp and cheek.

"I like you, though. You're easy to be with."

"I am?"

"Sure. You're jaded. Funny. Smart."

"Smart?" Dawn said.

"You like sex, don't you? I can tell you do. You give off a vibe. I'll do anything sexually. I feel like you're like that."

"I don't know what I'm like."

"I think you do know."

It seemed important he thought she knew what she liked, who she was.

He slid behind her and massaged her shoulders. She sighed and closed her eyes. After a while, he moved her hair to kiss her neck. It was easy to like it when she couldn't see him. But later, when he'd finished taking her clothes off and pulled her around so she faced him, sitting on his lap with her legs around his back, he wouldn't break eye contact. He managed to unbutton his pants and slide them down. They were fucking. She liked it, but she wanted him to look away. He wouldn't so she closed her eyes and leaned back and moved and listened to herself—and to him—until she started to come. He squeezed her nipples. She came harder and louder than she'd ever come with Terry. He came too, which she and Terry never did at the same time. When she opened her eyes, he was still looking, had probably been looking at her the whole time.

"You're beautiful in a way I've never seen."

She stood and put her clothes back on. She drank the rest of the whiskey in Matthew's glass.

"Stay," he said. "It doesn't have to mean anything. I want to sleep next to you."

She held up a hand. Sleeping beside another man was un-fathomable. She'd never spent a whole night with Terry, not really anyway, without having to sneak in or out or be quiet be-cause of someone's parents. This man—Matthew—probably assumed she conducted herself like an adult. He buttoned his jeans and sat comfortably on his couch, waiting for her to act. His chest was pale and peppered with hair. She couldn't believe she'd been turned on by someone who'd never lifted a weight in his life. Every way she had betrayed Terry deepened at that moment.

She left and decided she'd never remember. No matter what details stayed with her, she'd never acknowledge them. If it meant she wouldn't be friends with the photographer anymore, fine. But Matthew was easy. He didn't push. He didn't come on to her and, eventually, he stopped asking: You *really* don't remember? They became friends because he was the kind of guy who didn't let past discretions muddy up a friendship. He liked her, thought she was smart. She saw the way he watched her every once in a while, at least at first. She liked it a little. But he really wasn't her type. Not then.

Last night, though. When she admitted she remembered, their friendship changed. Shock, that's what she saw. And hurt. She'd hurt him. Hurting him hurt her.

She grabbed a blue bucket from the top of the stack and tossed it into the cart. She could skip the kneepads this time. Those cheap foam gardening cushions were as good and cost less if she could find one this time of year. The store had an outdoor section somewhere.

"Dawn?"

She turned to see Katelyn Rice. Katelyn and Nick had both worked at the Superstore back in the day and it didn't appear much had changed except that Katelyn's belly swelled and, even if she weren't pregnant, she'd clearly given up trying to be cute as a button. Her brown hair had been bleached to the color of old piss around the base of someone's toilet. She carried herself with such weariness that the sight of her exhausted Dawn, but that was probably because she knew Katelyn had one kid already and the thought of that much sex with Nick could put anyone to sleep.

"Hey, Rice."

"Pew. Nick and Katelyn Pew, remember? What are you doing here at this hour?"

"What time is it?"

"Before eight because that's when I get off. I hate working nights."

"At least you get to go home and sleep soon," Dawn said.

"Like hell. I walk in the door and Nick hands me the baby so he can come to work."

"What about sleeping?"

"When the baby's napping. And then for a few hours once Nick gets home."

"Christ. That's awful."

"Yeah," Katelyn said, playing with the nametag on her apron. The apron ties dangled since they could not span her girth. "You're lucky you didn't settle in like we did. You have no idea."

"Nope. I certainly do not."

She did feel lucky though. As Barb Turner pointed out, they were too young to make big life decisions about marriage and kids. At least she and Terry weren't working opposite shifts at shitty jobs. It would have been another hassle to fight about. It was easy to picture them growing apart, like Bridget and Mitch. She'd be the one trying to pretend their relationship was okay, like Bridget. Terry would be like Mitch, saying one thing and doing another. Dawn spent too much time during their relationship thinking of ways to make him happy. Plus, if she and Terry had gotten married, she never would have gotten to know Matthew. She might not have figured out people existed, men existed, who enjoyed conversation and got drunk without passing out. The idea of not knowing Matthew seemed worse than being in Katelyn's position.

"Nick and I are talking about moving. Down south to Tennessee where his family is from. You know, get away."

Dawn, who had been remembering the way her friend's eyes squinted when she spoke, snapped back to attention. Katelyn would never move. She couldn't. Her mother had MS and needed constant help. Katelyn was the one who liked routine to stay the same. Dawn had been the daring one. She took a few steps from the cart, finding it hard to believe she'd been the person to fill it up.

"I'm not going to buy any of this crap after all."

"Are you still a cleaning lady?"

Katelyn leaned forward and reached underneath her stomach. She clasped her hands and leaned back to hold some of the weight in her arms. Dawn was overwhelmed by the desire to see Katelyn's other daughter and to know if the new baby was a boy or girl. She missed Nick, stupid Nick who liked to run his mouth.

"I'm thinking about moving too," Dawn said.

She wished she could ask Katelyn to come with her to Key West. Together, it would be easy and fun.

"You should. I don't know why you didn't leave ages ago. The rumors. Lies. I know now it was all bullshit. Nick never should have freaked out on you like that."

"You're right, Rice. I am lucky. You seem to have a lot of regrets."

"Not that I don't love my kid," Katelyn said. "It's great. I'm just tired. Did I say you were lucky?"

"Yes, you did, missy."

She reached out and messed up Katelyn's hair, which she used to do as a joke when they were friends. She messed it up good and gave Katelyn's head a little shove as a send off. The girl finally woke up.

"Everyone says you turned rotten. Mean."

"Fuck that. You knew me before. Bitches, both of us."

Katelyn picked up a box of Brillo pads from the shelf and fiddled with the cardboard corner. She set it back down and smoothed her hair.

"You were fun. We were."

She yawned and gazed over her shoulder, as though someone might be there to take over or at least lay a sleeping bag on the floor and hand her a pillow. She laughed as though an old memory had come to mind, a few seconds too late because her brain was running slowly.

"I have to get out of this store," Dawn said. "I don't want to do this anymore."

"Maybe we can get together. After the baby's born and I can really drink."

"If I'm still in town."

"Are you going to the candlelight vigil? Did you hear about it?"

"I heard from Mrs. Folly. But no. My dad, he reminded me it's time to stop allowing people to place blame. I'm not going."

"Oh darn, it would have been nice to have…"

Katelyn trailed off as Dawn walked up the aisle without her cart, past the abrasive sponges and Mr. Clean Magic Erasers, through the line of customers waiting for the one check-out line open so early, and out the automatic doors into the cold sunshine.

Dawn pressed her cell phone against her cheek and swung left on Park Street. The car swayed a little, but she liked the control. How random to run into Katelyn. And, even stranger, that Katelyn came so close to apologizing she may as well have said the words. Too often in life, you reminisced and wondered how much of it you had gotten totally wrong. Katelyn didn't hate her, or if she had, not anymore. Going out for drinks actually sounded like a decent idea. Now there was the pressing need to speak to her dad. The phone rang a third time, then a fourth as she hung a right at the house with the inflatable Santa Claus crumpled onto its side. The Santa had been standing fat and tall yesterday when she drove past it. It looked dead now, the victim of someone not in the mood to be festive. They must have unplugged it overnight to save energy.

Being uptown seemed weird for a Friday, but she couldn't be this close and not drive by to check. The street and driveways were lined with cars still home as people woke up and got ready for work. The vibration of the ringing phone against her head pulled her out of her thoughts. Her father might still be asleep, her call trying to sneak into his consciousness like an alarm clock.

"Dad," she said, when he answered.

"What's up, sunshine?"

She let the easy tone of his voice flow through her body. His mood never varied and, if she had woken him up, she didn't need to worry. He always sounded cheerful to hear from her. Like Matthew, but she forced the thought of him out of her mind. Certainty was so rare she didn't want to spoil it. This was it, *the* moment. The enormity of it left her breathless.

"Hi, Dad."

"What is it?"

"I'm coming. I'm going to drive."

Saying it gave her a sense of lightness, as though each word weighed ten pounds as it left her lips. Of course she'd need the car. It made sense, just like it made sense to go to Key West and give it a try.

"Well. Slap my ass and call me Shirley," her dad said.

"Nice one."

"Well, I'll be a monkey's uncle."

"I want Shawna's job. You held it for me, right?"

"I have the help-wanted ad ready to post later today if I didn't hear from you."

"I want it. I'll take it."

"When are you coming?"

"I'm going to finish up with my last house of the week and leave tomorrow morning. I'll drive straight through if I can or stop at a cheap motel to sleep. Sunday night, possibly Monday."

"Your mother know about this?"

"She's got Davis. You know."

"Susan has always been better at being taken care of than taking care of someone else," her father said.

"It's fine," Dawn said. "I told her you had a job opening."

"I'm sure I'll get a phone call."

"Don't let her tell you she's missing her daughter. I hardly ever see them."

"I know what she's like. Passive aggressive in slow motion."

"I did a lot of thinking this week. About how mean she was to you. She's always tried to have me on her side. There are no sides here. She's my mother. You're my father. I can move wherever I want."

Her father didn't answer.

"I'm done. That's my speech," Dawn said.

"You know what is the best part of having kids?"

"You can make them clean your condo when they move in?"

"They grow into adults who figure stuff out. There was no winning with your mother. I tried as long as I could. Then I tried to be your dad apart from her. I didn't want to quit, kiddo, but I had to have some kind of life."

"I don't blame you for moving."

"Ricki has told me for years, just wait till she's grown. She'll figure out what's what."

"That Mom is impossible?"

"We don't need to go into specifics."

"I'm heading to the Letwinskis', my last house of the week. Once I finish, I'll pack up."

"You okay a few days on your own? I'm heading to the Bahamas for the holiday. Leaving Sunday morning and won't be back until New Year's. That okay by you?"

The idea of her father's empty house brought forth the feeling of sitting in a sanctuary. It would be like her own version of church, but without the prayers or worrying that Mrs. Folly was thinking this or that, or waiting for the perfect moment to assault her with fresh questions about the accident. Christmas at home also meant waiting for her mother's last-minute call telling her what time to come over. She'd go, have her elbows inspected, debate cream versus ointment, answer a few inquiries from Davis about her business, and head home to the trailer.

Going for a walk in the Florida humidity would be a glorious holiday. People watching. Window shopping. Sitting on a bench with her eyes closed and face to the sun.

"Yeah, sure. As long as you don't care. Maybe I'll have a place by the time you get back."

"Up to you," he said.

"I'm going to get a place. Try it for a year. See what happens."

"I'll leave the key under the pot. You remember the spot?"

"Yeah. I do."

"Ricki could use the help while I'm out of town. She'll be thrilled."

"Tell her I'll stop in as soon as I'm there. I'll only need a day to regroup."

"Drive safe. Text me when you get here. Not sure I'll have reception on Bimini, but I'll tell everyone to expect you."

"Thanks, Dad."

"You okay, kiddo?"

"I'm tired of it. This accident. I'll never be able to feel guilty enough. Staying here for so long was stupid."

"It didn't seem to me like praying with Sandy Folly would help matters."

Trying to breathe past the sudden lump in her throat took some effort. How she'd wanted to feel Mrs. Folly's light touch against her shoulder and be close enough to smell her lavender-scented hand lotion. She'd considered buying a bottle of it for herself—it was an off-brand because Mrs. Folly was never extravagant—but always reached past it to the unscented variety.

"She might have forgiven me. She might not have."

"You've had a rough road. I've got your back, you know that."

"I do."

"The sunshine will be awaiting your arrival."

Ahead, up the street, Dawn couldn't believe what she was seeing.

"Shit, Dad. I have to go. Call you back. Bye!"

She tossed her phone onto the console and pumped her brakes to a stop in front of the Chens' house. Her purse launched from the front seat onto the floor, dumping her cigarettes, lighter, and spare tampons onto the plastic mat. Outside on the curb, her bucket of supplies sat as she'd left them by the front door. The ceramic bottle lay next to it on the driveway, cracked in half from where it had fallen over.

She slid the gearshift into park and got out. She couldn't help glancing around to be sure Wei or Meng (or a hired hit man) wasn't waiting in an upstairs window to knock her off with a spray of bullets. The mop handle collided with her forehead when she lifted the bucket by its metal handle.

"Mother bleep!"

But she couldn't help laughing as she dumped the armful into the trunk, scrambled back to the driver seat, and got the hell out of there.

"That's going to leave a mark."

The adrenalin coursing through her arms and legs reminded her of driving around with Katelyn in high school, past curfew when the streets were black and slick, past Terry's house or Nick's house or, if one of them happened to be in a fight with her boyfriend, past the house of some other cute guy to prove other guys were in the realm of possibility, and damn if either one of them—Dawn or Katelyn—would be stuck feeling lonely or sad at such an hour because of that stupid sonofabitch.

Then and now, Dawn remembered that she was in charge of what happened next.

Karen and Mike Letwinski lived on the edge of town flanked with tall trees, ravines, and air so cold and clean it hurt to breathe. Dawn pushed her cigarette butt out the car window before pulling into their driveway. It wound for at least a quarter mile before the house came into full view. The exterior of the house wore a weird contemporary feel with angular windows and slanted frames, but the inside resembled a lodge in a western mountain town. Dawn loved it. It helped that the Twins were cool in pretty much every respect, from their Native American throw rugs to their all-wood décor to the water bong in the basement, complete with a small stash of weed. Their bathrooms were moderately clean and the DVD collection included a dozen high-end porn movies. Their bedside table held a couple sex toys and a bottle of lube. Karen kept a grocery list on the chalkboard in the kitchen, which, in addition to items like *apples, granola bars,* and *deli ham,* sometimes included *lady things, roid cream,* and *Mike's toe jam.*

Healthy, the Twins. Not too uptight for a clit stimulator, but classy enough for a full bedroom set of mission-style furniture from Crate and Barrel. She'd seen the catalog. Fresh fruit in the crisper drawer of the refrigerator, but still cuckoo for Coco

Puffs. Dawn found remnants of whole wheat bagels spread with Nutella in the kitchen sink some mornings. The sugar dispenser was always half-empty. The milk jug, half-full.

She let herself in the side door, which afforded a partial view of the cedar deck behind the house and the woods beyond. Sometimes she went back there to smoke and sat so still on the built-in bench it seemed like she became part of the scenery, like only God could see her and only if he happened to be searching. Rare were the times Dawn believed herself completely alone, unwatched.

That she experienced it at the Letwinskis' made her automatically like cleaning there, though if she sat too still for too long, her stomach would flip and drop and she'd become nervous, like she'd finally disappeared and didn't know how long it would take for anyone to notice.

Tossing her keys on the counter, she went for the notepad. She wanted to write a gracious letter to the Twins to explain why she was leaving. They were the only ones who deserved it. She planned to put in calls to the McIntyres and Rileys. She doubted Barb expected her to show up again.

In the end, no one would really care. A cleaning lady was a cleaning lady, even if she did bring an enchanted elixir that smelled of oranges or lemon or grapefruit depending on the week. They'd call Molly Maids and would grow accustomed to the scratch and bite of Clorox, the mind-numbing fumes from Pinesol, and the eye-burning vapor of Tilex. One day, while shopping in a specialty boutique, Barb Turner would be reminded of the woman who used to clean her house with a special concoction smelling like citrus.

She pushed the tip of a pen onto the paper.

Dear Karen, she began. She could have addressed Mike, too, but why waste the ink when everyone knows the men could give two shits.

This is my last day. I am moving to Florida. It was sudden. I enjoyed your home. Thanks for the job. Dawn.

The sentences didn't seem long enough, taking up only a

fraction of the page. Because it didn't seem right to leave so much white space, she added to the bottom:

> *Dawn's Magic*
> *1 empty bottle dishwashing liquid*
> *1 full bottle dishwashing liquid*
> *Fill empty bottle with warm water*
> *Add squirt of dishwashing liquid, at least 3 seconds*
> *Add 2-3 drops essential oil*
> *Swish*
> *Squirt*
> *Wipe dry*

She read it over. It seemed way too simple to work so well.

She decided to start with the kitchen. She tied on the paper towels and reached for her bottle. She fired Magic across the countertop with the enthusiasm of a kid holding a Super Soaker. She'd miss that part a little.

She barely noticed what she cleaned and kept her eyes on the length of windows against the kitchen wall. Whoever designed the house understood how much a view could help a person stuck in front of a sink washing dishes. Scraping burnt toast down the disposal barely mattered when you had all of nature's glory in your face. When winter left the trees bare and landscape colorless, the world still presented itself as whole and worthwhile. A patch of pale blue sky breaking through the clouds made her heart soar. Matthew may have wanted a life like the McIntyres', but not Dawn. She'd take a house in the woods any day.

She finished the counter and moved to the wall of photos. Sometimes she stood back and examined the details of the Twins' lives, but not today. Too much to do. And anyway, she'd practically memorized the timeline of their travels, the blue sweater Karen wore in Paris when Mike snapped her photo in front of a big church, how the Arizona mountains grew from the back of their heads, the weird shape of Mike's bellybutton on some beach in the Caribbean. They'd been married for decades. She could tell by the off-the-shoulder lace gown and the way Karen's tiara had been inserted to give the back of her hair some lift. They'd weathered all the trends pretty well, Dawn thought. They left little to make fun of. She gave the photos a light once-over with a damp towel. Matthew might be disappointed by the lack of ammunition the Twins provided. *If* she decided to call him. How could she call him? Matthew didn't deserve this last day. Then again, how could she not? Blowing off the last day of the shoot and skipping town, as appealing as it seemed from the perspective of avoidance, was about the biggest bitch move she could imagine. Matthew might improvise for his exhibit, but Monday through Friday had been the plan and she couldn't be responsible for a failure in execution. She couldn't believe she was considering it, but it boiled down to work ethic: do your best. It didn't seem right to give up on Matthew now.

She paused at the photograph of Karen and Mike on a motorcycle in front of some country store in the middle of nowhere. She didn't mean to.

Karen sported blue jeans, cowgirl boots, and a white tank top. She sat behind Mike with her hands grazing his waist. They were parked. There was no need to hold tight. She wore a helmet; he did not. In sunglasses, they were pretty hip for a couple in their early forties. Except for the two of them on the motorcycle and the store, the rest of the picture spread out to desert and sky the color of sand. This gave the motorcycle weight, in the photo and also in reality since Dawn understood the heft of the machine and how it could take you or throw you depending on the angle.

The bunch of paper towels in her hand fell to the floor without Dawn realizing she'd let go. It hadn't been on purpose. Not really.

She'd only been doing what Terry wanted. She remembered the weight of him when they had sex for the last time in his parents' basement a few days before the accident and the way his hipbones poked into hers. After he came, he pushed his upper body from hers and regarded her from above. She hadn't come, but wanted to and could if only he'd pull out and use his hands a little or his mouth. The expression on his face was unkind.

"You should be better if this is going to be forever."

She sat up and glared.

"What's that supposed to mean?"

She crossed her arms across her chest to shield herself from his scrutiny. She wished she'd remembered to do some sit-ups and pushups to give her arms and abs more definition.

"It's boring. Like, if this is going to be it forever, it's not going to be any good."

"Oh, thanks. I'm boring. Thanks a lot. What do you want me to do?"

"Surprise me out of the blue," he said. "Like pull me into a dressing room and suck me off when the saleslady isn't around."

She smacked his shoulder to get him to move, pulled on her clothes, and stormed out the side door.

"You're an asshole," she screamed from the driveway, burning more when she noticed the next-door neighbor staring from his porch.

She went home from Terry's that day, to her bedroom at her mom and Davis' house, and cried on her bed. Within minutes, she decided: if he wanted her wild, she could be crazy, uninhibited. She liked sex. She'd try positions and toys he wanted. He wouldn't need to fuck the girl from the Superstore or anyone else. For good measure, she got on the floor and did twenty pushups followed by one hundred sit-ups and waited over a day for Terry to call.

Terry's motorcycle hadn't been nearly as big or nice as the one in Karen and Mike Letwinskis' photograph. Not much larger than a mini-bike, the thing could have been an army reject with its flat green paint and leather case to hold wallets and sunglasses. The seat was narrow and short enough that Dawn easily reached around and stroked him during their next ride.

She'd wanted him to pull over to the side of the road and do her in the long grass. Or she'd have done him. Instead, the machine wrenched underneath her as it began to skid. Her arms pulled away from Terry's middle and she remembered being glad for the weightless feeling of falling as she watched the machine go over. It lurched because of its heft and she knew it was better to be falling than to be underneath, like Terry. When she woke up later in the hospital, there were only vague memories. Gravel on the roadside. Feeling grit when she ran her thumbs across the tips of her fingers. Fire roaring through her body. Flashing lights, but no sound as she lifted from the ground. She knew, though, exactly what she'd done. When she thought back on it, she'd considered it could be dangerous. The element of danger was why the plan was so great.

Dawn untied the twine and let the roll of paper towels drop into the bucket. Eying the note she'd written to Karen Letwinski, she soaked it with more Magic than was required. The page melted into the puddle and adhered to the granite. She peeled it from the counter, squeezed out the water and tossed it in the garbage can. Some secrets were meant to be kept. Her bottle was heavy, still almost full, when she set it on the floor and pushed it with her foot to align with the rest of her cleaning paraphernalia. It occurred to her to dump it down the sink, or better, over her head. She could use a baptism. Not the religious kind. More like a spiritual bath, a cleansing to mark the end of her cleaning career.

She pulled her pack of cigarettes from her purse and stepped outside on the deck.

After she lit up and took a few long drags, she called Matthew, hoping the deep breathing had calmed her enough to speak.

"Hey," he said when he answered.

"Hey."

Her hands started to tremble.

"I knew you remembered, D-luder."

"Shut up."

"Fine. But I knew it."

Silence filled the connection between them. Dawn took the opportunity to smoke some more. She heard Matthew light up on the other end and the snap of the Zippo as he somehow closed it with one hand the way he did. She'd never thought to ask him the story behind his ancient lighter or how he became an expert at using it. Sometimes he flipped it open and closed mindlessly, the way a person clicks a pen when they're thinking about what to write. It seemed terrible she'd never asked him the story about it. There must be one. Matthew never spoke about his father. Maybe the lighter had belonged to him. Perhaps his father gave it to him as a gift. Matthew might have stolen it or found it after his father left. She wished she knew the full story, that she'd asked him more questions and listened to the answers. He exhaled audibly the way he did with the first drag, as though smoking a cigarette brought a certain kind of relief.

"Where are you?" she said.

"Nico assigned me to a house fire on the west side. Boring. Mostly smoke. Everyone is out."

More silence, until Matthew finally spoke. "Why is it so bad to remember?"

"Dude. Shut the fuck up."

"I'd really like you to answer me."

"I don't want to."

Her voice caught in the middle of the sentence and she knew he'd heard. Talking about it wasn't going to help, was it? She couldn't begin to imagine what there was to say or what Matthew wanted to cover. Like two people couldn't have sex without rehashing the details or debating what it might mean. The naked branches of the trees waved in the breeze like the stiff jerks of a mime. She wanted to throw the cigarette into the woods so it razed the scene in half.

"Dawn."

"Don't say my name. Oh my God. Call me something else."

"D-ceiver."

"That's better."

"D-presser?"

"That's okay too."

"D-cider?"

"I have decided."

"On what?"

"On moving. I'm going. Tomorrow. I'm really going to do it. I called my dad to take the job."

Dawn smoked. She heard Matthew smoking too. His silence stung like a slap. It only figured she wanted him to protest. Women always wanted what they didn't get. Terry pointed it out all the time. She'd refused to answer Matthew's question and now here she was irritated that he wasn't sad and sorry she was leaving. Relationships were impossible—boyfriends, friends, all of them—and Dawn wanted to cover her ears and scream into the silence of the woods. She wouldn't, of course, because she never managed to say or do what she really wanted to. She acted one way, felt another, and never fully understood whether she meant what she said or did.

"Do you want to come over and do this or not?" she said. "It's Friday. I'm here. You may as well come so we can finish the week."

"Yeah, sure. I'll come." She gave him the address. "I should be able to get there within the hour," Matthew said.

"No rush. I'll be here, cleaning my heart out."

"Got it. Bye."

The notion and predictability of his parting words filled her with nostalgia; she liked how they came out in a rush. Friends were good for rituals and routine. Delivering the expected. Matthew had always been the friend to reassure her, to offer logical perspective and set her straight. She wanted him to miss her before she left. He should beg her not to go. Because if Matthew said it, he meant it.

As far back as day one, the photographer—Matthew—who walked into her hospital room seemed worth listening to, even

if it initially had to do with his casual mannerisms and nonjudg-
mental demeanor. Dawn had never known anyone to think out
loud, which is what he seemed to be doing.

"I wouldn't be here if it weren't my livelihood," he'd said,
dropping a business card onto the tray by her bed. "I know that
it's bad form to bother someone who's traumatized. My editor
has no boundaries."

He let the camera drop against the side of his thigh and ran
a hand through his tousled curls to hold them off his forehead
for a long moment.

"They gave Barnes the funeral. We flipped for it. I lost,
obviously. You'd think it'd be harder to shoot the funeral, but
it's not. It's always easier when you're among a crowd. Even if
everyone is thinking you're a son of a bitch, you know at least
one person there understands it's a job."

Dawn had pulled the sheets closer to her lap. She envisioned
Terry's mother standing in the rain near a grave, surrounded
by the rest of the family and their classmates from school.
Terry's coworkers from the Superstore would be there. The
other woman would be there. No one would pay attention to a
photographer because they'd all be watching her—Dawn—and
wondering.

She couldn't tell whether the photographer in her hospital
room was a boy or a man. He seemed older, definitely a man.
He had a real job. She considered he might be talking to her out
of pity, like a grown-up might were he to feel sorry for someone who'd been in a motorcycle crash. He brought the camera
to his waist and rested it against his belt buckle while adjusting
some of the settings. He met her stare.

"Don't look at me," she said.

Her voice dropped off into the otherwise silent hospital
room.

"You probably wish you were at his funeral," he said.

"No. I don't wish I were at a funeral."

"Where do you wish you were?"

"I wish I were a goddamned smear on the road."

"I can understand that. After four years with someone I'd want to be smeared on the road too. I'm agnostic so I can't get my head around the concept of God's plan when it comes to accidents. It's agony for the people left behind who have to endure the fallout, people like you who don't deserve it any more than anyone else. You know that, right?"

She'd stared at him, face numb, and for a minute the pain subsided like she no longer existed. The world went blank, as though the enormous thumb of God emerged from the heavens and smudged the bed until she blended with the room. When she blinked, pain crashed over her like a wave. She wasn't gone after all.

Matthew had the gift of pulling you directly into his logic, so much that you forgot yourself for a moment. For Dawn, being able to forget had become more important than ever. No one could resist a friend like Matthew, one who transported you to better, less painful places. That's how she ended up following him to his apartment that night after seeing him at the liquor store. That's why she ended up running into him at the art festival a couple weeks later. Maybe she'd hoped to see him there and purposely stayed near the booths displaying photography, but who wouldn't want to be around a person who made you feel better about yourself?

Dawn sat on the Letwinskis' deck for a long time, waiting for him, deciding she was done cleaning their house. She pulled her knees close to her chin. In a few days it wouldn't be so cold. She hadn't showered so the smell of Justice's cologne clung to her hair and skin. The image of Justice standing at his front door blended into one of Matthew stepping into the room. He'd come for her to make sure she was okay. She'd hurt him; he'd left.

Tonight would be packing, tomorrow simply driving away.

She flicked her cigarette over the edge of the deck and watched it hit the rocks and twigs below. It sparked, then smoked and finally kept to itself, a lifeless stick of cotton wrapped in paper. She bit her thumbnail and thought about leaving right now. Matthew, of all people, wouldn't be surprised to knock on the Twins' door and find no one there. Really, it was a perfect revenge strategy since Jen cost her a job. Someday, years from now when Dawn came home to visit her mom, she'd bump into Matthew at the liquor store and they'd laugh about the whole debacle. *It served me right*, he'd say.

She wondered if his hair would become gray as he aged or fall out entirely. She wondered if Matthew would still split the grant money with her if he won. Probably not. He could keep it all as a downpayment for his house on Bird Lake. A ring for Jen.

She reached for another cigarette and lit it with shaking hands. She dug through the contents of her purse to keep herself busy. She pulled the stack of business cards, stray receipts, and notes jotted on little slips of paper from the zippered pocket. Starting with the receipts, she reviewed each one to be sure it was safe to purge: one from the laundry where she took the McIntyres' clothes, this time for $35.75. She understood why she hadn't bothered trying to wash all that in one day. One from the Starbucks next to the cleaners from the same date back in September. She remembered now, a blindingly bright fall day and a Makers hangover. She, Matthew, Jen, and some of Matt's work friends had gotten loaded at the bar the night before, after a charity event. She'd spilled whiskey all over the secondhand flapper dress she'd bought for the occasion. The next receipt was folded into a tiny square that took some time to undo: $6.99 for the chicken shwarma lunch combination at the restaurant on the way home from the Rileys'.

Dawn balled the pile of receipts and tosse them next to her feet. She moved on to the cards, starting with the purple one from a trainer named Rex at the twenty-four-hour gym. She'd never been to the twenty-four-hour gym, but the guy approached her at the grocery store and encouraged her to join. She'd been holding a bag of tortilla chips and a container of onion dip at the time. Get sex with Rex, Matthew had joked when she'd arrived at his apartment. She tore the card in half.

She tore the cards from the community college, the technical training center, the massage school, and an appointment for a facial she never remembered making in the first place.

Her heart thumped when her fingers came across a lined-yellow page folded into quarters. God, it had been ages, almost a year. She'd written it on the top of the dryer in the Turners' mudroom after taking all of Barb's cleaning products from the cabinet and lining them up with price tags showing. It startled her to see the figures jotted on the page in red ink. She could have sworn she wrote it in blue, but it went to show how a person could imagine an actual situation in a way that never happened.

Windex: $4.94

Scrubbing Bubbles: $ 4.37

Lysol kitchen: $3.94

Murphy's Oil: $4.41

Pledge: $3.97

Comet: $3.99

Total: $25.62 x 5 houses = $128.10 x 6/x per year = $768.60 annual

+ $181.59 x 5 houses = $907 extra for Pledge

= $1,676.55 annual for supplies

The idea of Magic came to her as she pondered spending so much. Sometimes she used a little dish soap and water to wipe her counters in the trailer. No reason she couldn't do that for everyone. She hadn't thought to use the essential oils for fragrance until a couple months later. All her customers noticed and began asking what she used to make it smell so nice.

She'd gone into the cleaning lady business with such hope. She hoped to create distance from the trailer. And move on with her life. Sure, she made housekeeping easier for people like Barb Turner, but she couldn't make Barb happy. She couldn't help Wei Chen want to stay in the United States. She wished she'd never seen the lives of these people, these damaged, hurting people. Not only was it too easy to compare yourself to them, it was too easy to picture yourself as them, to see your future self living under the same set of circumstances. Magic didn't have the power to rinse off all the grime. Perhaps it wasn't living up to its name after all.

She lifted her sweatshirt to inspect the scabs. Twisting made them ache and stretch, but two days had made a big difference and pretty soon they'd be faded skin. Until she put on a bikini and got a tan. Dawn vowed to heal with the wounds. She wouldn't have to hide in Florida. This was the time to make sure she didn't end up as messed up as Barb Turner. Knowing what you didn't want to be could be as helpful as knowing what you did.

"What are you doing?" Matthew said, stepping from the asphalt driveway onto the deck.

Dawn dropped her sweatshirt. "I didn't hear you drive up."

"I saw you sitting there while I unloaded."

Both his camera bags were slung over his left shoulder. He wore a pale brown sweater with a hood. The shirttails of the plaid flannel hung beneath.

"Are you wearing a sweater?"

"I went shopping," he said. "My shirt has a hole in the elbow."

"A sweater?"

"Yes," he said, setting the bags on the ground. He reached into his back pocket for his cigarettes. "It's the Northeast. In December." He walked over and lifted her sweatshirt.

"What the fuck?" she said, swatting his hand.

"What did you do?"

"Don't touch me."

"I shouldn't be surprised you lied," Matthew said.

"I was too embarrassed to tell you."

"Tell me what?"

"I taped that money to myself. I don't know why. It was stupid. I had to rip it off."

"You had to?" he said, laughing. "You could have gotten into the bathtub."

"Shut up, know-it-all. What if the money ripped?"

"Uh. Tape."

He reached for her sweatshirt again and grabbed her wrist when she tried to swat him away. "Let me see." He put his cigarette between his lips for a free hand and wrestled her arm behind her back. She put her cigarette in her mouth and tried to punch his arm. "Stop it," he said.

He leaned over, revealing the hood on his sweater and how his hair curled into it, as well as the view of the woods over the top of his back. She stopped struggling. His hand grazed her side and he ran a thumb over the widest scab.

"Damn. I can see why you weren't moving much."

"I was never so happy to get drunk in my life."

He stood, closer to her than normal. All the boundaries she'd set, the barriers, the unspoken rules: none of it mattered. Worse, Matthew didn't seem nervous or uncomfortable. She knelt to collect the pile of paper and torn cards from the smooth cedar and headed for the side door.

"I was cleaning my purse," she said over her shoulder.

Matthew picked up his bags and followed her.

"I can't leave a mess on my last day," she said.

"I should hope not."

She opened the cabinet beneath the sink and shoved the papers inside before pulling the garbage bag from the can. She replaced it with an empty bag from the box in the drawer. He watched her tie the top of the bag and carry it to the door leading to the garage. She tossed it on the floor, went back to the sink, and washed her hands. She dried them on her jeans so she wouldn't add a paper towel to the fresh can.

Matthew took a step in her direction.

"Let's scout the house," Dawn said. "Get some inspiration to finish this."

He followed her while she narrated like an idiot, like he couldn't see the sights without explanation, but it seemed dangerous to invite quiet or give Matthew a chance to initiate a discussion.

"Upstairs," she said, pointing. "Their room is incredible. I love it. You'll see. The Twins have good taste. It's like the pieces of the house go together to make it feel like a complete home."

"Lead the way," he said, patting both camera bags.

She reached back and pulled the elastic from her ponytail. "Sorry I didn't think to primp like the other days. I wasn't sure we'd be doing this."

"Every day is different. That's good."

"It's your fault anyway," Dawn said.

Matthew thumped back down the stairs and disappeared around the corner.

"Where are you going?"

He reappeared with the Magic bottle in his hands. He inspected the soapy water and shook the bottle until foam appeared. He flipped the top with his thumb and aimed.

"Don't you dare!"

She ran as the foam dribbled out, making room for the stream of water that came next. He sprayed the back of her T-shirt and didn't stop. He took the steps two at a time and gained on her. Turning toward him did no good, despite her best efforts to knock the bottle from his hands. She gave up and stood there while he emptied it.

"That's what you get for blaming me for yesterday. And for lying about remembering."

She couldn't think of a response so she went into the Twins' room. He followed her through the doorway.

"Ah," he said. "Easy. Ceilings."

"What about them?"

"They're high. Majestic. The room can breathe."

"Right. But see the windows. Look at the painting. The bed frame. You step in here and it's all good. There's oxygen."

"You're not going to say one word about being soaked?"

"I smell Magical. At least there's that."

"Magical?"

"That's what I call the stuff. Magic. My cleaning Magic."

"Shouldn't you take off those wet clothes?"

"No."

"I don't believe you don't want to," he said. "Now that I know you remember."

That sweater! The goddamned thing unnerved her with its impeccable knit or whatever the hell it was that made it attractive. Amazing how a person's whole appearance changed by adding one garment, a stupid sweater, with a hood that somehow made his hair long and mysterious, and his neck graceful. The white T-shirt revealed the soft place between his collarbones. The plaid shirt, exposed where the collar framed his face and the tails hung against his jeans, combined with the sweater gave him a sexiness she hadn't known she'd be drawn to having been engaged to someone like Terry.

And if she'd heard correctly, he'd just asked her to take her clothes off. Her soaking wet clothes from yesterday, not to mention her unwashed hair that only grew more unruly and curly when it got wet. She almost laughed at her panic and self-consciousness. This was Matthew! Matthew. Her friend. A friendship she dictated. Or maybe that had changed.

Two thoughts occurred to her at the same time: first, that Matthew didn't care what she wore, and second, that she'd look way better without her clothes on. She wanted them off. "Why don't you do it?" she said.

"I'm a little concerned you're going to kick me in the nuts."

He set his bags near the door.

"I'm not."

"You're known to lie."

He pulled his sweater over his head and tossed it on the floor. He took off the flannel too.

"Hot?" she said.

"Always."

"That's my favorite T-shirt."

A cartoon crab with the caption *I'm Crabby*.

He walked to her as casually as he might have to inspect the photo on the McIntyres' bed. Before she realized, he'd lifted her shirt over her head in one swift motion. His mouth was on hers, but then he backed away. She remembered that about him:

Matthew didn't maul you, he took his time so you wanted him to touch you, backed off enough to make you really want it. His lips were inches from hers and he fingered the edge of her bra.

"You can tell me to stop," he said, sliding his hand inside the cup.

"You're sucking up because you know I'm mad at you."

She held the back of his neck anyway.

"Will you at least let me say I'm sorry? That I fucked up? That I misjudged Jen?"

"It was for the best. Losing that job helped me decide to go."

"You know I would have hidden until the situation was clear, right?"

"You said she understood."

"You act like I could have predicted any of what happened," he said. "There was no stopping it once it started."

He rolled her nipple between two fingers and Dawn wished her bra were off so she could see. He squeezed—hard—and his mouth found hers again.

"What happened wasn't cool," she said.

"It wasn't. It changed a lot."

"What changed a lot?"

"Watching the scene unfold. How you reacted. How I reacted. How Jen did. Everything changed. And it changed more when you finally admitted it."

He reached back and opened the clasp of her bra, pulling it off with the other hand. His leg wrapped behind her knees and it didn't hurt when she hit the floor because his hand was already behind her back. He pulled it free to work the button on his jeans and reached back to pull them down before doing hers.

"It did, didn't it?" he said.

His gaze held her, trapped her. She remembered why she'd been so upset the last time. She noted the gold flecks in the hazel and, having now known Matthew as long as she had, recognized his ability to get lost. He was looking at her, in her, through her. He snaked his fingers—gently—into the damp hair around her face. He closed his eyes for the briefest second and pushed into her.

She pushed back, against bulk and muscle she was sure hadn't been there a year earlier, but who knew what she knew back then. Memories grew thinner over time, assuming she'd remembered specifics to begin with. She'd hated Matthew then for trying to see her, refusing to like the intimacy. Now, though, she realized she had changed. It didn't hurt to be seen anymore and, this time, she wanted to see him too.

He gripped her thigh and slid his hand behind her knee, lifting her leg alongside her ear.

"I remember you being very bendy," he said, stroking her inner thigh with the backs of his fingers, then licking the length of her calf.

"No one has ever licked my leg before."

"No?"

He rested on an elbow and scratched his cheek with his middle finger. He paused to close his right eye and brush his eyelashes with his index finger.

"Matthew?"

"What?"

He opened his eye and she could tell by his face how much he wanted to move inside her.

"You're so hard."

"You're so wet."

She closed her eyes and a tear rolled toward her left ear and into her hair.

Matthew brushed the damp trail with his thumb.

"We better do this before I screw it up," she said, keeping her eyes closed. Louder, she said, "God, Matthew, I want you. Have I always wanted you this much?"

She'd forgotten how Matthew managed to put her in the right positions in smooth, seamless motions, as though painting on a canvas with vibrant colors filling the space exactly how he wanted. Toward the end, she opened her eyes to the earthy red and gold triangles on the Twins' bedroom rug, feeling Matthew's hand on her breast in the front and pushing up against her elbow in the back. She was close and didn't care he might come inside her. He mustn't stop. It wasn't until she started to come she realized he'd been holding back. She listened to the intensity of their culmination and right when she finished, he pulled out, a warm and satisfying confirmation he cared about not getting her pregnant.

He gently pulled her onto the rug and tucked her into a spoon. She felt soft fabric wiping her back. In the quick glance over her shoulder, the sleeve of Matthew's flannel came into view. He tossed it aside and moved his arm into the space between her breasts. It took a long time for their breathing to slow to normal and for her to stop feeling his heart pounding against her scapula.

"My God," he whispered. "There's something right between us."

She may have dreamt it, but right before she dropped off to sleep, she swore he said, "I don't want you to leave me, Dawn."

Not just leave, but leave me.

Maybe she dreamt it.

He touched her shoulder a little while later. Instead of watching him stand and get dressed, she watched the clouds blowing outside the circular window high on the wall.

"Please don't move," he said.

He reached for his bag and pulled out his camera.

"Look right at me."

With Karen and Mike Letwinskis' beautiful rug beneath her naked body, Matthew took her picture. He must have seen the rough red of her elbow and the self-inflicted scabs through the lens. She wanted him to see. All of it. A slice of sunshine warmed her arm and breast.

"I feel peace, Matthew."

"I see it."

After a while he stopped circling and put the camera back into the bag. He sat on the edge of the bed.

"I'm going home to work on the photos. I know exactly what I'm going to do."

"I'll be home packing."

"Do you remember all of it, D-pleter? What we talked about that night?"

"I said Terry was dead because I tried to give him a hand job."

"All this time. I had no idea if you remembered that I knew."

"Matt. You're the only person who knows. You're the only person I told. Ever."

"You can't be serious," Matthew said.

In the hospital, the police came and went. They asked whether she'd noticed anything out of the ordinary that caused the crash. Another car cutting in front of them? A pothole in the road? A muscle spasm or leg cramp? No, she'd said. The truth lodged itself somewhere in her throat and wouldn't budge. Had she wanted to tell, she wouldn't have been able to. Not that she wanted to. Mrs. Folly's face, pinched and pained, assured her to keep quiet. Being dead was bad enough. Her mother and Davis never asked for specifics, leaving it to Dawn to offer them if she chose. Speculation among their friends floated above their heads like a cloud that eventually blew over. Terry was practically a pro on the bike, Nick had said. He wouldn't have crashed driving a straight line going 45. No way. Dawn had found out, hadn't she? She'd found out about the cheating and wanted him to pay.

"I don't want to talk about it anymore," Dawn said. "It's enough that you know. No one else needs to."

A patch of blue appeared in the circular window, followed by a pair of clouds snaking through and around each other. Matthew knelt beside her and kissed her cheek.

"D-lightful."

She closed her eyes.

"I have such ideas for these photos. So many ideas, thanks to you. I'll see you later?"

She nodded and listened to him leave.

After a while, she got up, pulled on her damp clothes and left, taking a few gulps of the cold because she might not have the chance to do it again, at least not for a long time.

Dawn woke up at 11:37 with her head pillowed by her crossed arms on the kitchen table. She checked her phone. No calls. No texts. It did not surprise her since she'd left the volume up, an action she couldn't remember doing since she and Terry dated. They'd go for days without talking after a fight and she never wanted to miss a call if he caved first. Sliding the mute button to activate the volume when she got home from the Letwinskis' seemed like taking a step back in time.

Pinpointing the exact moment her friendship with Matthew had stopped and restarted held a complexity similar to viewing a slide under a microscope in chemistry class. What she'd thought was a simple spot of color pressed between plastic was, upon magnification, a world unto itself with life and detail and nuances she'd missed. Not only had her naked eye been blind to the patterns and colors, the layers and textures had also gone unobserved. There was a book like this she remembered from childhood about a speck of dust. It wasn't dust at all, but an actual planet with little creatures living and working.

This person, a friend she'd slept with once, now consumed her. He'd had her phone number for over a year and called often enough to be regular but infrequent enough to be inter-mittent. She'd never really thought about it. Now, alone in her trailer, she wished she could remember every conversation, the specific words he'd used, the tone of his voice and—oh God, yes—the sound of his laugh. His laugh always made her laugh, too, in a way that required shaking her head first and literally shedding bad thoughts from her day or tension from her neck or residual grouchiness or bitchiness. Matthew's laugh took you with him, like holding hands and jumping into water.

Her silent phone on the table, a lifeline that could connect her to Matthew, was reduced to an outdated electronic device with a tiny crack on the top corner of the glass in a worn-out plastic case. She needed it to ring so she could zoom in on his voice to remember him: the crinkle on his forehead, the smell of his neck, the softness of his hair against her cheek. That she didn't know if and when he'd call filled her with—what was it, desperation? Not exactly, but the ache of it felt familiar enough to need it gone. She recognized the frustration, too, of knowing she might be in for a whole night of waiting. Not because Matthew was stubborn like Terry, but because he was an artist.

Sometimes, when Matthew got involved in an art project, he worked all night and part of the next day without realizing how much time had passed. Especially when there was a deadline involved. She pictured his floor covered with prints, a burning cigarette in the ashtray on his coffee table. He'd toss some away, dig around some more, pull some to the forefront. Part of her wanted to drive to his apartment and watch him work. The very idea of him—his hair, his worn-out T-shirts, the taste of his neck—seemed magnetic. She'd watch him until she couldn't stop herself from hooking his belt loop with her pinky. Once he got close enough, she'd get ahold of the buttons on his jeans. She could make him stop working.

How she wanted to.

Her mind had been turning these thoughts over all night and, every time, landed on the possibility he wasn't working, he was with Jen. Or that Jen was over while he worked. Dawn didn't think so, she doubted it, but the worry prickled just enough to keep her from calling him. She hated the hot flare associated with jealousy. Plus Matthew knew she intended to drive away the next day. If he wanted to be with her, he would be. So why wasn't he?

The trailer rang with silence. Outside she heard hushed traffic from the road beyond the park and the hum of the nearby street lamp. Her clarity surprised her. She got up to pour herself another drink. A clear head could be dangerous. Plus, drinking meant it was still last night, not tomorrow morning.

Six boxes, a giant suitcase stuffed to capacity, and a travel tote

lined the wall near the door. The only cup she hadn't packed
was one she'd acquired from Matthew, a white plastic cup printed with pictures of a guy dressed in grape leaves sipping from
a gold chalice. The words said *Krewe of Bacchus*. Behind the guy
was what Dawn believed to be the sea. Matthew got the cup
from a Mardi Gras parade in New Orleans, where the people
on the floats hurled beads and cups and other trinkets into the
crowd. He'd come home with a welt on his forehead after being
nailed by a decorated coconut. Some guy snatched it up and ran
so all Matthew brought home was the injury.

She'd seen the photos in Matthew's album of masses of
people in the streets with beads piled around their necks and
drinks lifted. Some of the women weren't wearing shirts, but
had them painted on. Others wore costumes like doctor and
nurse uniforms with cutouts for butts and boobs. Masks painted in all colors with feathers and plastic sparkly trimmings.
Matthew had dumped his bag of souvenirs on the floor of his
apartment, mixed it around with his boot and taken a photo
before dumping it all into the recycle bin in the hallway.

Dawn needed cups so she'd taken one. The cup signified a
souvenir from Matthew's Mardi Gras photographs. Pretending
to be interested in the art—which she supposed she was a little—her main interest in the album had to do with Matthew
having seen so much through his camera lens. Dawn had seen
none of it. Cities she'd never visited like New York, Nashville,
and Portland. Trends like body piercings and leather lingerie.
What a homeless man looked like close up: so dirty that his
image appeared faded against the background. Whatever Matthew had said must have amused him, as a single dimple on the
scruff of his cheek accompanied the half-smile on his dusty
lips. The only part of the man that didn't seem faded were his
eyes.

Dawn sipped the cold whiskey. She wished she were wearing
her bathrobe and slippers. Changing clothes, though, implied
the end of the day. Tomorrow, moving day. Her right elbow
twanged so she pressed the cup against it. She liked the leaves

in the guy's hair, as though he'd been standing underneath a tree and a few fell on his head. The water in the background reminded her of her dad, of the ocean in Florida.

Florida, the first place she'd go since the accident. She hadn't considered going with her dad when he moved away. Back then, the idea of leaving Terry for the ocean seemed absurd. Senior year of high school trumped a beach. All days included Terry. Giving that up wasn't an option. Dawn knew they wouldn't force her to go. Her parents were cool like that and let her make her own choices. Even now. They didn't interfere.

None of the boxes across the room were filled to the top. It hadn't taken long to pack. She'd barely paid attention. One held her kitchen stuff—an incomplete set of dishes, silverware, a couple pans. Random plastic cups. A few little juice glasses that doubled as barware.

Next to that was the box of bathroom stuff with her towels and washcloth, shampoo, and toothbrush. The makeup bag her mother got as a bonus when she purchased some eye cream. Her hairbrush was the same one she'd used to get ready for school dances. Despite being a little worn around the edges and the rubber grip having softened over time, it worked as well as any expensive brush she might buy at a salon. Each bristle still had the plastic nub on its tip. She'd double-checked to be sure none had fallen off, which was pretty miraculous considering how much abuse it had endured tearing through her curls and being dropped about a million times. She'd thrown the brush at Terry once during an argument. It gave a satisfying thwap when it had hit his bicep.

Her clothes filled up two boxes, plus the suitcase. She probably didn't need the mountain of old T-shirts, two formal dresses, an old pair of snow pants. But who knew how long she'd live in Florida. Instead of sorting through them, she'd decided to deal with purging later, once she got settled and knew for sure.

One box held her extra blanket and sheets.

The last consisted of leftovers: an old camping flashlight, extra cigarette lighters and ashtrays, a keychain from New York

City she'd somehow acquired. An envelope of pictures of her and Katelyn Rice in Katelyn's yellow bedroom, acting silly and making faces. She, Katelyn, Terry, and Nick at school dances. On a trip to the Adirondacks to Nick's parents' cabin for a weekend.

She checked her phone again though it seemed certain it was asleep for the night.

Dawn cracked the remaining ice cubes from the tray in the freezer and poured the last of the whiskey over them. Kind of a bigass drink for midnight, but hell. Who cared? She navigated to her gmail box filled with spam. No real messages, so she set the phone facedown on the table and tried to ignore it. The empty shelves and cupboards in the trailer left her with a calming sense someone else would deem it a better place to live.

The boxes of her life taunted her, especially the last one filled with leftovers. Everyone had a junk drawer for the possessions without a place, all those belongings you thought you needed or would need someday, but probably wouldn't. Her rubber-band ball, for example. It seemed wasteful to throw one away and they came more than you realized: around the weekly coupon roll inside her mailbox, snapped onto the top of a container of berries at the grocery store to hold the cellophane wrapper, on the cheap bouquet of flowers she bought once and a while near the pharmacy checkout. Her collection had grown to golf-ball size. Who knew whether she'd ever need or use a rubber band, but those giant balls in the office supply section cost close to ten bucks. No one needed to waste that money.

So the ball ended up in her kitchen junk drawer along with the pen from the Native American casino a few towns over, a cheap pair of free sunglasses, and a plastic baggie full of random nails and screws from who knows where.

The Turners had several places containing leftover items, including a drawer in the kitchen, a basket in the laundry room, and a bureau in the living room. They held paper clips and stray batteries to old teething rings to rolls of undeveloped film. Carryout menus at the McIntyres', along with pencils, Post-it notes and a clay mold of Robert's teeth. Duct tape at the Rileys' mixed in with the stapler, oven mitts, and knitting supplies. Studying the items told you the facts you needed to know. Wei Chen also collected carryout menus and kept them in a drawer with their passports, a sun visor, individually wrapped Chinese candies, and an old screwdriver with white paint all over the blue handle. The Twins' junk drawer held little votive candles, pens and pencils, a couple rubber thimbles, a lint roller, and a worn-out leather wallet. For a while, there were condoms in there too.

Dawn knew her customers' junk better than her own. She eyed the box and was overcome with the same feeling as going to a thrift store: she might find an amazing and valuable prize if she searched hard enough. Of course not everyone had an old engagement ring sitting around.

The little black box was in there somewhere. She'd kept the ring on her finger for a while, a couple weeks after the accident, but began imagining Terry could watch her through the sparkling stone. She swore she could see his face somewhere in the diamond's reflection.

Jesus, Dawn, you should have used your head, he'd say.

What were the chances he wouldn't hate her for killing him? Not to mention destroying his bike. He'd saved for it, over $400, and had to spring for helmets, gas, and insurance.

Dawn swirled the whiskey a few times to make sure it was good and cold. Her possessions condensed to one nook of the house made the trailer less threatening. She believed for the first time she might be able to walk out of there and not be afraid anymore. In fact, she didn't feel afraid now. She took a few swallows, set the cup on the counter, and went to find the ring. She found it wedged between the cardboard wall and the red silk bag that held her vibrator. The top of the velvet box creaked when she flipped it open.

She almost laughed. The narrow gold band could easily be bent. The prongs practically swallowed the diamond.

Dawn put it on, wondering how she could have been so

stupid to think Terry watched her through its glint. Katelyn was right about being lucky, even if Katelyn only saw it through her eyes. Dawn doubted she and Terry would be on their second kid. She didn't know if he'd wanted kids. And Dawn would have surely tried to go to college, at least community college, so they wouldn't be dirt poor.

They might not have ended up getting married at all.

She put the ring back into the case and snapped the lid closed. She took a shot, arcing it toward the ceiling and making it into the correct box. She half-wanted to throw it into the trash. A pawnshop might take it. Or a donation center. Maybe someone in love needed a ring but couldn't afford to buy one.

The magnitude of being ready to be rid of it struck her. How could she not want Terry's ring? It didn't feel like a deception. More like a revelation: they'd be broken up, but not because he was dead. Just because they'd have broken up. She'd have ended it. Nick and Katelyn might still hate her, but not because he was dead. They'd be broken up. That's all.

Dawn would have moved on and met someone better.

She dumped the rest of the last drink down the sink, switched off the lights, and headed to her room for bed.

SATURDAY: ZOOM

YOU'VE SEEN IT, YOU'VE CLEANED IT,
NOW MOVE ON TO THE NEXT MESS.

Waking up early on a Saturday usually annoyed her, but today Dawn received it like a gift. She found her shoes and pulled them on. She lugged the suitcase to the car and hoisted it into the trunk. The tote bag fit snugly next to the suitcase. One box next to that. The rest she piled on the seats and floor of the back seat. It fit perfectly, like a puzzle. Mornings seemed full of possibility, as though the new light on the Earth was softer at that time of day and breathing nourished the lungs. Getting on the road at dawn, she knew, meant making the most of weekend traffic, road conditions, and hours of daylight.

Soon she'd have nothing left to do but stop to say goodbye to her mother and Davis, and leave Matthew behind. She slowed on the final walk back to the trailer to confirm she hadn't forgotten anything. Instead of locking up and leaving, she lingered in her bedroom.

Her stomach rumbled at the thought of going to Matthew's and Jen being there. She would never take the chance. She'd rather be the one who decided to leave than to go over for more and be rejected. There was no reason to believe Matthew wanted more than what happened at the Letwinskis'. Otherwise, he would have called.

Dawn sat on the edge of her bare mattress like an intruder in the room. The place was practically empty; she belonged nowhere. She wanted to wish herself into nonexistence, but more than that, she wanted Matthew. If she gave it five more minutes, he'd walk in to find her. He'd barge in with determination and wrap his fingers around her hair to tip her chin. His cock would already be hard when she pressed against him. Hope reignited when her phone rang. She sprang up and ran to the kitchen.

The number on the screen had no name attached, but she recognized it from before: Barb Turner. A groan escaped her. She answered with an unenthusiastic hello.

"Is this Dawn?" A man's voice.

"Yes, it is. Who is this?"

"This is Fred Turner. You clean our house on Mondays."

"Right. Indeed I do."

"There's a serious situation. My wife is very upset. She's missing a pretty important item."

"What is she missing?" Dawn said, sitting up straight.

"She said you'd know. She seems sure you took it. Positive, in fact."

Dawn knew exactly where the psych report was: in the dumpster with her other trash. Throwing it away had been easy. She'd been quick to disregard its meaning and significance—a mistake, it seemed, as big as taking the paper out of the Turner home. When you packed everything you owned and intended to drive away, it didn't seem necessary to worry about giving it back to someone you'd never see again. Barb Turner would be over and done with. Like so many other chores and tasks on her to-do list, moving gave her permission to cross them off.

She'd added the psych report to the pile of old bank statements right before she tied the last garbage bag. Hearing Fred ask for it back caused panic to spread through her like a prickly poison.

"I'm calling on her behalf because she's upset," Fred said. "She wants her property back and she wants you to bring over our house key."

"I'm moving this weekend. I was going to let you know."

"Moving where?"

"To be with my dad down south."

"We have a problem here. You have access to our home. It's irresponsible to leave town without returning our key first."

Dawn heard fussing in the background, the urgent and angry sounds of a woman. "I'll mail you the key," Dawn said. "I'll find a post office when I get there."

"She wants to mail the key," Fred said, not into the phone.

"She will not mail the key! She will bring the key right now and give me my property. Today!"

"I'm assuming you heard that," Fred said.

The next voice on the line was Barb's. "I trusted you, Dawn. This is serious."

"Take it easy," Dawn said. "There's a solution to every problem. We can figure this out."

"I will not take it easy! Here I was trying to help you. I'm a good person. You better get over here with our key and property before I call the police. I mean it, I will. It might not seem important to you, but it is to me."

"I decided to take your advice. To deal with my accident. You were right. So I decided to move near my father."

"You're a thief!"

"I'm not. You have to understand."

"I understand you're not the person I thought you were. Those are my children. They are the only ones who matter to me. Five children, five shoes. I don't care how screwed up I am. Do you hear me? You have no right to go through my bedroom. You shouldn't be digging around in there. This is my house."

Dawn stopped herself from correcting Barb. Five children needed ten shoes, but rational thinking seemed not to apply. She wondered about hospital privacy laws and whether it was serious to read a piece of paper in your employer's home. But she took it—God, why did she take it?

"I'm moving today," Dawn said.

"I'm calling the police. You have invaded my life. Jesus Christ, what is happening? To think I wanted to help you. I'm calling the police right now."

Barb hung up.

"Shit," Dawn said aloud.

"Shit," she said again.

Time held. She fought the urge to get in her car and start driving. It became clear now, all those times she'd judged other people for hit and run accidents or fleeing the scene of a crime. She understood the other side of it. Doing something wrong brought trouble. Getting caught confirmed stupidity. Human nature said to get the hell out of there. Why stay and admit you were wrong when there was a chance you could get away from it entirely? But come on, she reminded herself. It wasn't like she'd killed someone. This was not that. This was a piece of paper.

The trailer park didn't have garbage pickup until Tuesday. Dawn doubted anyone would take out the trash today. Her bags might be right there, front and center. It wouldn't be hard to sift through, mostly just paper, to find the psych report. The hospital logo would make it easy to spot. Getting in there was another matter. The mouth of the dumpster was tall enough to keep most people from trying to toss their bags inside. They left them on the ground for Justice to deal with later. Not Dawn; she enjoyed hurling her weekly bag of trash over the steel lip and listening for the whiskey bottle to smash against the bottom.

She rested her head on the table and contemplated the likelihood that Barb would really call the police. Her unfortunate conclusion was that she probably would, perhaps already had. Whether the police would actually respond was another matter. With all the real crime out there, what would it matter if a hysterical woman wanted a house key and piece of paper? From a cleaning lady.

Her phone rang, this time with a strange number illuminating the screen.

"Hello?" she said.

"Hi," said a man's voice. "This is Detective Ronald Haas. Am I speaking with the housekeeper for a very upset woman named Barbara Turner?"

Papers rustled on the other end.

"Yes," Dawn said. Her heart began pounding.

"You are…" the detective said, pausing for a long second. "Dawn? Is that right? I am speaking with Dawn?"

"Yes."

"I don't have the best sense of the situation, Dawn, but your client is highly upset. Something about you having access to her home. And taking an article or two? Is that right?"

"Yes. That's what she said."

"Without having the full story, I'm going to make a suggestion, Dawn. This client of yours doesn't seem like the type of person who takes loss lightly."

"No."

"If you do have her key, I suggest you return it. If you did take property, return it. I'm hoping to not hear from Barbara Turner again. It's not the sort of case we like to prioritize, you understand. I'm hoping you can deal with it personally to resolve the situation. Does that make sense?"

"Yes."

"Excellent," the detective said. "I hope this is the last time we'll speak. Goodbye."

"Bye."

Dawn walked out of the trailer without her coat and up the footpath to the dumpster. She stopped halfway there and turned. The neighboring trailers seemed closer together, almost cozy in their closeness. Hers had white siding, way brighter and cleaner than the others because of its relative newness. Warm light illuminated her kitchen window as though someone new had already moved in. She imagined a young family living there, a wife in the kitchen simmering ground beef for chili and the father and baby napping in the bedroom. It seemed like she hadn't lived there in years, but she could see why she'd wanted to live there. For a mobile home, it was far from dumpy.

She pictured the owner's paperwork, stuffed in a folder in the box wedged next to her suitcase in the trunk, and the way she'd signed her name in very small letters. As soon as she got settled in Florida, she'd find the statement of ownership and send it to Justice. She'd tell him: the first family who comes in that really needs it, give it to them. Tell them the previous owner took a great opportunity down south and wanted someone else to have a home. No strings attached.

The temperature had dropped considerably and her fingers ached. The lid of the dumpster was open, but Dawn had no way of knowing how deep the garbage piled inside nor whether the raccoons had chewed through it.

She reached up for the lip and wondered whether she had the strength to lift herself as a gymnast might on the high bar. She jumped and strained, only to find her cheek flat against the rusted surface and her feet still planted on the ground. Her left temple pulsed so she let go to rub away the impending headache. She eyed a stack of old milk crates and wondered if they would hold her.

"You lose your purse, little girl?"

Across the crumbling lot stood Justice with his hands on his hips. She motioned for him to come over.

"In a minute," he called.

Dawn hadn't noticed earlier that someone had run down the entrance sign again. This time it had fallen face first like a malnourished drunk in the weedy grasses along the street. She knew by the way his head swung from side to side that Justice was probably muttering about punk-ass fools. She laughed when he threw his hands up. He climbed into his pickup and drove toward the storage shed. He loaded the stepladder into the bed before crossing over.

"I'm not going to ask what you're doing," he said, sliding it out and leaning it against the garbage receptacle.

"Dumpster diving, what else?"

She smelled the compilation of the products on his bathroom counter: Axe body spray, Old Spice deodorant, generic mint toothpaste.

"You go off and make amends with Matts-his-name?"

"You think I'd let him off the hook that easy?"

"Yeah. You would."

He reached out and gave her arm a pat with his thick glove.

"I decided to move. Packed all my stuff."

"Really? Key West?" he said.

"Yep. Cleared it with my dad. I'm there."

"Good for you!" Justice said. "See? Trailer trash has goals too."

"We'll see. Can you help me with whatever I need to do to unload my trailer?"

"I can do that."

"I appreciate it. Really. It's time for me to get the hell out of here."

He peeked over his shoulder at the sign and sighed.

"Can you believe the motherfuckers?" he said. "Leave this here when you're done."

He kicked the ladder with his boot as his phone rang. He clamped his arm over his glove to release a hand.

"You've got to be kidding me?" he said to the person on the other end. "All right. I'll be there."

He slid the phone into the pocket of his coat.

"Emergency service call. Give you some time to think up an excuse for making a pass the other night."

"I'm sorry about that," Dawn said.

Justice only stared so Dawn laughed.

"What?" she said. "I am."

"You be careful. You're on a slippery slope."

"It means a lot to me that you told me about your brother. I'm really sorry. I can't imagine."

"My brother watched you make that pass at me. He says I should have tapped that."

"Terry watched me make it and said I've really lowered my standards."

"Who'm I gonna bullshit with when you leave?"

"I'll be in touch, I promise. It might not seem like it, but I'm a good person. I am now, at least. I will be."

She watched him climb into the service truck. He drove away and, just before he rounded the corner, honked and waved out the window.

The ladder opened easily and locked into place. She climbed up and peered inside. Like a gift, the last bag she'd tossed in sat on top of the heap, top side up, so she was able to reach over and untwist the tie. The bag fell open so she quickly sifted through to find the report and let the rest of the papers cascade down the pile to the bottom. She jumped to the ground and folded it into her purse.

☙

Dawn stepped onto the Turners' porch with their key in her hand. Her mind raced from trying to recalibrate a new schedule for the day. Because the policeman told her to return the key to Barb, she should also return the keys to her other customers. She'd been warned. She didn't want to get to Florida with loose ends back home.

Soon she'd be a person living in a different place, not where she came from. Looking forward was all she wanted to do, not look back. So, she'd make quick stops at the McIntyres', Rileys', and Letwinskis' to drop off keys; if they weren't home, she'd toss them in mailboxes with notes. Not the most professional move, but she doubted anyone expected two weeks' notice from a maid.

These detours, she insisted to herself, were essential to how she wanted to conclude her business. Doing her best. They were not excuses to lag in case Matthew called. She could not wait around for Matthew. Noon. She could finish by noon and still drive at least twelve hours before needing sleep.

Her key slid easily into the lock of the Turners' front door and she'd pushed it open before realizing what she'd done. She stifled her instinct to curse and slowly and carefully pulled the door closed. Next they'd call the police on her for unlawful entry. The adrenaline coursed through her body as she stood there. She waited the longest sixty seconds of her life before lifting her hand to knock. She held her breath to hear anyone who might approach on the other side. Finally she released a long, slow exhalation. The oxygen she pulled in seemed to save her from collapsing. She knocked twice, hard.

Fred answered. She'd only seen his pictures around the house, but he was easy enough to recognize. Chubby enough to be the husband who sweated all over the bed. His balding head gave him the appearance of a cartoon character whose face was drawn into a long oval. He leaned into the doorway with his hand clasping the molding. A gold wedding ring, hairy fingers. Scary fingers.

"I'm your cleaning lady, Dawn."

"Oh for heaven's sake."

"The police said I should bring it." She handed him the key. He clasped it, then put it in the pocket of his jeans, the dorky dad kind that pulled up too high. She couldn't find the courage to unzip her purse and hand him the psych report.

"Listen," he said. "Come in for a second."

"I don't think I should. I'm just doing what the officer said." The silver tab on the zipper of her purse was cold between her fingers when she tugged to open it. She realized her hands were sweating.

"No, come in. Come in," Fred said.

He waved her in, almost frantically, so she stepped through the threshold. His butt resembled an oval that matched his head. "Sit, sit, sit."

She sat on the couch, noticing the layer of dust that had accumulated on the coffee table since Monday. Colorful toys, empty juice boxes, Nerf bullets, and broken crayons were strewn about. A package of construction paper had been eject-ed from the plastic package like a deck of playing cards fanned for display. A pink laptop computer butted against the chest of drawers next to the front door as though someone had kicked it across the floor. Dawn could barely believe the mess. She'd never pictured the Turner kids playing in the living room, but it seemed they had free range. Across the room, the shine of little fingerprints dotted the wall near the light switch. Fred stood there, swaying from side to side, holding his chin, perplexed. "Uck," he said. "I don't know what to do."

"I should go. I'm not sure why you invited me in."

The zipper opened with a cheerful swish. The psych report remained folded between her wallet and cigarettes.

"Let me get Barb. She's going to want to talk to you."

His white socks buzzed with little zaps of static electricity against the carpet as he crossed through the children's wreckage to head upstairs. All the furnishings she wouldn't be cleaning on Monday sat before her: the piano, the vase over the blob. Someone had dumped Legos nearby, leaving half a pirate ship surrounded by blocks and bits. It didn't appear that any additional gifts had been added under the tree. No one had moved the holiday packages to their correct piles. Perhaps Barb liked her approach. She heard Fred go into the bedroom and voices as they talked. Muffled shouts and laughter of kids floated up from the basement. Dawn considered slipping out the door and leaving it at that. But then she heard footsteps on the stairs and both of the Turners were coming.

She slid the psych report between the couch cushions.

Barb followed Fred with her head down. She wore the plaid flannel nightgown and fat suede slippers. Your face didn't get that red and swollen unless you'd had a good, long cry. She sat down in the velvet chair with her hands in her lap. Her fingers were bare, no ring, and her fingernails were chewed. Dawn couldn't remember whether her customer's hands were in such a state last week at the pharmacy. Fred stood next to her, a hand on the back of the chair. He probably knew better than to touch her.

"Barb," Fred said.

"I owe you an apology," Barb said to her lap. "It wasn't my place to get involved with your life. I shouldn't have done that."

Fred raised his eyebrows hopefully.

"Okay," Dawn said.

"You don't understand how much I want to go back and do it all over. You think you can skate through life unscathed."

"Uh-huh," Dawn said. She couldn't help picking at a dry cuticle.

Barb's eyes glittered with tears ready to spill down her face.

"It took me years to get help. It was too late. And you, you're so young with your future in front of you. You need to be in therapy. You need to learn coping mechanisms. There is so much you can do before it's all so deep you can't find the roots."

"Barb, I think you're talking about you, not Dawn," Fred said.

"Maybe I am," she said, as the tears fell. "But can't you see why I want to help her? Her fiancé died in a terrible accident, Fred. How does someone get over that?"

"Barb," he said, putting a warning hand on her shoulder. She twisted out from beneath his touch.

"You're projecting," Dawn said. She'd learned the word from, of all people, Davis. "You're treating me like I'm you. I am in therapy, did you know that? I've been in therapy ever since. And I go to support groups. My parents help me. I have friends. You're assuming I'm dealing with this on my own, but I'm not. That's where you're wrong."

Barb wrung her hands. "You seemed so alone at the store the other night."

"I was buying cigarettes. You were the one who was alone, standing there staring at Christmas decorations. In your pajamas."

More tears fell. Barb nodded. "I was, I was."

"I'm not a *thief*," Dawn said, louder, aware of how stuck she was on that point.

Barb squeezed her fingers; Fred rocked from foot to foot.

Barb fumbled around and reached into the pocket of her nightgown. She extracted a gold necklace, the one with the five baby shoe charms. The birthstone jewels sparkled in the light as Barb arranged each shoe, sole down, on the palm of her hand.

"I found it," she stammered. "I thought you took it, but you didn't. I found it in Sofia's room. She was playing, I guess."

Dawn gripped the seat of the couch and pushed herself to standing. The transition to vertical left her dizzy. Barb appeared small and miserable enough to crumble. Her customer wiped her nose with the length of her sleeve and cried into the crook of her elbow.

"I'm supposed to be moving right now," Dawn said, "and I came here because you accused me of stealing."

"We're very sorry," Fred said. "We can give you this week's pay for your trouble."

Dawn watched Fred pivot on his heel, searching. His face

wore the expression of bleakness. He patted his front pockets, then his back pockets as though a solution might appear. He gripped Barb's forearm. Barb's presence in the room radiated around it like a painful pulse. A few days earlier she'd seen Wei Chen break. Now Barb had broken, too, in the same sorry manner with heat and tears and sorrow. Not all because of Dawn, but partially.

The indignation of having not stolen the necklace faded into the realization the Turners were correct in thinking she'd taken from them. She had no right to take Barb Turner's medical documents. She shouldn't have been digging around in there. A closet, a jewelry box, what was the difference? Barb had trusted her.

"I'm moving," Dawn said, clasping Barb's arm, "because you were right, Barb."

Barb sniffled. Dawn understood the point of upset when a person looks so awful from crying that it was impossible to picture her any worse. Her eyes were swollen slits. She let go of Barb's arm and stood there, as though watching her future self in the mirror.

A little girl rounded the corner, a tiny human wearing striped tights and a blue jean skirt with cowgirl boots. She stopped when she saw the three of them standing there, grimacing at her mother's face. She tiptoed away, as though they wouldn't see her if she were quiet enough.

"You were right that I need help. I *was* alone the other night. You helped me not be so alone."

"If you decide not to move you can have your job back," Barb said. "I love having you clean for us. If you stay." She observed the condition of the room and gave a weak laugh. "I haven't picked up for you yet. Obviously."

"I'm going to go. I have to."

"Wait, please," Fred said.

He opened the drawer of the table in the hallway, the one with the nicked leg, and got the checkbook. It shocked her to realize she'd never opened that drawer before. Not that she cared where they kept the checkbook, but she'd never noticed its absence. What else had she missed? Fred flipped to the right page and scribbled on the paper. He tore a check and gave it to Dawn.

She took it and headed for the door.

"Dawn," Barb said.

She stopped. Her customer's face was slick.

"Please forgive me," Barb said. "I'm getting help. And I'm so glad you're getting help too. It makes me so happy to know I was projecting, that you won't be in trouble or suffer like I did. Good for you, I mean that."

Barb reached for Fred's hand and squeezed it. He leaned over and kissed the top of her head. Dawn stared for a second at this unexpected display of affection. She felt like a child, as small as the little girl, so she pushed past the coffee table and out the door.

Dawn pulled into the McIntyres' driveway, paying attention to the evergreen trees that lined the curved stretch and the bed of rocks circling each tree. She'd never encountered other domestic workers, though surely they had gardeners, pool people, personal assistants. Hilary probably tried to schedule everyone on different days of the week to prevent fraternizing. The last thing she needed was the help conspiring to trick her into higher wages or bigger Christmas bonuses. Dawn parked in her usual spot and noticed two bouquets of pink and white balloons tied to the base of each mini-evergreen on the front porch.

Crap, a party.

She began to back out. The key could just as easily be mailed.

A line of cars filed into the driveway: Robert's Mercedes, followed by four or five others. She intended to sit as still as possible and drive out once everyone had gone inside. Robert noticed her when he and another man got out of the car. He waved her over so she quickly unwound the McIntyres' key from her keychain. She tossed her keys in the center console and stuffed the house key into her pocket.

"Come in, come in," Robert said, opening the garage and walking in so Dawn had no choice but to follow him into the house. Behind her, she heard car doors slamming, kids and people unloading and talking.

Robert wore a black wool suit. His white shirt practically crackled from the starch. Sometimes Dawn sprayed them a little stiff on purpose. The rows of tiny blue octopuses on his silk tie leapt off its yellow backdrop.

"Hilary will be in shortly. She rode with Wendy to help with the baby. You know how they love to help with the babies."

Dawn nodded. Robert tossed his wallet and car keys into the drawer.

"No caterers yet?"

"No," Dawn said. "I guess not."

"All right, well. Excuse me for a moment. They'll be in."

He disappeared down the hallway, past the library so she could only assume he was heading upstairs.

More people came in through the garage door, women wearing bright coats and colorful silk scarves. Men in long wool coats, scarves untied.

Finally, Hilary walked into the house carrying a baby in a flowing white gown. Her squat customer was practically lost in the mass of ruffles and tulle. The baby had a fist in its mouth and slobbered down the front of its dress. The dress seemed better suited for a wedding than an infant and probably cost more than her car.

To Dawn's surprise, Hilary walked to her and handed her the baby. Dawn took it—her—and the baby mouthed her shoulder. The baby kicked and wobbled so Dawn adjusted her arm to get a better grip. She smelled like sweet, powdery drool. The baby crushed her face into Dawn's sweatshirt and rolled her head back and forth as though using it as a Kleenex.

Hilary removed her coat and hung it in the closet. She took coats off the arms of the other women, then the men. Dawn stood there with the baby.

A photographer dressed in a white blouse and black skirt

appeared from the hallway. She spotted the baby and headed over. "Smile," she told Dawn. Dawn did. The photographer took about ten pictures in a row, stalking Dawn in a semi-circle like an animal. On the heavy side, she smelled fresh and clean, like lemongrass and a drawer full of makeup. "Finally cried herself out, I see," the photographer said.

"I don't know. I just got here."

"She's cuter when she's not screaming," the photographer said close to Dawn's ear and gave her a knowing, servant-to-servant gape. "The homeowner's kind of handsome. I'm a sucker for a crisp white shirt. Do you know him? He should be in a magazine."

Dawn considered Robert's features, his beady eyes, trim stomach and Euro fingernails. Without the expensive clothes, he'd be average at best, but knowing him led to the impossibility of forgetting the condescension and superiority complex.

"He has a twisted porn habit. Can't get enough of it. I clean here. I know."

"Oh my gosh," the photographer said. The woman's face went purple and just as quickly lost its color. She walked out of the kitchen. Someone else might have laughed, demanded to know more or taken offense by the language. A photographer like Matthew would have lowered the camera and asked how she knew. Dawn would have told her about the photograph she found had the woman asked. She wanted to tell the photographer that Robert McIntyre liked to belittle her. The conversations he started with the guise of being friendly were intended to put her down and make her feel low-class. Were she not holding the baby, Dawn may have followed the photographer to tell her everything.

Once Hilary finished hanging coats and closed the closet door, she came to Dawn and took the baby away. "This is embarrassing, but I can't remember hiring you for today. I'm sure I told you what your job would be? Did I not tell you the uniform?"

Dawn started to explain that she hadn't been hired, but the

garage door opened again and a line of people in white chef
coats came in carrying covered silver trays.

"Oh dear," Hilary said. "Here."

She gave the baby back to Dawn and got busy telling people where to go. Dawn stepped to the windows to get a better
view of the child's face. She slid her into the crook of her arm,
not unlike the China doll at the Rileys', and bounced her a few
times. The infant had milky blue eyes and tiny pink lips. Despite not having much hair, she had a cowlick front and center
that resembled a backward L and made her prettier and smart.
Not the cutest baby in the world, but not horrid except for
the drool. Heavier than the China doll and so warm that heat
wafted from Dawn's sweatshirt when she shifted and bounced.
Bouncing a baby seemed instinctive.

No one noticed her standing there. She had no idea which
was the mother. Robert walked into the kitchen with a drink
in hand. To her surprise, he approached. "I hate these gather-
ings. Church. Food. Conversation. They'll be here for hours."
He sipped his drink, which smelled strong and good. Bourbon.
"You the nanny for the day? Guess you're the right age for that."

"No. I'm not. I'm not working today at all."

"Oh," Robert said, swirling the drink around the glass.

Her words must not have registered or perhaps he thought
she meant taking care of someone else's rich baby was too en-
joyable to be classified as work. Robert smiled, amicably almost,
and Dawn got the sense the tables had turned on him. When it
came to a baby's Christening, Dawn somehow became an ally.

"Set your drink on the table," Dawn said.

Robert did. Dawn handed him the baby. He hugged her to
his chest like a sack of sugar. The baby swung her head side to
side like the blind singer Stevie Wonder. Dawn reveled in the
baby's gesture with a laugh.

"She drooled all over your nice tie."

Dawn lifted Robert's drink and sniffed it while he gaped at
her. "Dammit. Take her."

"No. I stopped by to tell you and Hilary I'm moving. I'm

here to give back your house key." She pulled it from her pocket and extended it to him. He stared at her palm and didn't let go of the baby, who began fussing and thrashing.

"Dammit!" Robert said.

"Not around the child!" said Hilary, swooping in and pulling the baby from Robert. "What in heaven's name is going on?"

"Our maid is here to quit." He noticed the front of his shirt and groaned. "Christ," he said. "Look at me!"

Hilary ignored him. She wore one of her tweed suit jackets with a matching skirt. The shoes may have been the ones Matthew picked for Dawn. She clucked at the baby and swayed from side to side. "Why are you quitting?" she said. To Robert, "What did you do to upset Dawn? You're incapable of feeling empathy for another human being."

"I did nothing!" Robert said. "I figured she was the nanny, but apparently not." Robert's face reddened before he stormed off.

Hilary continued swaying and cooing at the baby. "Are you really leaving us?" she asked Dawn.

"I'm moving. Your house key. I didn't realize you were having a party."

"That is disappointing," Hilary said. She pulled open the drawer and motioned for Dawn to drop the key in there.

"Thank you," Hilary said. "You will be hard to replace."

"Uh, sure. And thank you."

But Hilary had focused her attention back on the baby. Dawn only got a few words out before Hilary slowly stepped away and bounced toward the living room and the other guests. Dawn stood alone in the kitchen, save for half a dozen catering staff. She watched a woman plug in an espresso machine and unload a box of tiny cups. Another poured champagne and orange juice into crystal flutes.

Dawn took a breath and walked out through the garage and to her car. Before she got in, she took a moment to admire Bird Lake. It hadn't frozen yet and small waves lapped at the breaker wall near the McIntyres' dock.

❧

Any doubts about whether she and Bridget Riley might be friends in another life dissolved as Dawn watched her bounce around her kitchen making tea that no one wanted.

"It's so much fun to be in the Christmas spirit," Bridget said, opening a tin of peppermint tea with candy cane stripes. She frowned as she stared into it, then shrugged. She tossed a handful of teabags into the kettle on the stove.

"We finally agreed on a Christmas tree," Bridget said, sliding in socked feet across the oak floor and gesturing toward the white artificial tree. The thing was only about five feet tall, narrow and covered with white lights. Bridget plucked another gold bulb from the box on the table and plunged her arm so deep into the branches she almost fell over on top of it. "The trick is to use the whole branch to give the appearance of depth. You know what I mean? So the bulbs are three-dimensional and not just hanging off the tips of the boughs."

Dawn nodded from where she perched on a stool at the breakfast bar, wondering what the hell a bough was. She cast a sideways glance toward Mitch, who sat somewhat miserably at the dining room table. He wore black track pants and a Syracuse University T-shirt. Maybe he'd been at the gym.

Bridget wore gray lounge pants and a white long-sleeved shirt. Her hair, long and silky, was down today. Perhaps it only seemed shiny because of the tree lights. Her mood definitely outshone that of her husband, who kept eyeing the third-floor staircase as though he wanted to bolt.

"We can never agree on decor," Bridget said. "What I like, Mitch says it's too busy. Too frilly. Too whatever. But I love this tree. Don't you, honey?"

"It suits both of us," Mitch said.

"Compromise is about bending as far as you can for another person without breaking. That's the trick."

"I'm sure Dawn is far too young to be interested in marital advice," Mitch said.

Dawn laughed because she thought he was making a joke,

but Bridget's smile fell away so Dawn tried to cover it with a cough.

"I wasn't giving marital advice. I was talking about relationships in general. Compromise happens everywhere, you know, not only within your personal connections."

"Yeah, silly," Dawn said.

Bridget faced Dawn, who gave her a wide, genuine smile with teeth.

"Compromise is, like, the key to success," Dawn said. "You have to be willing to see from the other person's point of view. A lot of times, the answers are right there under your nose."

Bridget nodded, beamed, and ran on tiptoe to slide the kettle, which had started to whistle, from the burner. "See?" she said to Mitch. "Dawn gets it. It's a female intuition."

"Probably." He rolled his eyes, though it didn't seem like he meant to, kind of a natural douchebag move.

She poured tea into an enormous white mug and handed it to Dawn. Dawn hated tea so she set it down and blew into it. She breathed through her mouth so she wouldn't have to smell it.

"So," Bridget said, coming around the breakfast bar to sit on the stool next to her. She patted Dawn's arm. "Tell us about this move. How exciting! To be able to go anywhere in the world you want."

"Not anywhere," Dawn said. "I only have five hundred dollars saved."

"That's great!" Bridget said. "Isn't that great, Mitch?"

"Fabulous."

"I worked hard for it. Although I'll admit I had the good fortune to get a little bonus recently."

The color in Mitch's face drained.

"Really?" Bridget said.

"One of my customers. Very generous. Too generous, really."

"Tell me, tell me!" Bridget said, bouncing up and down in her seat.

"I guess they wanted someone to be discreet, you know, because that is important to them."

"I'm, uh, not feeling too good," Mitch said. Perspiration gleamed on his face. Dark half moons hung underneath both eyes. He swooned in his chair.

"Oh, honey! Are you all right?" Bridget ran over and clasped her husband's arms. He shook her off. "I'm trying to help."

"I might puke."

He stood and shuffled toward the stairway with his head down. The way he clasped the handrail and coughed, the distance from the bottom to the top seemed insurmountable. Dawn watched his chest rise and fall as he took a breath. He walked slowly up the stairs.

"I better make sure he's okay," Bridget said.

"I should get going. Key West, by the way. That's where I'm heading."

Dawn took the Rileys' key from her pocket and snapped it down on the counter.

Bridget walked her to the stairs. When Dawn paused to say goodbye, her customer grabbed her and hugged her so tight Dawn squeaked.

When Bridget held the embrace for a couple seconds, Dawn reached around and patted her back with one hand. The other arm was wedged against her side. Bridget's hair smelled like flowers. She wondered what it would be like to be hugged by Barb Turner or Hilary McIntyre. Barb would smell like day-old perspiration masked with deodorant. Hilary would have that old-lady smell, a mix of stale breath and hairspray. Dawn stood there patting until Bridget let go.

"Good *luck*. I'm so *excited* for you. You have the world at your feet. Make the *most* of it."

"I will. You have a really nice place. Thanks for hiring me to clean it."

"I know it's a little bare," Bridget said. Tears suddenly appeared in her eyes. "I'm sorry," she said, blinking the tears over the tops of her fingers. "I guess the idea of moving away, starting fresh, got to me. It's amazing to have a new chance ahead of you."

"Believe me, there's a lot behind me too."

"Oh, right. I'm sure. That's true for all of us."

She pushed her hands into the pockets of her pants. Searching with hopeful eyes, she stopped at the Christmas tree. Dawn heard her draw a breath through her nose.

"By the way," Dawn said. "Can you tell me about your doll? That one on the hutch?"

She pointed down the stairs.

"Clara Jean. She belonged to my grandmother. My mom and my grandma both died so she means a lot to me. She's a symbol of the women in my family. I see her every time I walk in and out of the house. She reminds me to stay true to myself."

"That's cool."

"I miss them."

"Well, bye. Thanks for the opportunity," Dawn said.

She headed down the stairs, keenly aware that Bridget didn't go up. Dawn went out the door and onto the porch. She stopped to take in the tree-lined street. A noise perhaps, like a creak on the stairs, caused her to look back.

Bridget Riley's silhouette disappeared into the French doors of the hoarding room. She'd come down instead of going up.

Mike Letwinski opened the door wearing jeans and one of those waffle-knit shirts you see in the men's department. In his hand was a half-eaten apple. He smelled of soap and cologne, organized. It seemed he had the whole day before him. A good husband, Dawn noted, should probably have this quality.

"We're not changing religions," he said.

"What?" Dawn said.

Despite being in his forties, Mike had a youthful vibe. His jeans were slim with an indigo wash. Not like the dorky dad jeans Fred Turner wore. Mike lacked any sign of the spare tire that so many older men seemed to develop.

"I never understand why you bother to come up the driveway. Did you walk? No," he said, leaning out the door and spot-
ting her car. "At least you had the sense to drive. You realize
you're never going to convince a person to convert to your
beliefs. Religion and politics."

He tapped a socked foot and crunched into the apple. Dawn
half-expected him to shut the door in her face, but he didn't. He
stood there chewing.

"I'm Dawn. I clean your house every Friday. Is Karen
home?"

"Oh my gosh."

He brought his hands to his face, including the one holding
the apple. He had nice hands with tidy fingernails. The guy appeared mortified.

"I am so sorry. I assumed you were one of those religious
zealots. She's not here. She's at the grocery store."

His hair was slick with a little gel, but it worked. Like his
jeans and his shirt, it gave him a subtle sense of style without
trying.

"I didn't have time to call ahead. I'm moving to Florida and
thought it might be rude to take your house key. So here I am.
Here it is."

She took it out of her pocket.

"Of course you're not one of the religious people," Mike
said. He reached out and took the key. "No. Definitely not a
bible beater. I'm so embarrassed."

He relaxed enough to continue eating. It figured the Twins
ate the bright red apples, Dawn's favorite.

"Can you tell Karen I stopped by? I was hoping to say goodbye to her."

"Oh gosh. She's going to want to see you. She loves you,
you know."

"She's not home when I'm here," Dawn said. "We've only
met a few times."

"She talks about you. How well you clean and how it helps
her stay sane."

"Thanks. I try."

Mike pressed his foot on the doorplate so that it rattled a little.

"Can you come in for a few? She'll probably be back in fifteen or twenty minutes. I know she'd really like to say goodbye."

"I'm sorry, I really can't. Someone is expecting me."

"I understand." He lowered his voice, as though someone might overhear. "She's pregnant, that's all. I thought she might want to tell you. And I don't want her to be upset about missing you. You know how those hormones bring on the mood swings."

Dawn laughed.

"Not really," she said.

Mike laughed too.

"Yeah, I guess not. You're a little young for that."

"Congrats, though."

People like the Twins should have babies. They had a nice house, good jobs, and liked each other. Katelyn and Nick didn't take time to prepare. They'd never have a wall full of photographs documenting vacations and good times. Their pictures would be kids' birthday parties in cramped apartments. Their jobs would only be the kind you can get without an education, with set hours and shifts. Dawn wished more for her friend. She wished more for herself.

"I am elated," Mike said. "Over the moon. We've been trying for a long time. We'll find out the sex of the baby next week. I'm almost hoping there are two of them in there. Don't tell Karen I said that. I've wanted to be a father forever."

He took a few more quick bites and threw the apple core far across the yard between a couple pine trees. He pointed.

"Swing set, right there. There, a trampoline. Over by those trees, a swimming pool. We're going to have everything we ever wanted."

"Great," Dawn said.

"Does Karen have your number? In case she wants to call you and say goodbye?"

Dawn nodded. He reached out and rested a hand on her shoulder for the briefest second.

"Thank you for all you've done for us."

"You're welcome. You're very welcome."

"Don't tell Karen I mistook you for a religious freak. She'd kill me. Being rude to solicitors is one of her pet peeves."

"I won't," Dawn said.

She heard the door close as Mike went back inside. She sat in the car, enjoying the sunshine on her face through the window. Driving away seemed sad, like leaving new friends from camp.

She pulled a cigarette from her purse and lit it. She'd never heard a man talk about being a father before. It figured Mike would be that excited. He'd be the dad who jumped into the swimming pool in the shape of a cannonball, wearing that bathing suit from the picture on their wall. His weird bellybutton. Pretty soon, they'd have a new wall of photographs of kids, family pictures, and trips to Disney. She imagined Mike standing in front of the Christmas tree with a screwdriver, trying to put together a toy from Santa. That kid would be lucky.

Dawn drove to her mother's house, keeping an eye on the inconspicuous bungalows leading up to theirs on the corner. Only one had left on the Christmas lights the night before, leaving an unimpressive swirl of colors around the pine bushes and the trunk of a small tree. Each house was different, some boasting all-brick and awnings hanging over the front porches. Others were built from aluminum siding with brick faces. No one on the street had much time for gardening or yard work. Lines of moss snaked through the cracks in sidewalks and driveways. Someone hadn't bothered to bring their flowerpots inside so they stood like frozen weights on the front corners of a concrete porch. They'd crack come spring. Large trees hung overhead, but not enough for the road to be described as tree-lined and, without leaves, the wiry branches offered no illusion of protection.

Dawn pulled into her mother's rocky driveway, two long

strips of cement sandwiching frosty grass. Old snow, now dirty and closer to ice, served as proof that neither her mother nor Davis had bothered to properly shovel after the last snowfall. They weren't unusual in the neighborhood. Certain chores— pulling weeds, shoveling more than a walkway to the front porch, bringing the trash barrels back from the curb—seemed unimportant here.

Her key slid into the lock like second nature. Her hook on the wall now caught the hood of Davis' winter coat so she tossed her jacket on the floor and went to find them.

"Hello?" her mother called.

"It's me," Dawn said.

"You're early. I thought you said noon."

"*Before* noon."

Dawn went into the kitchen, where her mother and Davis sat with their beer, a pack of Camels, lighter, ashtray, newspaper, and a deck of playing cards. The only space was the narrow path where they slid the cards back and forth. Her mother leaned back in her chair and extended her arms. Dawn walked between them for an awkward reverse hug.

"My daughter is moving to Florida. This is hard to believe," her mother said to Davis.

"Yes, it appears she is. Good news. Great news."

"How are your grafts?" her mother said, grasping Dawn's arm. She pushed up the sleeve of Dawn's sweatshirt so Dawn bent an elbow in her mother's direction.

"Tight. But not terrible. You know."

"Great. They're great. Aren't they great?"

Her mother twisted her wrist to redirect her elbow toward Davis and nodded as though Dawn were modeling a new outfit or pair of shoes. Dawn tolerated it because it seemed that Davis had convinced her mother the move was a positive, not a negative. She almost expected him to wink at her, but he maintained his neutral expression.

"Oh," he said, squinting in the dim light. "Yes. They're elbows."

"Is your father expecting you?" her mother said.

"Well, yeah. Duh."

"Be nice to Susan," Davis said. "She cares."

"She asked a stupid question. Yes, he knows I'm coming. If you're going to work for someone, you have to let them know you're taking the job."

"I hope you've thought this through," her mother said, pulling a cigarette from her pack and lighting it. "It seems so, I don't know, rash."

Dawn helped herself to a soda from the refrigerator. She cracked it open. A beverage gave the visit more of a celebratory feel. A fresh start should be celebrated, she thought. Besides, her mother and Davis were drinking before noon. She nodded at the cigarettes and her mother handed her one. "What are you playing?" Dawn said.

"Gin," said Davis.

"Always gin," said her mother.

"What reason is there for me to stay here?"

"Oh, thanks a lot," said her mother. She took a drag of her cigarette and tapped it over the ashtray long after the ash had fallen.

"That could hurt Susan's feelings," Davis said.

"How many weeks until Ft. Meyers? We'll visit," said her mother to Davis.

He thought for a moment with his lower lip curled and his eyes fixed somewhere on the ceiling. "Five, I think," said Davis. "Wait, no. Four and a half."

"I want to talk to you guys before I leave."

She hadn't expected to say it and her heartbeat quickened. The announcement, she knew, was intended to draw their attention out and away from themselves. Though she'd come over to say goodbye to her family, it never seemed to be about her. Not really. Not this time or any other time in the past. This redirecting of focus was selfish and reminiscent of her mother. Her mother sat back in her chair and regarded her as though settling in for a long and boring presentation.

"About what?" her mother said.

Dawn's throat tightened. It hadn't been on purpose, but she'd caused the accident. Not because she'd wanted to hurt Terry, but because she wanted to please him. Not that she ever would have made him happy. She wanted to say she'd been trying too hard to make the relationship work and that, she knew now, Terry criticized much of what she did and her appearance.

It seemed like she could have this conversation with her mother and Davis—adult to adult—and they'd all feel a sense of unity or at least understand each other. At the very least, she might stun them into empathy. This was her family, after all, and Davis was her mother's husband now so he counted. Her mother would be pleased at the inclusion.

But her mother shook her head. She discarded a queen of spades. Strangely, her hand included a pair of jokers. She and Davis had their own rules for everything. "No," her mother said. "We're not going to do that. There is absolutely no point. Not now."

Davis nodded. "I agree. We don't need to dredge up old pain. You make your way. You're going to start a new life with your father."

Dawn opened her throat and let as much soda down as she could before the carbonation affected her eyes. She heard Barb Turner's words from the picnic bench outside the pharmacy: *People don't like it when you suddenly have wounds you never had before. In fact, they hate it. They hate you for it.* She set the mostly empty can on the table with the others. "I don't see why you two couldn't smile and nod for five minutes. Just bullshit your way through it. Give me some closure or peace of mind."

She put a hand on her mother's shoulder and gripped it until her mother met her gaze. Davis stood, but her mother held up a hand. The crease was there, between her mother's eyebrows, that suggested anger despite her lackadaisical manner. Dawn had always wondered whether the crease proved her mother's meanness. She liked that she could squeeze harder if she chose. She could bring tears to her mother's eyes or make her flinch.

"Terry died, Mom."

"You say that as though I had a hand in it. I didn't tinker with his brakes if that's what you're implying. I liked Terry."

Dawn released her mother's shoulder.

Her mother leaned forward in her chair and reached across the table. Davis cupped her hand. Dawn headed for the door. She thought about telling them Mrs. Folly had called. She wanted them to feel guilty for not listening. It had always bothered her mother when Dawn called Mrs. Folly *Mom*.

She decided to tell the truth. "It will be nice to put some effort into my relationship with Dad. It feels like a void in my life. I think my dad is a nice person, a caring guy whose focus is happiness. I love that. The people who work at the bar, they all love him."

"Dawn?" her mother said. She stopped and waited. "You could have died. I can't think about that anymore. I know Terry died, but I'm just glad you didn't. Davis understands. He knows that after your father left, you and I only had each other. Didn't we spend all our time together?"

Dawn heard herself exhale and stopped before it became a sigh. "I know, Mom. I'll call you when I get there. Let you know my address. All that."

"Drive safe, Dawn," her mother said.

"Goodbye, Sunny D," Davis said.

Dawn headed toward the door and heard her mother murmur words she couldn't decipher.

"It's okay, Susan," Davis said. "Everything is fine."

The car was still warm from the drive over and the heat blew warmth when she turned the key in the ignition. She sat watching water droplets fall from the dirty black-and-white-striped awning over the side door. The awning had been there ever since Dawn could remember. It seemed like Davis should take it down and scrub it; the slick mark on the pavement below was streaked with dirt.

People let things go for far too long, the sure way to ruin anything of value.

৵

Dawn sat in the parking lot of the McDonald's and drank from an enormous cup of Coke. She sucked it down in long, freezing gulps. The ice had melted to dilute the syrup enough to take the edge off the sweetness. She unwrapped the breakfast sandwich in her lap and took an enormous bite. The egg was fresh, still hot. So were the hash browns. Whoever happened to be working the fryer today understood the importance of salt.

She watched people walk in and out of the Superstore in the adjacent plaza, people of all colors and sizes. Big people, small people, people wearing sweatpants, and people wearing dress clothes, as if for a wedding or baby shower. Moms pushed babies in strollers and held the hands of toddlers. Some didn't hold their hands and you could see them yelling and waving their arms when the kid took off in the wrong direction. Idiots. The moms, not the kids. They'd grab the kid by the bicep and drag said kid into the store on tiptoe. Katelyn probably did stuff like that. People were crippled by their own stupidity in moments of frustration, by mistakes they couldn't see.

She finished the sandwich and wiped her hands on her jeans.

A trim woman in expensive yoga clothes exited the store pushing a shopping cart with three children attached to it, one on the front and one on each side. They were bundled in jackets and the smallest had a green balloon in his mittened hand. The kids were smiling and so was the mom. She stopped behind a minivan and the kids stepped off. They got into the van while the mom unloaded the groceries in the back. The mom didn't notice an action figure sail out the van door and roll under the tire of the neighboring car. She closed the kids' door on her way to the driver's seat.

Dawn pondered the relevance of an action figure. Did it matter? One mother might punish the kids later for the waste of a toy. Another wouldn't notice. One might notice, but not really care. There were enough toys and way more important worries, such as whether the kids would get into college, get married, and have families.

Dawn sat up in her seat and watched the van back out of its parking space. She wanted it to rock to a sudden stop and for one of the kids to get out to retrieve the toy. Someone would surely miss it later. Dawn hoped none of those kids got sick or hurt or, worse, died too young. The mother might think back to this day at the Superstore and how all three kids wanted a ride on the cart, and they were all having such a good day until later, when the green-balloon boy cried for his action figure and admitted he'd launched it right out the van door. She'd wish she hadn't yelled.

Being someone's mother, you'd never be able to get through it without mistakes. Without guilt. Whether you meant to be a good and caring mother or not.

Dawn remembered a time in the hospital when she woke to her mother sitting beside her. She took up so little space on the edge of the bed. Sometimes Dawn felt giant in comparison, like their roles had been reversed. Dawn had watched her mother whisper to herself, thinking how strange it was to see her with her hair down. They looked more alike this way. She couldn't make out what her mother was saying. Maybe she'd been pray-ing. Pain took away Dawn's ability to speak, but the suffering in her mother's eyes affirmed she should keep quiet. Her mother patted the bed covers, repeating the word: "Okay, okay, okay, okay."

Mrs. Folly hadn't visited, not once. It never occurred to Dawn to feel angry, at least not until right now. She'd believed that Mrs. Folly, as Terry's mother, held the right to feel the most loss, the most hurt, to search wildly for anyone to blame for any reason.

Dawn noted the mileage on her car and reset the trip odom-eter to zero. The static strip from the auto place confirmed she wasn't yet due for an oil change. Her tank was full of gas. She'd topped off the wiper fluid. She lowered the volume on the radio to think. How wholly unsatisfying, to simply pull onto the road and start driving toward Florida. She'd handled her business with her customers and at least tried to leave her mother and Davis having shared her pain. It couldn't be helped that they were unwilling to take some of her burden. People always expected such climactic endings, like Dawn thinking her farewell visit would be different than any other time. Yet she couldn't pull away. Unfinished business remained with those who mattered the most.

&

She'd only planned to drive past Terry's house. If she meant to stop, she had no idea what she'd say. *Say goodbye*, she told herself. *Isn't that why you're here? This is what you need to say goodbye to.*

She couldn't remember if the Folly's house had always been so rundown. It probably had. Mrs. Folly was the kind of woman who grew tomato plants in old buckets on the front porch. They used to sit in mismatched plastic chairs on the front lawn on the weekends and play badminton with bent racquets. Dawn always won. Instead of getting mad about being beaten, Terry bragged that his girlfriend could beat his father. Not that Mr. Folly seemed to care much, but Terry loved teasing his dad about it.

Dawn sat in her car, parked neatly in the space across the street from the house. Her spot—the neighbors had probably thought hers was one of the Folly's cars. She'd spent far more time at Terry's house than her own. Terry's bedroom with its Buffalo Bills blanket across his bed. He collected pennies in a giant souvenir mug from Niagara Falls. She'd liked to compare the brand names in the family's refrigerator, like Hunt's instead of Heinz. Mrs. Folly bought generic cans of green beans and sliced peaches. They always had a bag of oyster crackers, which Terry had liked to pour into a small glass dish and top with a spoonful of peanut butter.

Dawn could hardly believe it when her feet touched the street and she found herself crossing the brown lawn and using the wobbly handrail to step onto the porch. The Folly's doorbell always seemed to be broken so she knocked on the storm door.

The front door opened with its familiar squeak and swoosh.

Craft supplies, Dawn thought, as the smell of the house flooded her memory. It reminded her of a basket full of yarn and knitting needles. Gypsy, the old lab-mix, was nowhere to be found. Mrs. Folly wore her old black jeans with the tiny bleached mark above the knee and the pale blue sweatshirt from a trip to the Finger Lakes. For as much as life had changed, Dawn realized it was very much the same. Her slide-on granny slippers were the same rusty red.

"Well, well, well. Len said you'd be by once I called." Mrs. Folly's voice carried a nasally tone she'd almost forgotten that blended into a low-pitched song. It was still the most adult-sounding voice Dawn could remember.

"Hi."

"You've grown. You look like your mother with your hair like that. Did she tell you I saw her at the garden supply?"

"I wanted to thank you for inviting me to the prayer vigil for Terry," Dawn said.

Mrs. Folly seemed to flinch at the mention of his name, as though Dawn were a stranger who wasn't supposed to know she'd lost a son. She still wore the ruby ring, her birthstone, small on her long fingers as she stroked the thin skin on her neck. Mrs. Folly never painted her fingernails.

"Len says it's bad when we don't include you. As if it matters. I can see you're a woman now. You're grown."

"My father gave me a job down in Florida so I'm moving there. Today is my moving day."

"Of course you get to have a life."

"Mrs. Folly."

"Oh, honey, for God's sake. My name is Sandy."

She reached for the doorframe and clasped it.

"I wanted a life with Terry. I got one without him. We both did. Thank you for inviting me, but I can't come."

"That's fine. You're not the one I want anyway."

"I know. Trust me."

"I used to trust so much, Dawn. Now I don't know who or what to believe."

"I wish you didn't feel that way, but you do."

"Good luck with your new life in Florida."

"Goodbye."

Dawn expected to hear the door close.

"Did you cry about it?" Mrs. Folly called. "Did you ever cry?"

"My God. Yes."

"I'm sure you think I raised a terrible son. He was only twenty, you know. He deserved the chance to test the waters. He had every right."

"That doesn't mean I liked it."

"No. You didn't like it."

"I planned to fight for him. You know I would have. I wanted to be your family."

Mrs. Folly, still clutching the frame of the door, seemed to swoon as if on the verge of fainting. Her temples pulsed. They stood there—two women—and Dawn understood. Enough time had passed that they'd both changed. It was impossible to anticipate how a person might age or grow. Now that they'd seen each other, all that remained certain was they'd never know how Terry would have ended up. His memory, frozen like the cold earth, would always be a twenty-year-old man.

Neither of them had known him fully. Maybe he'd disappointed both of them. The certainty of death meant never getting to ask for answers or clarification, to know what he really wanted or whether he wanted Dawn or the woman from the Superstore. Probably, he'd have ended up with neither. Mrs. Folly might not care about her anymore, but not because he was dead. They'd be broken up. That's all.

"I pray to God every day for answers," she said.

"I don't think there are any," Dawn said. "But I still love you, Mom."

Mrs. Folly took a breath. When their eyes met, Dawn's chest hurt so much she dropped her gaze to her feet. Mrs. Folly shifted and a hand brushed Dawn's sleeve. "Goodbye, honey."

"Goodbye."

She crossed the street and got into her car. Numbness made it difficult to feel her fingers and toes. She managed to slide her key into the ignition and drive away. The further she got from Terry's house, the lighter she became. She hoped some of the weight was lifting from Terry's mother too.

Dawn knocked on Matthew's door. It only took a few seconds before she heard movement and the lock sliding. The smell of him—smoky, warm, sleepy—drifted to her as he leaned into the doorway. His hair was tousled, his face patchy from not shaving. He wore faded jeans and a T-shirt with an old Pepsi logo. He hadn't been working, at least not for a while. The faraway glaze in his eyes was gone, the disorientation so clear on his face when pulled out of his imagination or whatever dreamlike place he escaped to while creating art.

"Everyone knows what time it is except me," he said. "I'm glad I didn't miss you."

She nodded, though it didn't give her any information of value except that perhaps he'd lost track of time like she'd suspected. Whatever he'd been doing, she knew to give up the fantastical notion he'd pull her inside and take her clothes off. A different scenario, collapsing into his arms in tears and admitting she'd gone to Terry's house, also faded as a possibility. Reality presented itself, as solid as her feet on the landing outside his apartment door.

"Barb Turner accused me of stealing. They said I had to return the key today. Then they found what I stole."

Matthew's expression was impossible to read, but when he stepped aside, Jen sat on the couch with her elbows against her knees. Happy, no, but not upset. Her coat and bag were on the floor beside her boots, which she hadn't removed, as though she hadn't been there for long, or wasn't planning to stay. Dawn came inside.

She wanted to believe Jen hadn't spent the night and was now heading out. This was a quick visit.

Or maybe her visit would be quick and Jen would be the one staying. She should have kept driving.

"I thought you were moving," Jen said.

"I am," Dawn said. "I got delayed. I just said to Matthew."

"Well. I'm sure it won't do any good to tell you I'm sorry about getting you in trouble."

"Probably not. But hey, I'm moving so who cares, right?"

"What can I say? I freaked. Well," she said to Matthew. "Are we done?"

"Yeah. Think so," he said.

She stood and pulled her purse over her shoulder, the big burgundy tote Dawn had seen and coveted at Kohl's. Definitely better suited for Jen and her office work environment.

"Do you want to tell her or should I?" Jen said.

She didn't wait for an answer.

"Matthew and I are taking a break," she said to Dawn. "At least for now."

Dawn's face warmed.

"You don't seem surprised," Jen said. To Matthew, "What, you told her ahead of time? That's great."

"I'm not surprised," Dawn said. "But he didn't tell me ahead of time. I'm never surprised."

"You're never surprised?" Jen said.

"When Matthew ends a relationship, I'm not. Friends can tell when it isn't a perfect fit. No offense," Dawn said.

Jen began pulling at the strap on her purse as though it were slipping.

"It amazes me Matthew would be friends with you in the first place. All he talks about is how you need to get your head on straight. How you create your own problems and screw everything up. Almost like you do it on purpose."

Hearing the truth—because, of course, it was true—about herself from Jen didn't sting as much as she expected. She lingered on the idea of self-sabotage. Having someone point out the obvious cause of the obvious misbehavior lifted all of it up so it seemed to hover like a cloud, but instead of raining havoc,

240 Beth Uznis Johnson

the cloud dissipated. Maybe she did act that way on purpose, but not for attention or out of desperation like Jen probably assumed. She did it to punish herself. Recognizing it, or rather having Jen enlighten her by stating the facts, eliminated its effectiveness. Punishing yourself on purpose when you knew that's what you were doing did not work. The human mind was happy to trick itself but could only do it to a point. Jen had outed her. It stung a little, yes, but cleared up so much confusion in her own mind that her next inhalation seemed to fill her body completely with fresh air.

"What's really crazy is that either one of you would be seen with me. Let alone spend time talking about me when I'm not there," Dawn said.

"My head is fine. I'm not the one who's a mess," Jen said.

"You're the one who created the problem and screwed up at the Chens'," Dawn said. "Maybe you did it on purpose because you don't like me."

"Dawn, she's pissed off," Matthew said. "You know I don't think that about you."

"You both convinced me that breaking and entering was okay," Jen said. "That's how messed up you are. Who breaks into people's houses for the sake of art? That's not art. It's stupid. And, Jesus, Matthew, I didn't really say it, but those photos are far from artistic."

"You showed her the photos?" Dawn said. "How could you do that?"

"Why wouldn't he?" Jen said.

"How could you show her?" Dawn said.

Heat flooded her face with the kind of anger there was no controlling. Like everything Matthew had said was a lie to shut her up so she'd be a good little model and do what he wanted. She pictured him with Jen over his shoulder at the computer, laughing at her inexperience. Pointing out her scars and discussing their ugliness. Matthew telling Jen exactly why Dawn's thigh had a Frankenstein-like scar and how the skin was used to patch what the asphalt burned off. And if Jen thought that was bad, she should see Dawn from the back. The project was supposed to be theirs. Just theirs. No matter what she tried to have and keep, it always got taken away.

So Jen simply had to ask to see them and Matthew relented, or he didn't think twice and simply agreed. Sure. Why not? They were just another batch of photos from another project.

"Why *wouldn't* he?" Jen repeated.

"You're an asshole," Dawn said.

"Dawn," Matthew said.

"No, not Dawn. I told you. Not Dawn."

Matthew said to Jen, "So you're that person who has to destroy my most important friendship."

"Your most important friendship? She's not even nice to you."

"That's bullshit. You know Dawn is one of my best friends, that we met under impossible circumstances and I'm lucky she understood Nico gave me a horrible assignment. You know what she's been through. You've said how hard it would be."

Jen studied Dawn's face for way longer than was comfortable. Dawn wanted her to think the tears were because she was angry. She inhaled deeply in an effort to suck all the emotion back inside. Jen's eyebrows raised. She tipped her head back and closed her eyes

"I'd actually convinced myself you didn't want him," she said, opening them.

"How do you know I do?" Dawn said.

She blinked away the tears that filled her eyes, hating herself for being weak in front of Jen and Matthew. She didn't want either one of them to know.

"Of course you do. I'm leaving," Jen said, and she did, taking big strides and clomping down the stairs two at a time. Dawn felt incredibly young and small in comparison.

Matthew stepped over to close the door.

Dawn tried to imagine Matthew wasn't there. This was her apartment in Key West. She closed her eyes for a picture. It took a moment for the idea of Matthew's strange kitchen setup to fade, the way it simply appeared on the far end of the room without a doorway or change in flooring. She'd never liked how you had to lean into the counter and peek beneath the cabinets to talk to someone in the living room. Her place would be open and airy. There might be painted tiles on the kitchen wall over the sink. They'd be white with blue, or yellow with bright flowers. Her floor would be tile, not carpet. No one in Florida cared about carpet.

The thump of the front door of Matthew's building tried to bring her back as Jen reached the bottom of the stairs and left. Her place wouldn't have a front door; it wouldn't be an apartment building at all. The beauty of Key West was how the neighborhoods spread out to tree-lined streets with individual houses. A house might have an apartment off to the side, or one up a flight of stairs with its own balcony. How lucky if she could get a luxury like that. Or, better, if the landlord owned a pool and didn't mind her using it.

She didn't need to be a head case anymore. Work at the bar was waiting. Her father was counting on her to help Ricki over the holidays. Maybe her father put up Christmas decorations, like wreathes or garland decorated with flip-flops instead of candy canes. Patrons would be happy to be in a tropical location. Who wouldn't be glad to be away during that time of year? Everyone would be in a good mood, eager to spend money on drinks. Think of how much money she'd make in tips. She'd open a savings account.

Jen's burgundy tote bag would be unnecessary and absolutely wrong there. Dawn would need a canvas tote. A knit backpack. Anything else besides a fancy leather monstrosity with silver zipper tabs and accents.

"Don't get stuck in your head," Matthew said. "We should talk about this."

"What do you know about my head?" Dawn said. "Apparently you think I'm insane."

"That's not the word I'd use," he said.

"You don't know me at all."

"You won't let me know you. I tried to know you fourteen months ago."

"You don't understand. I didn't know anything else besides Terry."

"Not to disrespect the dead, but that guy sounds like he was an asshole," Matthew said.

"We'll never really know now, will we?" Dawn said.

"It doesn't have to be bad to get over it," Matthew said. "The guy wouldn't have wanted you to mourn him forever."

She leaned forward to rest her cheek against the counter. Matthew stared straight ahead.

"I don't want you to think Jen and I sat around gossiping about you. It wasn't like that."

Weariness overcame any remaining anger, but there wasn't much anger anyway. Dawn sat on the couch. He sat next to her and sighed, pushing his hair off his forehead and letting his hand fall to his knee with a slap.

"I'm so tired," she said.

She covered her face with her hands.

"What are you doing?" he said.

"She wanted to help me," Dawn said through her fingers. "The lady from the first house, Barb Turner. She's way more fucked up than we thought, Matthew. I told her I was already getting help."

"And?"

"Well, I'm not. I've never gotten help and obviously I can't help myself. You and Jen are right about me. It's no big secret. I probably do it on purpose in a way, to punish myself. We both know I'm partially to blame for what happened. Accident or not."

She clasped her arms across her waist and didn't care. Tears rolled down her face, but inside she barely felt emotion, just tired.

"I need help," she said. "So I don't end up like that lady. I don't want to end up like that lady, Matthew. She's so bad. What if I get that bad?"

He extended an arm so she leaned into him and cried. She'd forgotten what her own crying sounded like. She listened to it and was grateful even if she didn't feel it. Matthew's hand wrapped around her bicep, his fingers gently squeezing every few seconds. He lowered his face into her hair. She sat up and watched his chest rise and fall against his T-shirt. The curve of his knees looked just right in his jeans.

He leaned forward, a little, and his hands slid up her thighs, which he squeezed, a little. He studied her face and drew her to him like a magnet, like her insides were sucked out and into him. They sat like this for a long moment until she noticed the little white scar on his bottom lip, a narrow line. Probably a split lip from childhood or a time he fell and cut it against his own teeth. She reached for his face and kissed his bottom lip. He closed his eyes, but didn't move. She left her mouth on his lip and found the scar with her tongue. Matthew inhaled, and held it. "Why not?" she said.

"I don't trust you. Why go down this path?"

"It's all I can think about. It's all I want right now."

"That's because you're leaving. It feels enticing. I'm not up for your games."

"I'm tired of my games," she said. "I'm tired of me."

"Now that doesn't sound like the D-voider I know."

"The idea of you being with Jen last night drove me insane. I got jealous."

"That really doesn't sound like you," Matthew said, with a laugh.

"Terry hit me once. He made me feel ugly. Self-conscious. He said mean stuff."

"Dawn," Matthew said.

"Really, it's okay. I might as well admit it. He used to twist my arm behind my back to overpower me. He probably would have broken it by now."

"That's not how a man is supposed to treat a woman."

"All the feelings, Matthew, they were sucked down the drain today. All that's left is me. Empty me."

"You're not empty, D-tail. That would be impossible."

"Empty except for you. All I can think about is you, Matt."

"Don't call me Matt," he said, but he reached around her and pulled her forward until she slid off the couch and stood in front of him. She slowly worked the buttons on his jeans and tugged to pull down his pants and boxers. He laid a hand on top of her head, so gently, when she knelt. After a few minutes, he slid his hands under her arms and stood, bringing her with him. He took off his T-shirt so she took off hers. He held her arms, somehow knowing that circling his thumbs around her elbows was the right thing to do. Tingles and zaps vibrated through her extremities. He watched her unzip her jeans and let go to allow her to take them off. He locked his arm behind her back and stepped around to lock his foot and leg around hers.

"We'll finish talking later, okay?"

"Whatever you say, D-flector," he said.

"Matthew. You're Matthew," she said, feeling his grip tighten.

She could tell she was about to get lost, gloriously lost, and was happy he was going to take her with him.

Matthew's bedroom was getting dark when she woke. His down comforter was heavy. She could tell from the draft on her back that Matthew had thrown his side off so she slid over and snuggled underneath it as the chills worked their way through. Her knees were warm against her stomach when she pulled them in. She couldn't remember ever having slept naked.

The shape of Matthew's body came into focus, his arm flung over the top of his pillow. She fought the urge to reach over and stroke his hair; it might be rude to wake him. He might have forgotten she was there and jump awake. But then, as though he knew she were watching, he reached around her waist and pulled her toward him until his chest met her back. She threw the comforter half over him and couldn't believe how much another person warmed you, and not just because he had decent heat and bedding.

Her move could always stop here. No one was forcing her to go. Her father wouldn't be surprised if she called to say she had reconsidered. Making contact with Mrs. Folly as a grown woman was enough. Nothing could be perfect between them, but they'd faced each other long enough to see their lives would go on, separately. Dumping the trailer would be easy. She didn't need it anymore.

She wouldn't be the first person to change her mind because of an important relationship. She knew Matthew as well as any woman knew Matthew, including Jen. She probably knew him better. Couldn't her toothbrush just as easily replace Jen's? If she and Matthew started dating, they'd already be years ahead of his relationship with Jen.

Her cleaning career was over, but that didn't mean she couldn't stay and find a different job. Bartending, for instance. Women like Dawn got great tips, especially when they wore tight yoga pants and white T-shirts to work. Or white button-down shirts with the front tied into a little knot above the navel.

She and Matthew could date. She and Katelyn could be friends again. Katelyn and Nick might want to go out with her and Matthew. Dawn could babysit Katelyn's kids to see if she liked kids after all. Who knew. That baby at the McIntyres' hadn't been so bad, save for the slobber. Mike Letwinski acted like having kids was the goal.

Matthew draped his arm over her hip with fingers barely brushing her skin.

Freeze time, she thought. When she was little, she used to tell herself this on special occasions or happy moments, like on her birthday when all her elementary school friends sang to her in silly voices or visiting Nick's cabin when she'd joked around the campfire and they'd died laughing for hours. And now, definitely the first time wanting to freeze time since Terry died, all because of lying in Matthew's bed with his warmth surrounding her.

It seemed incomprehensible that Barb Turner didn't like being held, touched, wanting someone to reach for you. No wonder she wore flannel. Thick enough to muffle a stray hand. Thick enough to be warm. Thick enough to be not the least bit sexy. The barriers people created to protect themselves. Dawn got that. She'd had plenty of days when taking a shower seemed like a marathon. No need to try.

That little girl's face had said so much. Maybe it was Sofia, who snuck the baby shoe necklace from her mother's room. Sofia knew she could be a better mother than her mother, one who didn't cry and wear pajamas and forget to do the laundry. If Sofia had five kids, she'd be sure to love them all and answer when they spoke to her. The girl was highly experienced in retreat, that was for sure. Like a miniature soldier, she understood she had entered dangerous territory. Her expression was not one of surprise, but of practiced response. Barb yelled at her when she came across the necklace in Sofia's bedroom and Sofia stood there, wondering how her mother got upset by such minor situations. When Sofia tried to hug her mother, her hands were slapped away because her mother never wanted hugs.

Yet Barb had reached for Fred's hand, a shock to Dawn. Fear must come in levels and values, in doses like medicine. In sizes like clothes. Or messes. So one day your house is clean and you're feeling pretty good about yourself, but the next day you attempt to bake muffins and don't bother to wash the pans or wipe the crumbs from the counter. For a while you don't worry about the mess. But then it starts to wear on you. The egg shells in the sink. The sticky batter that dripped onto the range. There is no choice but to go back to being a neat freak.

Barb took Fred's hand when she had no more to give, not even to the fear. The trick, it seemed, was to stay in the empty place in order to fill yourself back up with better emotions. To clean off all the dirt and grime, and more importantly, to keep it like that.

She stretched her legs and listened to her knees and ankles pop and click.

Matthew lifted his head. His hair was messy, falling over his forehead and sticking out and up. He rubbed his eye with a fist.

I never really loved Terry, Dawn thought.

"You're here," Matthew said.

"I'm here."

He laid his head on the pillow and grazed her stomach with his fingers.

"You've always been pretty," he said. "I mean, you're pretty. That's a fact. Now I see the parts that offer added hotness. Like this."

He ran a finger down the length of her neck to her nape.

"And this," he said, letting his index finger settle in the left dimple on her lower back.

"You come through like a professional in the photos. All the textures in the different houses, I hadn't realized what we'd see," said Matthew. "Nor had I realized how much emotion would come through. You really put yourself there. I don't know how, but you did."

"I thought about myself living in each house and how it would feel based on what we saw."

"Right, but they were regular houses. You wouldn't find them unusual if you walked in for a dinner party."

"That's the key," Dawn said. "The trick is to see. A lot of the answers are right there."

"That's why you're in my bed right now."

His breath was warm on her neck.

"Possibly." She pulled his hand between her legs and reached back between his.

"I have a lot of work to do," he said, working his fingers. God, he knew how to work his fingers. "Making choices, editing, thinking about exhibition, you know, the actual display."

"You're going to be busy. I wonder what I'll be doing while you're doing all that."

"You can do what you're doing. Or like this."

He repositioned her hand and wrapped his fingers around hers to apply more pressure.

"What else do you like?" she said.

"I like to feel it. Really feel it."

"I like to feel it too."

He pulled her hair until she rolled onto her back.

"Definitely tell me when," he said. "I have very few boundaries."

"You'll say when before I do."

"Doubtful."

"I want to sleep next to you all night," she said.

Dawn decided, one night. A good night sleep with Matthew in his bed, yes, with the sheets and comforter. In the dark with his warm body behind her. She could leave early in the morning and know exactly how it was supposed to feel. Maybe she'd sneak out so they wouldn't have to say goodbye. Matthew would understand. She'd roll down the street, her mind overflowing with gratitude because of hope and possibilities, because of the beauty that came with art, and because her father offered her the job.

MONDAY: PERSPECTIVE

LEAVE WHEN IT'S CLEAN
AND DON'T LOOK BACK.

Dawn woke up and took a moment to enjoy the silky-smooth pillow against her cheek. Her father had sprung for nice sheets in his spare bedroom. The tan background was adorned with tiny pineapples. The base of the lamp was shaped like a pineapple. The jagged, thorny decor gave it a sort of formal sophistication, despite the reality of it being a pain in the ass to extract the fruit from the husk and remove the core. Pineapples, the perfect fruit in its original fancy outer shell and in its neatly cut slices.

Her father had purchased a wicker dresser and matching bedside table. There were scented candles on a silver tray and a tissue holder with a gold pineapple etched onto the front. The candlewicks were still waxed over, having never been lit in the years they'd sat there. Nonetheless, they smelled as tropical and coconutty as the day Dawn had first seen them. The clock on the bedside table ran on a battery, but resembled the old-fashioned kind you wound every day. It balanced on a tiny silver tripod and told her it was almost three in the afternoon.

The golden light gave the room the elegant, yet inexpensive simplicity achieved at stores like Target. It went to show that good taste didn't have to cost a lot. Her father's guests most likely assumed they were being pampered. Dawn wondered who visited besides her. Probably everyone he knew from up north came down for a free place to stay. She took pride that he washed the sheets between visits and took the time to fold them under the sides of the mattress. They hadn't been ironed but smoothed over and still held the sweet aroma of dryer sheets.

Doing your best, Dad, she thought.

She'd slept in boxers and a tank top; she wasn't cold and her feet were on top of the sheets instead of underneath. She'd always liked waking up at her father's house, realizing how light and unburdened she had become. Whether it was from the

254 Beth Uznis Johnson

warm weather, the comfortable surroundings, being somewhere different or what, she didn't know. All she knew was that it was Monday and she would not be cleaning for the Turners. Barb may have straightened up last night—or not—and draped her arm around Fred while they slept, but today she'd have to clean her own house. Whether Barb had called in sick in order to mop the floor and change the sheets or if she went to work like normal, Dawn could make coffee in her father's small kitchen and sit and watch the news on his wicker couch, enjoying the cool Florida tile under her feet.

Aside from some bad traffic in Richmond the drive down was uneventful and easy. She had never taken a road trip alone and enjoyed the freedom to stop whenever she wanted, even if it was just for a pack of gum, or to drive a six-hour stretch without tapping the brake one time or letting the speedometer dip below 85. She left her phone powered off in her purse and relied on the radio for entertainment, no matter what station came through the static. Entering Florida was a victory, but she knew the state was long. The last leg through the Keys meant a lot to her, as the Atlantic churned with whitecaps and she powered on her phone.

Matthew had texted hours ago.

imy

She didn't know what it meant, but it had to mean something and that, alone, filled her with happiness. Her driving fatigue lifted and gave her the energy to know she'd make it the rest of the way without napping in any more McDonald's parking lots. She hadn't been unhappy up to that point, neither happy nor unhappy, just moving forward with her gaze alternating between the road in front, her speedometer, and the colors in the sky as the day faded into night.

She pulled off somewhere near Marathon Key and did a Google search.

I miss you.

She hadn't responded, but missed him too. She'd missed him since she'd merged onto the highway going south sometime during the quiet hours of early morning, preparing to cover some serious ground. Gradually the sun rose. The landscape for miles had been more of the same: grey sky, stretch of highway, signs to tell her what restaurants and gas stations were coming at the exits. The longer she drove, the brighter the colors became: green grass, flowers, ocean, the houses. As much as she wanted to see herself against the Key West backdrop, her forward motion kept drifting sideways for a second or two to conjure up an image or a feeling: Matthew's fingertips grazing the space between her breasts when he kissed her, the weight of his pelvis and surprising smoothness of his stomach against hers, how he kept his eyes on her face almost the whole time, though he moved and connected and touched her as though he saw everything. Something in Dawn, among the twists and turns of organs and ovaries, had awakened. Something Terry hadn't come close to rousing.

She'd pulled into her father's driveway at dawn on Monday morning and checked her phone again.

Will send u link 2 photos tmwr.

She'd gone inside and crawled into bed, too tired to think much about it, but noticing the way her teeth were cool from the air conditioning every time she brought her lips together; she kept smiling in the dim light as she fell asleep.

Now, in her father's kitchen, Dawn opened the cabinet beneath the sink and rummaged around. One small bottle of Palmolive, the green kind. She found a Tupperware bowl and mixed Magic with hot water from the tap. Her father used Bounty paper towels, which were sturdier than the cheap ones she normally used. Her dad seemed oblivious to crumbs and coffee splatters. Same as the Chens. Wiping the tops of his tables, counters, and desk made a huge difference.

Had Dawn known the better paper towels were so effective, she might have sprung for them. The whole concept of you-get-what-you-pay-for depended on circumstance. Take the McIntyres. Pretty much everything in their house was top of the line. Some of the brands, like the appliances, were foreign names she'd never heard of. The dishwasher started with a quiet, high-tech-sounding hum. It shifted from cycle to cycle as smoothly as Robert's Mercedes shifted gears. The napkins brought in by the caterers, though paper, resembled cloth. When you cleaned at the McIntyres', nothing broke and everything came clean, like window frames that someone had forgotten to wipe for months. Once, Dawn cleaned a patch of shoe-molding in the corner of the dining room—between the wall and the antique China cabinet—and, though her paper towel came back filthy, a few swipes with Magic was all it took for the smooth, thick paint to gleam. And that was using the discount paper towels.

She laughed out loud at the idea of using cheap paper towels to clean expensive artwork and expensive paper towels to clean the laminate counter and pressed wood cabinets in her father's kitchen. The coffee maker was a standard Mr. Coffee, the dish-washer a Whirlpool with a latch to swing in order to lock it, and plastic buttons for the cycles. His place was decent, but not upscale. The room was practically aglow after a few minutes of Magic. Clean made everything better.

Her father would be thrilled when he got home from the Bahamas. It all boiled down to expectations: who wanted what and how much it took to make them happy. All Dawn knew for sure was that Magic made everyone happy. Having created it gave her the certainty she could find other ways to make do on less. She wanted little and needed little, which right now seemed a good position to be in.

Dawn had decided sometime during the drive through central Florida that Barb Turner's problem wasn't that she wanted too much; her problem resulted from thinking she needed five kids and a husband in the suburbs when she could have used a better shrink and more time to heal. Dawn recognized the hysteria she'd heard in Barb's phone calls as her customer rambled. Dawn herself had done this plenty of times, trying to fight with Terry when she wasn't sure why he was upset in the first place or, worse, trying to make up under the same circumstances.

She found the Tupperware lid and snapped the container

closed, leaving the Magic on the countertop for later. She measured coffee and sat at the kitchen table. A check of her phone showed no messages, but that was okay. She lived in Florida now and she'd be damned if some guy from back home took all her attention. There were errands to run, places to see. Her father had a set of coffee mugs that said *Key Westerners know how to party*. She pondered this as she sipped. She also realized how different coffee tasted when you weren't drinking it to get warm. Already warm plus more warmth, a nice combination.

Her phone illuminated on the table. A link from Matthew. She touched the screen and waited. Expecting a basic slideshow from one of the sites Matthew used to store and share photos, the pale green background of his professional site appeared. That meant he'd worked over the photos carefully, including retouching and color correcting, and took the time to finalize the presentation of the art. He must have worked almost nonstop since she left. She wondered if he'd slept or eaten. Perhaps he hit send and collapsed onto his couch. Maybe he sat anxiously at his desk waiting for her response, chewing his fingernails or smoking cigarettes. Dawn wanted a cigarette, but she wouldn't smoke in her father's place and she wasn't about to go outside where the brightness of the afternoon would make it hard to see. The idea of finally viewing the photos was overwhelming. Her heart pounded as she clicked the play button.

The title appeared: Coming Clean.

A photo appeared showing a quarter of the left side of her face, only her left eye, the smooth skin over her cheekbone, the sweep of her hair across her forehead. The photograph faded to another that revealed the bottom right side of her mouth, the gentle arc of her neck and curve of her shoulder and collarbone.

Huh. Not at all what she'd expected.

Images rose and faded of her face, neck, waist, her hands resting on bare thighs. She recognized textures and colors in the background from her customer's houses: the Turners' quilt, half a Chinese fan next to her painted eye, the doll's white lace in her lap next to her hands. The final image, where the slide-show stopped, showed her stretched on the Twins' rug, her arm reaching toward the camera.

Watching the photos rise and fade a second time, she realized most of the shots were of her face, or pieces of her face. Every now and then, a part of her body. Feelings swelled with the memory of her discomfort at the Turners', her cheeks hot and red. The metal shaft cut across her cheek in anger at the McIntyres'. Sorrowful mouth at the Rileys'. The sad doll's hand next to her hands. Discontent at Wei Chen's. Peaceful Fridays at the Twins'.

The photos didn't tell a story about a cleaning lady or her customers. Matthew had seen a transformation of some kind. The slideshow repeated over and over. Every time it played, she hoped it would freeze and remain on the last shot. Every time it began again, her breath caught in her throat until it finished.

Dawn advanced the slideshow to Wei Chen's house. She found the photo she wanted and stopped. Matthew had focused on Wei's stuff and found a central point where the corner of the dragon picture frame met the cross of the paper fan. Both rested on the straw mat. Dawn hadn't noticed the leg of the bed frame, wood carved with an intricate pattern. The left side of the shot held the length of Dawn's curved shoulder and arm. She wished she could call Wei to explain and that Wei would understand. She'd show Wei the photos to see how beautiful her possessions came together. No one was making fun of her pain.

She called Matthew from her father's landline. It rang four times before he answered. "Hey," he said, realizing it was her.

"It wasn't about the people at all," Dawn said. "Or the houses."

"It could have been. I saw you. You were the interesting part of this experiment. There's a lot to you."

She left the final photo on the screen, the one from the Twins' bedroom.

"When I got out of the hospital, I went to Terry's grave and sat there all day. The cemetery was so peaceful and quiet. Sunny. I didn't feel guilty that day, only relieved. Like a big mess had been cleaned up while I wasn't paying attention."

"I like when we have sincere conversations," he said.

"You're a beautiful artist. You're lucky to see as much as you do. I wish I could."

"Thank you."

"I'll call you later, okay? I need to watch this a hundred more times and do some thinking."

"I wish you were here in my apartment. I want to hold you."

"I'm in Florida, though. I have arrived. Goodbye," she whispered, and powered off her father's phone.

She watched Matthew's slideshow one last time. She got up and warmed her coffee. She found a pair of cutoffs to wear with her tank top and stepped into flip-flops. Her father's bathroom sink had dried toothpaste in it, which she'd clean later. She had things to do.

When her phone vibrated on the kitchen table, she left it there. She couldn't help smiling, though. Matthew rarely disappointed her. Curiosity overcame her. *My body is searching for you.* Dammit if Matthew hadn't gotten under her skin. Matthew, an artist who liked to feel. He had a good chance of winning a Krindle grant.

She'd have a place of her own by the time Matthew did or didn't win the grant. Staying with her father very long seemed unlikely, as she couldn't wait to get to the library and search for online apartment listings. Best to get busy with the search. She picked up her phone and texted Matthew and asked him to send her a picture of Bridget Riley's hoard in a tumbled, colorful pile. She could have a print enlarged, a big one, and she could frame it for the wall of her new place. She could decorate around it. Matthew could autograph it. With his talent, it could be worth money someday.

She remembered a nearby shop right off Duval with beautiful tapestries to hang on a wall. She'd go—today—and buy her favorite one with Mitch's money. Between Matthew's photo and a vibrant tapestry, she liked her new apartment already. Hopefully it would have a place to sit outside, like a porch or patio.

One of the cruise ships in port blew its whistle. Another blew its whistle in response. Dawn rinsed her father's mug and put it into the dishwasher, which was full so she found Cascade and started the cycle. Again, same as the Chens.

Different people in different houses. Same lives.

The flip-flops sounded like summer as she stepped into the sunshine. Picket fences lined the sidewalk. Many had flowering bushes on the other side that grew taller than the fence and cascaded over to complete them, like a dot on top of an i or frosting on top of a cupcake. The fronds of the palm trees swished in the wind. A rooster clucked its way across the street.

She spotted the door to her father's bar ahead. He'd painted it red to draw attention. A wire snowman covered in Christmas lights stood on one side. Above its baseball cap, the chalkboard welcomed the cruise ships by name and explained the daily drink special. Her father had great ideas. She grasped the brass handle, took a breath, and went inside.

It smelled like dishwater and old beer. Someone had already cranked up the music. Dawn let her eyes adjust to the dim light. She scanned the room for anyone familiar, but only saw the faces of strangers.

"She's heeeeere!" Ricki stood behind the bar with a rag. She tossed it aside and came running. She'd dyed her hair pink. "Dawn's here! Dawn's here!"

Dawn watched the woman wave her arms as she clomped over in clogs. A colorful scarf around her head held the hair off her face. Ricki had managed the bar since the beginning. She stood taller than most women or men and commanded a room.

Ricki embraced her and didn't let go. Dawn smelled the dusting powder on her face. Her skin was warm and tan. Ricki rocked her around before releasing her.

"We are so happy you are here," Ricki said.

"Really?"

"We have been waiting for you. We've been waiting for ages."

She pointed toward the swinging door that led to the kitchen. Someone stood on the opposite side, a man whose red flip-flop wedged it open several inches and whose hand wrapped the top of the doorframe. The man who stepped out was tall and tan, with shaggy hair and a shark tooth necklace: her father. He waved. "Hello, daughter."

"Wow," Dawn said. "What happened to Bimini?"

"Cut short for my important houseguest."

He stood there grinning until Dawn walked over to hug him. He smelled like sunscreen and the ocean. She stepped into his arms and relaxed into his permission to take it easy. Her father had put her first. She savored the idea of being someone's highest priority. He squeezed her a couple times before standing back, dropping her hands last but not before noticing their overworked condition, for which he nodded and gave her a thumbs-up. Dawn slid her fingers into the pockets of her cutoffs.

"Now," said Ricki. "Now our little bar feels complete." She raised her arms and danced a little circle in time with the reggae music. Dawn's phone vibrated in her pocket. She danced a little circle, too, without using her arms. Ricki danced back to the bar and picked up the towel.

"It's so sticky. No matter how much I clean it. Must be the rumrunners. Damn pineapple juice."

Dawn stepped behind the bar and looked around for supplies. "I have just the solution. Cleans dirt you didn't know was there. All that's left is the clean underneath."

Ricki watched her make Magic in a plastic pitcher. Dawn went to work wiping the surface until she'd traveled from one end to the other. She flipped the paper towels and dried in the opposite direction. Her father stood there, nodding. Ricki ran her fingers along the grain of the wood and smiled. "Like I said, we've been waiting for you. Your dad tells us you're multi-talented and hard working."

"Do your best," Dawn said. "That's what he always told me."

"That's right, honey. We live by those words around here."

The song ended. Ricki moved the clean glasses from the rack to the shelf. "What are your plans?" Ricki said, dipping her rag into the pitcher of Magic and wringing it into the sink. She began wiping the sinks and faucets.

"Exploring. Shopping. Relaxing. And finding an apartment."

"We've been placing bets for years on how long it would take you to get down here," her father said. "It was only a matter of time before you came home."

"Home," Dawn said.

"You're home," Ricki said. "Don't you think so?"

She tapped them both a beer and motioned for Dawn to sit. Dawn hoisted herself onto a stool and lifted her glass to toast with her dad. Dawn tested the stickiness of the bar with her folded arms. Barely sticky at all after a wipe down. She swallowed some beer and pulled her phone from her pocket.

In response to her message about sending the photograph, Matthew had texted back:

May bring it myself.

A response came to her, one she wouldn't send, but one that pleased her just the same because Matthew would understand what she meant. She wanted to tell him to hurry home. Her father took a long pull from his beer and stood.

"You want to come back at seven to meet everyone? Nina, Christine, Sam, Marco. He's cute. You'll like Marco. Everyone likes Marco."

"Sure," Dawn said. She put her phone into her back pocket.

"Start tomorrow at five?"

"Sounds good."

"I've got to call the menu printer," he said. "Guy's trying to jerk me around. Finish your beer. See you later?"

"Absolutely," Dawn said. She stepped behind the bar for the pitcher of Magic and poured a thin line down the length of each of the four sides of the bar. Rags would actually be more efficient. She grabbed two from the top of the pile, using one to wipe and the other to dry. In between sections, she paused to take long swallows of the cold beer. Whatever Ricki had poured, it was dark and tasted like hops that crackled in the back of her throat. She'd need to get reacquainted with the flavors and descriptions of all the beers and cocktails. Satisfied by the gleaming wood, she finished her drink and washed the glass in the sink. It clinked in that pleasant way clean dishes sound when set on the drying rack. She folded the rags over the faucet to dry.

She almost wanted to stay inside the dim bar to polish the brass rails and make the whole place sparkle. But the cobbled streets and sunshine called, too, so she pushed out the heavy door to her first day.

ACKNOWLEDGMENTS

This novel wouldn't exist were it not for my former cleaning lady, Debbie. Thank you for always rearranging my silk flowers, generating the spark for this novel.

Huge gratitude to my teachers who provided guidance and feedback in workshop on early chapters: Pinckney Benedict, Fred Leebron, Jill McCorkle, Dana Spiotta, and Peter Ho Davies. Thank you to my Tinker Mountain, Sewanee, Tin House, and Bread Loaf classmates for your insightful critiques. And to my MFA professors, Susan Perabo, David Payne, and Elizabeth Strout for teaching me to be a better writer.

Thank you to early readers Carla Damron, Steve Eoannou, Dartinia Hull, Ashley Warlick, Jack King, Jeanette Brown, Shelly Drancik, Alissa Surges, Allison Krieger, Mickey Hawley, Maggie Duncan, Angele Davenport, Rita Juster, Heather Marshall, Henry Rozycki, Margarita Bauza, Mary Masson, and Jim Walke. The time you spent means the world.

Thank you to Barbara Jones for the generosity of your time and edits, which helped me draft the final version of this book. And thank you, Rob Spillman, for your support and mentorship. You said, "Good work rises to the surface," and I refused to stop trying. My gratitude to Jackey Chen for guidance on how Chinese speakers often reverse translate when learning to speak English.

Thank you, Facebook friends, for being so damn funny and helping me curate Dawn's top 100 list of ways to mess with customers. Our list is solid.

To my mom, Judy Silverman, and late grandmother, Evelyn Uznis. How amazing to have two strong women in my life who taught me you don't have to be tall or a man to accomplish your dreams.

And to my husband, Ken, and our sons, Alex and Kevin. Thank you for the time and space to be a writer and for understanding I was only kidding when I promised you a swimming pool if I ever got my book published.